THE TIME OF MAGIC BOOK I

THE WITNESS

AMIR SHEVAT

CONTENTS

PROLOGUE

Valor sat in the dark.

He closed his eyes. Rain dripped from leaves overhead, and the grass felt cold beneath his knees. A damp chill clung to him, thick with the scent of wet trees and earth. Around him, voices rose in soft chants–his father's, his mother's, his people's–rising and falling around him like a river of song. The smell of the giant, ancient woods surrounded him.

"Time to die?" asked the small voice in his head.

"My last son," his mother had called him as they'd shared yesterday's breakfast of fruit and nuts, his final meal before the fast that would prepare him for what lay ahead.

The words had burned into his soul. All of his elder brothers had failed and were believed to be dead, and now, it was his turn to risk the same.

"Are you prepared? Will you succeed or join your brothers in an early grave?" demanded that damn voice again.

A night owl hooted in the distance. It sounded almost happy. Was it a reassuring omen, or was nature just indifferent to his fears?

"Our only hope," his grim-faced father had called him over that same last meal together. "You are so young, and I'm sorry we are sending you to do this... There is no other way."

There is no other way... no other way! Valor repeated his father's words to himself, clinging to them for confidence.

A warm wave of bright light passed through him, visible even from behind his clenched eyelids, a sign that the Time Gateway spell was finally ready.

Valor opened his eyes.

The shining, round gateway stood in the middle of the forest clearing. The unnatural light cast shadows across his people's faces, hundreds of them, all focused on him.

Without a word, Valor stood, marched through the glowing portal, and instantly was engulfed by burning heat. His eyes slammed shut against the blinding glare. His skin screamed in pain. His mind reeled in fear, and his soul twisted with despair.

"Time to die? Will your story end here?" asked the pesky little voice in his head.

CHAPTER ONE

Waiting for a man to come out of a portal and die is one weird job description.

Sarah sat on a comfortable sofa in the Reception Room. Her mind went back to the first time her mother brought her here when she turned twelve. Her mother had been excited that day, telling her now-grown daughter about their family's secret mission.

Sarah remembered how shocked she had been by the story her mother told her, the thrill of entering a secret society, of having a life-mission, of owning a role in the future of the world. Most of all, she recalled the smell of the Reception Room: old oak and leather.

By modern standards, the large room was poorly lit, with no outside windows and dim light from the oil lamps on the walls and from a grand fireplace, embossed with silver and gold. The flickering light danced over the large furniture and the bookshelves which had fascinated her as a girl. At that time, she had not known the smell, as well as the lavish furniture, were all fake, meticulously engineered to mimic an ancient British royal reception room. Even the fireplace wasn't real. Behind all the wood and leather, there was a sophisticated system of surveillance cameras and climate control systems. Everything had a reason in the Reception Room.

"One day," her mother had told her, "you will take my place in the Brotherhood. You will have one of the most important roles in the history of humanity. Correcting a wrong done centuries ago. Making the world magical again."

The Brotherhood was the name of their secret organization. A Reception Committee member was the most sacred role in the Brotherhood, a role which had been passed down to her through the generations.

Sarah shifted on the sofa. At twenty-eight, she carried herself with the purposeful grace of someone accustomed to taking charge. She'd chosen her clothes deliberately. Her fitted charcoal wool blazer and straight-leg trousers struck the perfect balance between modern professionalism and timeless elegance, the kind of outfit that wouldn't look out of place in a Victorian drawing room or a contemporary boardroom. This was her outfit on this day, every year since she had taken her mother's role in the organization.

One thing her mother had not told her on that first day was that the role involved watching a man die in agony every year for the rest of her adult life.

Today was that day of this year.

The thought brought her back to the present, and she glanced across the room to Richard, who smiled at her reassuringly, even though she knew he was as anxious as she was.

Richard was her best friend, despite being almost twice her age. His silver hair had been perfectly styled. He had strength in his weary blue eyes, and his bearing carried the unmistakable stamp of military training—shoulders squared, spine straight, movements precise. The small bottle hanging from his gold chain seemed wildly out of place when compared to his elegant dark suit.

Sarah looked at her watch.

Five minutes to go. Chris better not be late like last year!

As if on cue, the door opened and Chris came in, huffing and puffing. He murmured an apology and took his designated seat between Richard and Sarah. He always reminded her of a little piglet of a man. Chris was in his thirties but looked older. His pale, doughy face glistened with sweat despite the room's careful climate control, and what remained of his thinning brown hair clung damply to his scalp. At thirty-something, he carried the soft bulk of a man who'd spent too many years behind a desk, his expensive suit straining slightly across his midsection.

Chris studied her. They had known each other long enough for him to recognize the look she gave him.

"I'm not late, Sarah. Not like last year," he said, answering her unstated accusation.

A strange static sound filled the room, as if two electric wires were clashing in the middle of a storm. They all tensed and looked at the fourth empty sofa in the middle of the room in front of them. For a moment, nothing happened.

Then, the air in the room suddenly shimmered, becoming thick and damp like a night mist in an ancient forest. Sarah's nostrils filled with the rich scent of wet earth, decomposing leaves, and old trees. The temperature dropped ten degrees in an instant, raising goosebumps along her skin.

Two feet above the central sofa, reality began to unravel. What started as a shimmer became a tear, not a perfect circle but a jagged wound in the fabric of space itself. The hole gaped dark, but its edges burned with flickering firelight that danced like living flames. The rim pulsed with an inner glow that cast shifting shadows across the leather furniture, making the familiar room feel suddenly alien. It always reminded Sarah of film reels burning in old movies.

For a split second, Sarah could have sworn she saw a gate made of light and runes shimmering on the other side of the rift. There was a sharp scream of pain, and a figure fell through the rift and landed on the sofa. In an instant, the hole vanished, but the man remained.

He convulsed violently, clearly in agony. Though he looked to be in his early twenties, his screams sounded like those of a starving week-old baby. He rolled off the chair and vomited onto the heavy carpet. Then he went terribly quiet.

Sarah sighed in sadness.

"Another dead one. God, I fucking hate this part," said Chris as he got up and pulled a black body bag from a hidden drawer next to his seat.

"Chris, show some respect," said Richard in his deep Army voice.

"Don't lecture me, Richard. I am not in the mood," said Chris. "Get the shovel, and we can get this over—"

"Bloch te mi?" came a young, angry voice from the figure on the floor.

They all froze.

The blood drained from Sarah's face, and her throat dried. Years of martial arts training had taught her to control her body, but nothing had prepared her for this moment. She pressed her palms flat against her thighs to stop them from shaking. Her breathing turned shallow, barely controlled. A cold shiver ran up her spine.

"Bloch te mi?" the man repeated, trying and failing to stand. "Pana me!" he cried.

Sarah turned to Chris then Richard. Chris looked like he might either bolt or faint. Richard turned ashen, his eyes full of both fear and awe.

They all knew it was Richard's moment to act. They had trained for this their entire lives. Richard had once admitted, on his fiftieth birthday, that he feared all the training had been pointless, just like for his father and grandfather before him. But now, it was happening exactly as foretold. They didn't understand the words the man was uttering, but they knew the response.

As they'd rehearsed a thousand times, Richard stepped forward to greet the man.

The new arrival struggled to his feet. He was taller than all of them, thin but not sickly. His long, pale blond hair hid his ears and most of his narrow face. A deep forest green tunic clung to his body, the fabric newly stained with his vomit.

Richard unclasped the bottle from his chain, pulled the cork for the first time in Brotherhood history, and bowed.

"Mok le Richard Palmer, istaloo..." His words faltered, uneven and low.

The tall young man was clearly confused and scared. He looked around as if searching for ways to escape. "Bloch te mi?" he shouted, waving his arms wildly and nearly knocking the bottle away. "Ne istaloo, Richurd," he added with a softer tone.

Sarah held her breath. The next few moments would determine the success or failure of their entire life mission. Only one other sentence remained in Richard's arsenal. If that didn't work, they'd have to use force, and she doubted they'd succeed against the strong-looking stranger.

"Mok le Richard Palmer, PARAMATE! Paramate istaloo," Richard implored, falling to his knees. The carpet muffled the thud. He raised the bottle high above his head.

The man stared down at him, his blue catlike eyes boring into Richard. The stranger stood silent for what felt like an eternity.

"Na me, Richurd," he said at last, his voice low. He took the bottle from Richard's trembling hands and drank it all in one gulp.

Nothing happened.

Then, as the man's expression began to shift toward anger, his eyes widened in surprise. "Kalamti Barvi? Ha!" His tone shifted, his gibberish replaced by smooth, deliberate words. "Hello, Richard, the Guardian of Memories," he said warmly.

The sound of his voice conjured a vision in Sarah's mind, one of a sunny garden full of butterflies. Love and peace washed over her, and she gasped.

"I can't believe I'm alive," the man added, brushing his hair back to reveal a long, inhuman ear.

Sarah smiled in wonder. This was really happening.

The tall man turned toward her. His features were sharply defined and unmistakably elvish. His catlike eyes looked young and old at the same time. Long blond hair fell across his face, revealing just enough of his pointed ears. With an elongated face and narrow chin, he was beautiful but unmistakably not human.

He wore simple travel clothes, a long-sleeved tunic in deep forest green and tan fitted trousers. The fine fabric draped his tall, lean frame perfectly, though the garments bore the worn look of a long journey. Wrinkled and now stained, they still carried an unmistakable quality.

"Are you Sarah, the Guardian of the Staff?" he asked, facing her.

Sarah's training kicked in, overriding her awe. This was what she'd been born for, what she'd spent her life preparing for.

"Mok le Sarah Bradford," she recited, bowing as she repeated the ancient words she'd learned at four. She pulled a small, black, rounded box from her pocket and offered it to him, bowing again.

She acted with practiced precision, her movements sure despite the unprecedented situation.

He took it and tapped its edges with one finger, and the box responded like liquid shadow. The metal flowed upward in a single graceful motion, stretching and reshaping itself with an elegant fluidity. In less than two seconds, a six-foot black staff stood in his hand, its surface gleaming. He struck the wooden floor with it, testing its strength.

His eyes swept the room, pausing on Chris. "And you must be Chris, the Guardian of Magic."

Chris didn't move. "They always die. I wasn't prepared for this," he mumbled. "Shit."

Richard glared at Chris. "It's in the blue cabinet," Richard growled.

Chris rushed to the cabinet in the corner, yanked the door open, and retrieved a glass sphere the size of a tennis ball. Nearly tripping on the carpet, he held it out to the man.

Sarah shook her head. *The fool forgot the ceremonial words.*

The stranger pressed the orb to the staff's tip and hummed a tune. The orb glowed faintly, then merged with the end of the black rod.

He smiled, holding the staff in his right hand. "My name is Valor, son of Valor the Third," he announced with regal pride. "I am the prince of the white elves and heir to the throne. Thank you for saving my life."

Butterflies fluttered in Sarah's stomach once again.

Valor scanned the room, searching. His brow furrowed. "Where is John, the Guardian of the Witness?"

"My lord, John and his entire family were wiped out in the First World War," Sarah said carefully. Seeing his confusion, she added, "It was a global war about a hundred years ago."

"That is most unfortunate," Valor said, his expression

mournful. “I fought beside his ancestors. I loved them dearly. The world is poorer without the Johns.”

He lowered his head, closed his eyes, and fell into a long silence.

Suddenly, his eyes snapped open. “Have we lost the witness?” he demanded. “Is all hope gone?”

“No, my lord,” Sarah said, shifting uncomfortably and bracing for the wrath she expected.

He didn’t seem to notice her hesitation.

“There’s a problem,” Sarah continued. “The witness doesn’t know she’s the witness. After the Johns died, we lost track of the bloodline. We only found them years later through a genetic screening program in the USA.” She paused. “Her parents weren’t cooperative. She’s completely unaware of her role... and honestly, we’re not sure she’ll be a willing witness.”

They all studied the elf prince with worried stares. They did not know how he would react to the bad news.

To everyone’s shock, Valor stepped forward and hugged her, beaming. “This is the first good news I’ve heard in years!” he said. “Don’t worry, Sarah. I’m sure I can convince her to accept her destiny.”

“Oh,” Sarah muttered, straightening her clothes and blinking away tears of relief.

“It’s even better this way,” Valor murmured.

“You haven’t met her yet, my lord,” Richard warned. “Brenda is quite a character.”

“Brenda? You mean Julia, surely?” Valor countered.

"They didn't enforce the Naming Rule," Richard replied. "They named her Julia, but she changed it to Brenda at some point."

The Naming Rule was simple. The name of a role-bearer in the Brotherhood remained the same throughout the generations. Sarah's mother's name was Sarah and so it was true for all her foremothers.

"Hm." Valor grew thoughtful, his eyes fixed on something unseen. "That's to be expected of those who do not know." His posture slumped, and the lines around his eyes deepened, exhaustion visibly washing over his features.

"You need rest, my lord. We'll talk more in the morning," Sarah said softly, guiding him to an armchair. Her touch was gentle but confident as she helped him settle into the chair. Her practical instincts took over. He needed rest, and she would ensure he got it.

Valor nodded, collapsed into the seat, and was asleep within seconds.

They stood above the sleeping prince, and the room fell silent other than the soft snoring of the elf.

"Holy fuck. I did not expect that," Chris said.

Crude, perhaps, but accurate.

History was unfolding before them. Everything they'd trained for was happening now.

I hope we're up to the task, Sarah thought, not for the first time and likely not for the last.

CHAPTER TWO

Brenda was having a very shitty day.

Her bank account was nearing zero, rent was due, and her roommate was MIA again. The job interview had gone badly. She knew it.

Damn it. I really needed that job.

In the last six months, she'd only landed three interviews, and every employer had wanted someone with twice her experience.

Maybe getting an anthropology degree wasn't the brightest idea after all.

A young guy passed by and smiled, and she returned the tiny polite smile that did not invite a conversation. *Doesn't he know that smiling is illegal in New York?*

Brenda had the kind of natural attractiveness that didn't require much effort when you were twenty-two. She had striking dark eyes, sharp cheekbones, and shoulder-length black hair that she usually kept loose and unstyled. Today, she'd thrown on her one decent blazer over a comfortable t-shirt and jeans for the interview, choosing function over fashion as always. Her worn sneakers had seen better days, but they were comfortable, and that mattered more to her than impressing anyone with expensive clothes she couldn't afford anyway.

Her thoughts spiraled. These weren't great times for grants or academic jobs, and she was stuck in the middle of it all. The cost of living in New York didn't help, but it was the farthest she could get from her parents, which was its own kind of win.

She sat down on the front steps of her apartment building. Her former apartment, depending on how next week went. It was a five-story brick structure that showed every year of deferred maintenance. Paint peeled from the window frames. The concrete steps had hairline cracks, and one lobby window was still covered with plywood from months ago. It wasn't the worst building in the neighborhood—the heat worked, and the locks functioned, but the landlord clearly spent as little as possible on upkeep.

She wasn't in the mood to trek up the creaky stairs. She especially wasn't in the mood to pass the drunk guy who always slept it off in the second-floor corridor.

She sighed. Confident she'd get the assistant-researcher job, she'd quit her waitress gig last week. Now, rent was due soon, and she had no way to pay it.

That meant the street... or going back to her parents.

She stood and kicked a chunk of broken concrete from the step. It clattered across the road and landed in a pothole.

I'd rather live on the street.

The thought of returning to her constantly bickering parents made her stomach turn. Their lectures about "learning something practical" and "doing something with your life" were bad enough. The "you should find someone" speech was worse.

Worst of all, they'd probably start calling her *Julia* again.

Names mattered. Her mother's name was Julia, and she was *definitely* not her mother.

Her relationship with her mom was complicated. Brenda loved her mother, sure, but she preferred to love the woman from several time zones away. Her mom drank too much and fought with her dad daily, often explosively.

Brenda's phone buzzed, breaking her spiral of thoughts. The screen lit up with a cracked-glass glow and an unfamiliar number.

Great. Probably the bank. She answered anyway.

"Hello?" said a woman's voice. "Is this Miss Mountain?"

Oh, fuuuck. Definitely the bank. Nobody calls me that unless it's bad news. Why did I answer? Stupid, stupid, stupid.

"Who's asking?" she replied in a deeper-than-usual tone, giving nothing away.

"My name is Sarah Bradford. I represent a research fund called BRHD. We read your article on the endangered Kachuka tribes in the Amazon. We were very impressed."

Brenda blinked, and her jaw slackened.

"Miss Brenda Mountain," the voice continued, "I'll get to the point. We'd like to offer you a position as a researcher with us."

What the fuck? Okay. Relax. Play it cool.

Brenda inhaled, held it, and let it out slowly. This would be her dream entry-level job. She could not believe her luck.

"Assistant researcher?" she asked, attempting a casual tone.

"I'm afraid we won't be able to provide you with an assistant in your first year," Sarah said smoothly. "The matter is still confidential. You'll work independently, though supported by others in the fund. Would that be acceptable? Would you be interested in meeting to discuss the offer?"

Brenda actually danced in place on the edge of the step in front of her shit apartment building. It was her private happy dance, one she rarely used these days. With effort, she kept her voice guarded. This had to be too good to be true.

"Where'd you get my number?" she asked. "I haven't applied to anything under BRHD."

"Let's just say we have our sources, Miss Mountain. You were referred to us," the woman replied with a smile in her voice. "Are you interested?"

"I'm willing to hear the offer," Brenda said, masking her thrill with a studied nonchalance.

"Excellent! We'll send a car to pick you up tomorrow at 9 AM. Please pack for a fortnight and bring your passport."

A fortnight? Was that...

"Wait, two weeks?" Brenda asked, alarmed. "Where exactly am I going?"

"Our recruitment headquarters are in London," Sarah answered confidently. "We'll cover all travel expenses and provide a thousand dollars per day for the duration whether you accept the position or not."

The words "a thousand dollars per day" rang like a gong in Brenda's brain. Still, this was bizarre.

"You do know this sounds like a scam, right?" she said.

"I understand your concern," Sarah replied, "but I assure you, it's legitimate. I recommend you research us, and you will receive a formal confirmation of your trip by email. If you accept the offer, you'll be able to work from anywhere you like."

Brenda was out of excuses. No job. No leads. No rent money. Just an increasingly loud voice in her head that said, *It's this or move back in with Mom.*

She looked around at the cracked steps, the peeling paint, the boarded-up window. She closed her eyes and took a deep breath. When she opened them again, her voice was steady.

"Okay," she said finally. "I guess I'll see you tomorrow."

"Wonderful!" Sarah said. "Don't worry, Miss Mountain. I look forward to meeting you soon in London."

And just like that, Sarah hung up.

In shock, Brenda stared at the crack running down her phone screen.

My life's going to get a whole lot better.

THE COOL NIGHT air slipped through the open kitchen window, carrying the sounds of the city with it, distant sirens, car horns, someone's music playing a few floors up. Brenda sat at her wobbly table, one leg propped up on a folded napkin to keep it steady, her laptop balanced precariously on the scratched Formica surface. The kitchen was barely big enough for one person, with cabinets that didn't quite close properly and a refrigerator that hummed too loudly, but the window faced west and caught the last light of the day, so it wasn't that bad.

The neighbor's cat pushed through the screenless gap in the window, sauntered across the chipped linoleum floor, meowed once, and jumped into her lap. Absently, she cuddled him close and began typing into the search bar. A moment later, her eyes widened.

BRHD was some kind of massive UK corporation that traded as Brotherhood PLC on the London Stock Exchange. It was one of those companies that seemed to own a piece of everything—food, energy, tech, and probably half the stuff in her apartment. Their research division was what interested her. They funded everything from biology to philosophy. Buried somewhere in that list was anthropology.

Apparently, BRHD accounted for twenty-eight percent of global research grants and made a fortune off patents.

Interesting.

She drummed her fingers on the worn Formica. A little flicker of hope sparked inside her. The cat purred on cue, clearly pleased with himself.

Brenda shut her battered laptop gently and leaned back, lost in possibility, then sighed. She was going to be able to make rent, and the passport her parents had inexplicably made her get was finally going to be useful.

Her parents were super weird that way. It felt like they were always prepared to leave at a moment's notice. They made sure the whole family had current passports but rarely traveled out of state. They told her to be friendly at school but refused to let her friends visit the house. They talked constantly about the merits of being brave and self-reliant yet never took any risks themselves, living the same predictable routine year after year.

"You're too special. We can't risk anything happening to you," they would say whenever she challenged their contradictions, and they would never explain what that meant no matter how much she pressed them. Just another smelly secret in a pile of garbage that had been her childhood.

The next morning, Brenda knocked on her neighbors' door to share the news and ask them to water her plants.

Josef and Petra Svoboda, the Czech couple in their seventies who lived next door, beamed with excitement when she told them. Josef still spoke with a thick accent despite forty years in America, and Petra had a habit of pressing homemade cookies into Brenda's hands whenever they met in the hallway. They were the kind of people who remembered her birthday and worried when she came home late, treating her more like family than her actual parents ever had. They promised to care for her plants and insisted on a celebratory dinner when she returned.

They even helped carry the bags to the taxi waiting at the curb.

Brenda hugged them goodbye and smiled as the car pulled away. She waved, even as a weird little feeling took root in her chest, a whisper she couldn't shake.

I will never see them again.

CHAPTER THREE

This elf better not die on my watch!

Chris stared out the window at the rain. Sarah and Richard were out on their “important tasks” and left him to babysit the sleeping elf prince.

He sighed. He was not the sharpest tool in the shed. He knew that. He heard it from his father, he felt it from his wife, and he saw it in the faces of his colleagues. Frankly, he was totally comfortable with that. Being smart was overrated.

Smart people were expected to do hard things, brave people were expected to do dangerous tasks, organized people were expected to lead things. He was none of that, thank God. His favorite shirt read, "If you do not try, you do not fail," and it described him perfectly.

Chris poured another double of the expensive stuff BRHD kept at headquarters, took a swig, and deposited the half-empty glass on the table, the same table he'd already filled with an assortment of food for the "new arrival." He dropped into the nearest chair, his back to the entrance.

The worst was to be considered competent. Chris tried to

avoid that the most. Competent people were given work, and that was absolutely devastating. Work was other people telling you to do something you didn't want to do for money. What a rotten deal that was. Chris's father was on the board of the BRHD and made sure his son had a job that matched his skills.

"Once a year, fly from Zurich to London, sit in a room, watch a man die, and report back if anything else weird happens," his father had said.

That was as good a job as Chris could have dreamed. Now his wife was texting him from their vacation house in Lake Como, asking why he hadn't come home already. What was he supposed to tell her? That he was at work?

His eyes wandered sadly across the dining room. This place did not resemble the family vacation homes at all. The place was dimly lit by the gray, oppressive light filtering through the windows. The oak table and chairs were the kind of solid, traditional pieces that could have graced any English manor house over the past five centuries—timeless, imposing, and built to outlast generations.

His thoughts went back to his father's instructions. Things had definitely gotten weird this time around. He'd tried calling his father ten times in the last five hours. No answer. Very unlike the man. Had one of those self-righteous colleagues of his already briefed him?

And then there was *the thing* with Valor.

Chris hadn't been able to wake up the bloody elf.

Before Richard had left to collect the witness, he had told Chris that Valor would probably sleep for two or three hours. "Like elves usually do," he'd said.

As if *anything* about this was "usual."

But Valor had now been out for six hours. Chris had checked on him repeatedly only to find him in the same stiff meditation pose. Chris made as much noise as he dared. No reaction. Was the elf even breathing?

What if he dies while I am in charge? His father, and the Brotherhood, would never forgive him.

"Not on my goddamn shift," Chris muttered, pushing back from the table. He'd better check on the elf one more time. Before he could stand, a cheerful voice spoke directly behind him.

"Good morning, Chris."

Chris launched out of the chair and nearly jumped out of his skin. He hadn't even heard Valor enter the formal dining room.

"I'm starving! Thank you for preparing this wonderful feast." Valor leaned on the heavy wooden dining table, shoveling handfuls of nuts and dried berries into his mouth.

Chris stared in disbelief. This couldn't be the same creature who'd been puking his guts out seven hours ago. Valor looked impossibly refreshed, as though he'd spent the last night in a spa. His clothes were somehow immaculate, the forest green tunic crisp and tan trousers unmarked, as if last night's mess had never happened. The elf practically glowed with energy and good cheer, making Chris feel even more pathetic in his rumpled, sleep-deprived state.

Valor looked straight into his eyes, and Chris's heart pounded. The elf really creeped him out.

In daylight, the prince definitely didn't pass for human. He was towering and wiry, like a young Olympic athlete, with long blond hair tied back in a ponytail. The eyes were the giveaway—catlike with slitted pupils and almost no white. He reminded Chris of the character Spock from the old Star Trek series.

Valor was handsome, sure, but in an *animal* kind of way.

"Wonderful feast," Valor repeated, his mouth full.

How can anyone call dried fruit and nuts a "feast"?

Chris had dragged himself all over the city hunting for these so-called "elvish necessities," as Sarah defined them.

"Good morning, my lord," he said dryly. "We were expecting you a bit earlier..."

Valor just kept humming to himself, eating with both hands and downing glass after glass of iced tea.

"I haven't slept so well since..." Valor studied the ceiling, thinking. "Since I was sixty, if I recall correctly." Red berry juice dripped from his chin onto the carpet. "I'm sorry I'm eating like this. I haven't eaten for a long while. Had to fast to prepare for the... travel."

Chris stared at him, slightly disgusted. *Chatty bastard.* Aloud, he said, "Enjoy your meal, my lord. There's plenty more."

God knows I spent my whole morning hunting this crap down. You'd better enjoy it.

Chris scowled, but Valor either didn't notice or didn't care. He kept eating and humming, perfectly content.

After a long while, Valor looked up at him. "I like you, Chris. I have a premonition that you will have a critical part in the success of this quest. I have a feeling you will save my life."

Well, that's awkward.

"You are confusing me with Richard, my lord. He is responsible for your safety. He is well trained for it and is very competent at that," Chris said, omitting the fact that he personally had no skill or intention of saving anyone, ever.

"Heroes are not always chosen by their skills, virtues, or even will. Most times they are just in the right place at the right time," Valor answered, his eyes looking at Chris with a weird intensity. For a second Chris thought he saw them glow blue. "Fret not, Chris, you will do the right thing when the time comes."

Don't bet on it.

Chris tried to keep the annoyance from his face.

"Chris, how long have you been an active member of the Brotherhood Reception Committee?" His tone was soft and almost sad.

How long have I been burying dead elves, you mean?

"Five years, your highness."

"Call me Valor or 'my lord.' I'm not 'your highness.' Not yet."

"Yes, my lord." *No way I'm calling him by his first name.*

Valor nodded then added, "I'd like you to take me to see them, Chris."

Chris's stomach dropped. He knew who Valor meant.

"My brothers. The ones you buried."

Cold sweat prickled at Chris's neck. "We should wait for the others. We can't just go out in the middle of the day and..."

He stopped when he met Valor's eyes. That stare didn't tolerate objections.

"And yet," Valor said, his voice calm and final, "you *will* take me there. Now."

IT WAS FREEZING outside when Chris opened the heavy door at the rear of the mansion. The sunlight caught Valor's pale face, revealing the faint blue veins on his temples. Valor gave Chris a look that said, "I'm not afraid of a little cold. Lead the way."

Chris stepped outside, shut the door behind them, and led the prince across the expansive backyard. A small hill overlooked a large, empty clearing. Chris guided him to the top.

Valor stopped. His eyes widened, clearly in shock.

Below them were six star-shaped grave markers spaced evenly like military headstones, their surfaces slick with moisture and darkened by patches of moss that had begun to claim the stone. The rich smell of wet earth hung heavy in the air, mixing with the damp and decay that seemed to rise from the ground itself. A chilly wind cut across the hilltop, striking them with icy fingers that made Chris wrap his jacket tighter around himself, while his breath came out in small puffs of vapor. If the markers had been crosses instead of stars, it would've looked exactly like a war memorial, which, Chris realized with growing unease, was exactly what it was.

Valor stood perfectly still. His blue eyes darkened until they were nearly black.

The temperature plummeted further, and Chris could swear he felt the cold coming directly from the elf.

A low growl, like something feral and ancient, rose from deep in Valor's chest, vibrating through the ground beneath their feet.

“There... are... no... trees,” the elf’s words hit like an icy wave. His pitch-black eyes locked onto Chris. “Why are my brothers buried like animals?” he asked, voice trembling with fury. “Why aren’t they buried beneath trees?”

Chris swallowed. “What does it matter? They’re dead. Trees or not... nothing’s going to help them now,” he said without thinking.

Bad move.

Valor tilted his head, inspecting Chris like a cat might inspect a trembling mouse. He didn’t need to say anything.

Chris suddenly realized how bad an idea it was to keep talking.

Can he read my thoughts?

Chris tried to backpedal, to explain, but time slowed.

Valor still stared at him, unblinking. Chris couldn’t look away. His thoughts grew fuzzy, cotton-wrapped, as if Valor was slowly turning down the volume on Chris’s mind. The last thing he remembered was the sensation of falling, not physically but mentally, tumbling down into a dark, silent place where his own willpower simply stopped.

And then, everything went blank.

The next thing Chris remembered was driving back from the nursery in a blue truck filled with six young trees. His mind felt muddy, but he knew he had one single important task to accomplish.

One tree for each grave.

Three hours later, Chris was still outside, mechanically digging the fourth hole. His expensive suit had been ruined, mud caked into the fine wool, the jacket torn at the shoulder, his usually lavish-looking appearance destroyed. His well-manicured nails were broken and bloodied from clawing at roots and stones, and despite the cold air that should have chilled him to the bone, sweat poured down his forehead in steady streams. His body screamed with exhaustion, but his hands kept moving, compelled by something beyond his control. His eyes were burning with sweat and fatigue.

But once the sixth tree was in the ground, he thought...

Maybe then I'll be allowed to sleep.

CHAPTER FOUR

Roy Valemont sat in the back seat of the black car, watching the streetlights blur beyond the rain-speckled window. He hadn't expected his day to end like this. It was nearly midnight, but he was on his way to work.

The evening had actually started off well. He'd been having dinner with a lovely young lady, a stunning blonde whose youth and curves served as the perfect accessory to his elegant suit, with the extra bonus that that lady was not his wife. Roy had always believed that beautiful women were like fine watches—meant to be displayed, admired, and frequently upgraded for newer models. She had been a fantastic upgrade to this evening.

They'd been sitting in a high-end French bistro, his opulent clothes immaculate and his silver hair perfectly styled, the heavy gold Rolex catching the candlelight as he cut his steak. His date had chatted about something. Her job, her roommate, he hadn't really listened. She'd looked perfect across from him, which was all that mattered. Her actual words had been just pleasant background noise while he'd enjoyed the envious glances from other diners.

Then his phone rang.

It had been set to silent, but it had rung anyway.

He pulled it from his pocket, ignoring the annoyed look from his date and the disapproving glances from nearby tables.

“It has started, sir. Please exit the building. The limo is waiting out front.”

The line had gone dead.

Roy's expression hadn’t changed. He’d calmly finished his last bite of steak, chewing deliberately while his date's voice had cut through the restaurant's ambient chatter.

"Who was that? Roy? Is everything okay?"

He’d ignored her completely, as if she hadn't spoken at all. Standing smoothly, he’d straightened his suit jacket with practiced precision, ran a hand through his already-perfect hair, and adjusted his cufflinks. Without a word, no goodbye, no explanation, no glance back, he’d marched out of the restaurant and slid into the black car waiting for him. He hadn’t even paid the bill.

Fuck it, he thought. *I never thought this day would actually come. If this is a drill, I will have someone’s head on a platter.*

James Webber, Roy’s chief of staff, occupied the seat beside him with the rigid posture of a career bureaucrat. James was dry as they came but alarmingly efficient. Thin, completely bald, and wearing another of his interchangeable gray suits that seemed tailored to match his equally gray face, James was red tape made flesh, and he wore that distinction like a badge of honor. While Roy couldn't be bothered with forms, protocols, and regulatory nonsense, James consumed it all with the enthusiasm of a man who'd found his true calling. He made the endless logistics of Roy’s life disappear as if by magic, which Roy greatly appreciated, even if he’d never say it.

Without a word, James handed Roy a paper brief. The document's cover was maroon and had the official Kildare Corporation logo. Roy had only heard about maroon-classified documents in theoretical briefings. He had never actually seen one in his fifteen years running the company. This was the color reserved for secrets so dangerous they couldn't be discussed anywhere outside Kildare headquarters.

The document was titled: "Suspected Witness #K25"

Roy raised his eyes to James with a questioning look, but his chief of staff's expression remained impassive. Protocol dictated complete silence on such classified matters until they reached the secure floors of Kildare headquarters, and James followed protocol like scripture. Roy knew better than to waste his breath.

Inside the brief were photos of a young woman in her twenties. Some had been taken from afar, others snapped from hidden cameras inside her apartment. Roy lingered on the more revealing shots. Might as well pass the time enjoyably.

The car eventually stopped in front of a tall, nondescript building. The rear doors opened.

Roy and James were escorted to an elevator inside by two men in dark suits with earpieces. They didn't speak. Didn't even nod. *Fucking zombies,* Roy thought. Kildare security was notoriously uptight, much less friendly than JFK security on a bad day.

The elevator doors closed behind them, and the carriage began its descent.

After about forty-five seconds, the doors opened to reveal a vast underground hall that looked like mission control for a shadow government. Multiple large screens lined the walls, their blue glow casting an eerie light across the space, while subtle white noise hummed from hidden speakers, sophisticated sound masking to prevent any electronic eavesdropping. At the center sat a massive mahogany boardroom table that probably cost more than most people's houses, its polished surface reflecting the light from the wall-mounted displays. The room felt like a boardroom that was designed by someone with unlimited funds and healthy paranoia.

Around it sat twenty-five people dressed in everything from evening gowns to gym shorts to what appeared to be pajamas, each yanked from their evenings just as abruptly as Roy.

Jack Morrison, the director of operations who usually intimidated people in thousand-dollar suits, sat slouched in a wrinkled Yankees jersey that made his thick frame look like an off-duty bouncer. The sight of Kildare's most feared department head looking like he'd been dragged from his couch without warning would have been amusing if the circumstances were different.

When Roy entered, the chatter died. Twenty-five pairs of eyes turned to him. Now that they were in a secure space, he could finally speak freely.

"What I want to know," he barked, "is which idiot decided to run *another* drill?" He glared around the room. "We had one three weeks ago. We do this crap once a year. What the fuck?"

Silence.

His chief of security, Mary Drechsler, looked up at him with that same unreadable expression she always wore. Her red hair was damp with sweat from what looked like an evening run, and her black athletic wear clung to her lean frame, but she sat in the boardroom chair like she owned it. There was always something unsettling about the way she watched him, not with the deference he expected from subordinates but with the calculating patience of someone who knew exactly what cards she held. Her green eyes held a zealot look of expectation, as if she'd been waiting for his predictable dramatics to run their course before the real work could begin. Truth be told, Roy had *never* seen her in anything but zealot-mode.

"This is not a drill, Roy," she said. "Our source tells us the

Brotherhood just made contact with Suspected Witness K25. They plan to move her to London."

Roy's stomach dropped. Cold sweat prickled across his back. "What?" he rasped. "Any sign of a Reappearance?"

"We don't know yet," Mary said. "Our source is low-ranking, the first one we've gotten into the Brotherhood in years, but now we've lost track of all their known members. They've just... vanished."

Roy sank into the big chair at the head of the table. He studied the gathered faces. *Do I trust these people? Hell no. They couldn't organize a bake sale without me. Even with instructions.*

"Okay," he said, projecting more confidence than he felt. "You all know what's at stake. We've been sitting on our asses for generations, but now it's game time."

He thought it sounded pretty damn grand, but they didn't look impressed.

Especially Mary.

"What exactly do you want us to do, Roy?" she asked flatly.

They locked eyes. Roy remembered the Christmas party two years ago. *If it weren't for that night, I'd swear she had no pulse,* he thought.

He closed his eyes for a moment. When he opened them, they were wide and blazing. "I want the Witness fucking dead," he snarled, slamming the table for emphasis. "Dead. Dead. Dead. Dead!"

The hiss of covered gasps echoed in the conference room.

Spineless bastards. Happy to cash their paychecks, but the moment I ask them to earn it...

"Apparently some of you need a reminder of what is at stake here," he said, his voice dropping to a dangerous whisper.

He swept his gaze around the table. Mary met his stare with her usual unimpressed calm. James kept scribbling notes like

Roy was discussing quarterly reports, and the rest looked like he'd just suggested eating babies for breakfast.

“I guess you do...” Roy said, half to himself.

His predecessor had told him that people in corporate environments had the uncanny ability of forgetting their core objectives and doing useless things instead. He had often encouraged Roy never to assume his reports were exempt from this tendency, no matter their seniority, and to constantly circle back to reaffirming the basics. These words struck home today with uncomfortable clarity.

He leaned forward, his voice low now. “The Witness is key to the Reappearance. Without her, they can’t complete it. I sure fucking hope I do not need to remind you that our organization's sole job is to save humanity from the Reappearance of magic.” He scanned the room, pausing on each face. "Let me paint you a picture," Roy continued, leaning forward until his knuckles pressed white against the table. "She lives, magic returns. Magic returns, civilization ends. Are we clear?"

A few nodded.

That will have to do.

“Gather your people. Cancel everything. Call your wives. Call your husbands. Tell them you won’t be home for a while.”

The attendees shifted in their seats, but none spoke.

Roy allowed the silence to grow heavy before he stood.

“The shit,” he said with finality, “has hit the fan.”

CHAPTER FIVE

Brenda passed through the tedious airport security without a hint of frustration. The air smelled of recycled air-conditioning mixed with fast food and too many bodies in too small a space. Announcements echoed constantly over crackling speakers in multiple languages, children cried, and somewhere a man was arguing loudly with a TSA agent about his confiscated shampoo. She was so excited about flying overseas, not even JFK could ruin it for her.

She hauled her carry-on in one hand. The damn thing was heavy, but she refused to check a suitcase. That was non-negotiable. Brenda hadn't trusted "systems" for as long as she could remember. The idea of handing over her belongings to vanish into some black hole and magically reappear in another country? Ludicrous.

She wandered through duty-free with the giddy enthusiasm of a kid in a candy store, sampling four different perfumes at the cosmetics counter until her wrists smelled like a flower shop explosion. At the toy section, she lingered over a ridiculously big

LEGO starship set, running her fingers over the box and seriously considering blowing her limited funds on something completely impractical. Then, she tried on a pair of designer sunglasses that cost more than her monthly grocery budget, making fashion-model faces in the small mirror while knowing she'd never be able to afford them. She was barely able to afford the coffee, and after tasting it, she regretted she had.

Her parents hadn't had the money, and even if they had, they never would've let her travel. Too risky, too dangerous.

And if they ever found out about the "random call" that had landed her this flight, they would lose their minds.

"You're too important," they always said. "You can't take these kinds of risks!"

What a couple of lunatics.

She was heading toward the gate when she heard her name over the loudspeaker, "Ms. Brenda Mountain. Ms. Brenda Mountain. Please proceed to the nearest white courtesy telephone."

Weird.

Why was security asking for her? Brenda's mind raced through possibilities. Was something wrong with her ticket? Had she forgotten something valuable at one of the duty-free counters? Maybe they'd found an issue with her passport or discovered some problem with her hastily packed luggage. She tried to remember if she'd done anything suspicious, but she'd been the model traveler—polite to TSA, patient in lines, hadn't even complained about the overpriced airport coffee.

She spotted a courtesy phone and picked it up. "Ms. Mountain speaking..."

There was a burst of static. Then, a raspy voice said, "Ms. Mountain, this is airport security. Please read the locator number on your phone."

She found it printed on the handset. “Uh, number 356. What is this abou—”

The line went dead.

Confused, she placed the phone back and glanced around, unsure if she should wait, but then the final boarding call for her flight boomed overhead, and she grabbed her bag, ready to make a run for it.

“Are you Ms. Mountain?” The deep voice stopped her short.

Two men wearing crisp airport security clothing stood behind her, both with the kind of disciplined posture that screamed of a military or police background. They weren't trying to look intimidating, no scowls or obvious threats, but everything about them suggested serious competence. Well-built without being bulky with alert eyes that missed nothing, they were the kind of professionals who could probably handle any situation without raising their voices or breaking a sweat. Not menacing, exactly, but definitely not the type you'd want to fuck with.

She considered lying, but it didn’t seem productive.

“Yes. What’s this about?” she asked, channeling her best boss voice.

“Please come with us. We have a few questions,” said the taller one. He flashed a badge too quickly to register then grabbed her arm.

“What the actual fuck—” she started.

“Don’t make a scene. Just come with us.” He glared at her.

They pushed through the crowd, one gripping her arm, the other flanking her. Confusion turned quickly into fear. Before she could ask anything else, they opened a nondescript service door and led her into a small, windowless room with a mirror on the wall, the kind they always used in interrogations. In movies, anyway.

"What did I do?" Brenda asked, her voice loud and sharp, but the men left without a word.

As soon as Brenda heard the door close, she circled the small room, taking in her surroundings. The space was clean but carried the stale smell of old cigarettes. A metal table sat in the center with four chairs bolted to the floor around it. The mirror showed signs of wear around the edges, and the fluorescent light above flickered with the kind of barely perceptible irregularity that had always bothered Brenda. She paused to stare into the mirror, wondering who might be watching from the other side.

A woman in a police uniform entered.

Brenda blinked, startled by the resemblance. The woman looked remarkably like her, slightly older but not by much, same height and build, same shade of dark hair, similar haircut. Not identical but close enough to be mistaken for the same person by someone who did not know her well.

What an odd time to find my doppelganger.

"Ms. Mountain, your passport and ticket, please," the woman said, all businesslike.

Even her voice seemed eerily familiar.

A chill spread through Brenda. Her gut clenched. Something was seriously off, but she handed over her documents. "I want to know what this is about. I have a right—"

"There's been a terrorist threat," the officer cut in. "I need to inspect your jacket. Now, please." The tone was cold and authoritative.

Brenda hesitated, but that uniform, and the hard edge in the woman's voice, left little room to argue. She slipped off the jacket and handed it over.

One of the men from earlier walked in, holding a carry-on. For a second, Brenda thought maybe she'd left hers behind, but her own bag was still right there, at her feet.

What the...

The officer put on Brenda's jacket. Then, without a word, she grabbed the new bag from the man and kissed him firmly.

What's going on...

"See you on the other side," the strange woman said grimly, and she dashed out the door.

Brenda just stood there, her mouth open. "What the hell just—"

The man grabbed her arm again. "Come with me. Now. We don't have much time."

His voice.

It was the voice from the courtesy phone.

She looked closer at his face. Were those tears in his eyes?

He grabbed her hand and started running.

"My bag!" she gasped, reaching for it, but she was already being dragged away. "Where are you taking me? Why did she take my jacket?"

No answer. Just that iron grip on her hand pulling her through a maze of restricted corridors she'd never known existed in an airport. He moved with the precision of someone who'd memorized every turn, pausing at each corner to make sure the next corridor was clear, glancing nervously over his shoulder every few seconds then confidently selecting the right door from rows of identical service entrances. It reminded her of that scene in The Matrix where Neo navigates the endless hallway of doors, except this was terrifyingly real, and she was being dragged through it against her will.

They rounded a corner and bolted down a long private hallway that led to a small waiting jet. Panic surged through her.

"STOP IT, you fuck! HELP!" Brenda screamed.

She swung wildly and hit him. Missed his face, but her fist caught his shoulder, and something strange happened. She was not sure if she imagined it, but a burst of heat flared from her hand.

He cried out in pain but didn't let go.

They stumbled down the hallway and into the plane. This was the kind of private jet celebrities used, all cream leather seats that looked more like recliners than airline seating, with generous space between each row and large oval windows that offered an unobstructed view. The cabin smelled of money and luxury, a stark contrast to the violence of her kidnapping.

He shoved her roughly into one of the plush seats, the expensive leather squeaking under her weight as she landed hard.

Another man appeared. She recognized him as the other security guy that took her initially. He slammed the hatch behind them and gave a thumbs-up to her captor.

He then knocked on the cockpit door. "We've got the Witness. Let's get the hell out of here."

The Witness? Did he just call me that? This has to be a mistake...

The plane started moving. Angry voices squawked on the radio.

Tears welled in her eyes. "Why are you doing this?" she sobbed.

To her surprise, the man who had just violently dragged her through the airport looked at her with unexpected kindness. His expression was deeply sad, almost pained, with something almost fatherly in the way his eyes softened. For a moment, he looked like he wanted to comfort her, to explain everything and make it better, but then his gaze dropped to her unfastened seat belt.

"Buckle up," he said urgently. "Please. We are taking off now!"

She sat up, barely buckling her belt as they accelerated.

Outside the window, she saw her British Airways flight still at the gate.

If only I were on that plane...

And then the British Airways plane exploded in front of her eyes.

CHAPTER SIX

"She's dead," Jack said, smugly standing in front of Roy. "We confirmed that she boarded the plane before we detonated the device."

The air in Roy's office was thick with the scent of old money and smuggled Cuban cigars, the kind of atmosphere that whispered of exclusivity. Rich mahogany paneling lined the walls, and the floor was polished hardwood so lavish it looked like a mirror reflecting the recessed lighting above. At the center of the room sat Roy's massive executive desk, a monument to corporate authority crafted from what looked like a single piece of dark wood, his high-backed leather chair positioned behind it like a throne. Everything in the space was designed to make visitors feel small and remind them exactly who held the power.

Today, Jack seemed completely at ease in the menacing office. He slouched in the chair across from Roy's desk like he was lounging on a beach, his legs stretched out straight and his muscular arms folded behind his head. His broad frame filled the chair, and his relaxed posture radiated the kind of quiet pride that came from completing a difficult mission successfully. He looked like a man who'd just accomplished a hard task and was savoring the moment, confident in his work and expecting recognition and rewards.

"You are a fucking degenerate. A *fucking degenerate*, Jack," Roy said, seated behind his desk, his eyes locked on the man. "You had to blow up the entire plane, right? Couldn't just poison her? Or put a goddamn bullet through her head? No, not Jack. Jack needs to blow shit up. No body. No confirmation. Just *boom*. Right, Jack? *Right?*"

Roy stood. He walked calmly to the closet, hung up his suit jacket, and pulled out a gleaming white coat, something between a lab coat and a ceremonial robe. It shimmered under the lights as he slipped it on. The pristine white fabric covered Roy from neck to shoes, transforming his appearance completely. He looked like a surgeon preparing to save a child's life in an operating room, only his eyes were lifeless and cold.

Jack's smirk vanished, and his face went pale.

"Oh, no," Roy continued, his voice rising. "*Fucking* Jack needs to make a goddamn mess, as always!"

Roy walked to the far wall where his weapons collection waited like old friends. The display was organized with the meticulous care of someone who knew each piece intimately, when it was made, how it worked, what it felt like in his hands. Swords, knives, whips, spears, and firearms were arranged not just as decoration but as tools he'd selected over years of collecting, each one earned or chosen for a specific quality he admired. He chose a long, heavy blade and unsheathed it with care. It shone in the office light.

Jack started backing toward the door, only to realize the two large bodyguards had closed it shut behind him. "No, Roy. No. Look, we confirmed it was her. She couldn't have survived! There were no survivors. None! It had to be her—"

The bodyguards outside must have heard the screams and the heavy thud.

After a few minutes, there was a soft *tap-tap* at the door. They entered, careful not to scuff their polished shoes on the blood-spattered floor.

Roy calmly removed his lab coat and handed it to one of the guards. He slipped back into his expensive dark jacket and buttoned it neatly. He moved to a small warming device mounted beside his desk and withdrew a damp, heated towel. With the same methodical care he applied to his appearance each morning, Roy wiped his hands clean then his face, erasing any trace of what had just occurred.

"Jack's such a fucking mess. In life *and* in death," Roy muttered. He glared down at the body. "Do you feel smug now, Jack? Do you feel like you did the right thing?"

Roy kicked one of the severed hands. He did feel a little better. A little less angry.

He handed the sword to one of the guards who held it awkwardly to avoid the blood on the hilt. "Clean it up, boys. I'm heading to the Blue Room. Take your time. Make sure it's spotless. I won't be back for a while."

He strolled into the hallway, humming to himself and dragging his soles slightly on the white carpet to clean the blood from his shoes.

Deep down, Roy suspected he might be broken in some fundamental way. He'd started keeping a mental list of the potentially psychopathic things he had done, and that list was getting pretty long. But on the other side there was Dorothea, his golden doodle. The fact that he genuinely cared about her well-being had to count for something, didn't it? Today's incident with Jack would definitely tip the scales, though. He doubted one loved dog could counterbalance his growing list of transgressions.

On the bright side, being oblivious to others' feelings was a wonderfully effective trait for getting what you wanted. Roy was absolutely convinced he'd landed this lucrative role precisely because he was willing to do what it took to get here, doing the things that would make others squeamish or guilty. He was fairly certain that his particular illness was actually a prerequisite for most successful top senior roles in large organizations.

He stopped in front of a blue door, took a deep breath, made sure his jacket was straight, and walked in.

Inside, the Blue Room felt like home to Roy. Bright white walls were accented by the cobalt stripe that gave the room its name, and the long blue conference table stretched under the even fluorescent lighting. This was his favorite room. This was where normal business happened—budgets, acquisitions, personnel decisions. The familiar corporate environment helped Roy slip back into his executive mindset, where everything was just another problem to solve and every decision could be justified through solid strategic planning.

Roy took his seat at the head of the table, pressed a blue button, and waited, still humming softly to himself. Since this morning, Monty Python's "Always Look on the Bright Side of Life" had been stuck in his head.

IT WAS AMUSING to see his team roll in with grim faces. Apparently corporate gossip traveled fast even in the most classified environments. Everyone knew what had just happened in his office, and no one wanted to make eye contact with a man who still had blood under his fingernails. The silence was thick and uncomfortable.

Good, Roy thought. *Smug bastards, all of them.*

"As some of you may have heard," Roy began, "we *assume*

Witness K25 is dead." He let the word *assume* hiss longer than necessary. He scanned the room. "Mary, any progress?"

Mary Drechsler sat at the far end. She didn't look smug. She didn't look anything. You would have sworn she was made out of fucking titanium, hard and cold, Roy thought, not a single emotion on her face or in her tone. What a zealous freak that one was.

"Yes," she said, her voice flat. "We believe we've located the Brotherhood's stronghold. Our source gave us a lead, and we tracked a phone signal. They're on the outskirts of London."

She clicked a remote, and the large monitor mounted on the wall flickered to life. The screen showed a satellite map that zoomed in smoothly on the appropriate suburb of London, finally focusing on a large, stately house surrounded by extensive grounds. The property had a sprawling backyard that extended well beyond what the neighboring homes possessed. Plenty of space for privacy and, Roy noted grimly, plenty of space to hide things from prying eyes.

"Send three squads," Roy said. "I want it discreet this time. I'll be very disappointed if I hear about a nuclear explosion in London." He glared across the table.

A few people looked away. Mary didn't blink. She didn't cower.

"How did you cover the fuck-up at JFK?" Roy asked, turning to her.

Mary glanced at James Webber with the kind of practiced handoff that came from years of working in perfect sync. They had the seamless coordination of two people who lived and breathed their jobs and probably spent more time in conference rooms than their own homes. As far as Roy could tell, neither of them had lives outside of Kildare, which made them extremely boring but invaluable employees.

"Religious terrorism," James said blandly. "We planted a few scriptures around the airport. Left a couple of bandanas in the bathroom."

Roy smirked. *Those two should really date.*

"What are the next steps?" Roy asked, turning back to Mary.

He knew from experience that she would be the only person in the room who had already thought three moves ahead. While everyone else was still processing the information, Mary would have a complete operational plan ready to execute. Her ability to anticipate and prepare while others were still catching up was one of the few things he genuinely respected about her. That, and her fine ass.

"We believe the London location is heavily fortified," said Mary. "We think it contains a live Traveler. The first ever confirmed living Traveler."

Roy scowled. *Living traveler. First ever.*

She stared at Roy. Unblinking.

He waited for her to continue, but she didn't. Her emotionless expression creeped him out more than usual.

"Do whatever you have to, but keep it quiet," he said finally. "The last thing we need is public exposure. The forefather of Kildare never predicted the fucking Internet or social media. Once something's out, it *can't* be contained."

He let that hang in the air. A few of the younger middle management nodded in agreement.

"I'm not sure any of us would be safe if this leaks. Humanity is at stake. You all know that," he added.

Mary's face didn't move, but for a moment, just a flicker, Roy thought he could read her.

Yes, Roy, her eyes seemed to say. *That's true, just like it's true that you're an incompetent and violent fool.*

CHAPTER SEVEN

Sarah observed Valor as he moved through the yard with his staff in hand, his body flowing with an inhuman grace that defied ordinary movement. What started like a martial arts tai chi would suddenly shift into something impossibly fluid—a leap that hung in the air too long, a turn that seemed to ignore gravity, steps that barely touched the ground. His tall, lean frame moved like liquid mercury, each motion seamless and precise in a way that no human body could achieve. Throughout the dance, he swept his staff in deliberate arcing motions, the black rod cutting through the air in perfect curves that seemed to follow some ancient pattern.

Sarah tiptoed slowly toward the yard, trying not to disturb his practice. It was a beautiful dance, and the first time in her life, she had seen real magic. Not the kind stage magicians perform and not the kind from fantasy books, no flying, no lightning. It was like watching a horse run or a cat leap. It was natural, subtle, and elegant.

As Sarah studied Valor, her breath caught in her throat. From childhood, she'd been taught that magic was beautiful, that it would one day return to heal the world and allow humans and other creatures to live together in harmony. For too long, those had been merely stories, lessons from the Brotherhood that felt more like fairytales than prophecy. Now, watching those impossible trails of light dance through the air, something deep in her chest unfurled, a mixture of wonder and delight. Her childhood hopes were literally coming to life before her eyes.

Valor kept dancing. Within the flowing motion, he made arcing gestures with his staff. Each sweep left behind a glowing trail in the air, each a different color fading slowly into the night. The arcs together formed what looked like a shining rainbow of light, though without the familiar order of colors found in nature.

Valor began to move faster, his pace accelerating to an astonishing speed. It was getting close to midnight, and glowing trails now surrounded him.

"Good evening, Sarah," he said without panting and without looking at her. "I will be right with you."

Sarah sat down on the grass, pleasantly surprised to find it dry despite her expectations given the late hour. Even in the darkness, she could sense the expansive nature of the backyard, large, green, and lush from what little she could make out in the dim light spilling from the house windows. The high privacy fence that surrounded the property was barely visible as a darker shadow against the night sky, creating a sense of complete seclusion. It was the perfect place for magical practice without prying eyes, a hidden sanctuary on the outskirts of London where ancient arts could be performed without detection.

Valor swung the staff several more times, completing a final set of swirling rainbows, and then dropped smoothly into a seated position next to her. He considered her with his large eyes. The light from the house behind her illuminated his face while probably casting her own in shadow, not that it would stop him from seeing her clearly, she knew.

"I have a question for you," he said with an almost childlike enthusiasm.

"Yes... my lord?" she replied, smiling, unaccustomed to seeing unabashed joy on anyone's face.

He seems so young, she thought. *In his late teens, if I had to bet.*

"Exactly that!" he exclaimed, pointing at her. "There is hesitation in your voice, just like the others, when you call me 'my lord.' Why is that?" He tilted his head like a puzzled puppy.

"All the people you've met so far come from modern Western cultures. We don't tend to use titles. We usually call people by their first names," she explained, speaking slowly and clearly, like she would have to an intelligent child.

He considered this, as if processing new and curious information. "People do not have titles? Does this signify anything? What is the cultural importance?"

"We consider ourselves equals, so titles are meaningless. Well, mostly meaningless. It's more complicated than that." She wanted to explain more, but he was thinking about it, his eyes now lowered to the grass.

"I like that," he said eventually. "It is a silly but very optimistic way to look at the world." He grinned, as if expecting her to laugh. When she didn't, he continued more softly, "Please call me Valor from now on."

She nodded gently. Though she still couldn't quite believe she was sitting next to a living elf, she felt oddly comfortable. It was like sitting with an old friend, one with whom silence was allowed, even welcome.

After a long pause, Sarah spoke. "Brenda, the Witness, is on her way with Richard. They should be landing early this morning."

She didn't mention the ordeal with the plane. She wasn't sure how to approach such a subject with Valor and decided to leave it out for now.

Valor didn't seem to notice anything was missing. He smiled at her. "I am looking forward to meeting her. I have so much to learn and to teach her!" He sounded eager, as if he had been waiting a very long time.

Unable to remain stoic in the wake of such elvish enthusiasm, she felt the corners of her mouth turn up. "I'm sure she would be glad to learn about you," Sarah murmured, despite knowing the shock Brenda was about to experience.

"Every day, magic is coming back stronger. Two days ago, I couldn't light a candle. Today, I was able to do the *Dancing Lights* spell. Even so, Brenda is critical to our success. I'll need to guide her toward the right path as soon as she gets here."

"Valor, she'll be tired and frightened and confused. Remember, she knows nothing of our mission," Sarah said carefully. "She'll need time. I'll need to talk to her first and make sure she's ready for your meeting... Please try to understand."

His expression shifted from eagerness to something darker. He turned thoughtful then sad. *Sad like an owl,* she thought.

And then she understood, with relief, that he'd made up his mind.

"Very well, Sarah, Guardian of the Staff," the prince said formally. "I will trust you on this one."

"Thank you, Valor." Sarah smiled at the young elf.

They shared another long silence. Then Valor spoke again. "It's not fully back, you know."

"What's that?"

"Magic," he continued. "None of my defensive or offensive spells are working." He looked slightly embarrassed. "I can feel it returning, but for now, I'm completely defenseless."

Sarah gave him a reassuring nod. "Have you wondered why

the glass doors in your room's shower are so thick?" she asked. "Your shower doubles as a panic room. It can stop most calibers of bullets."

He seemed confused. "What are bullets? And... shower? Do you mean the fountain with the lever? And what is a panic room?" He brightened. "I do not tend to panic," he added earnestly.

Sarah was slightly amused. "Sorry. Modern words. Yes, we call that a shower, and a panic room is a secure room that protects the person inside. Bullets are small metal projectiles fired from weapons called guns. Guns and bullets are very common these days. The panic room will protect you from most of them, though very large guns or explosives might be able to break through."

She didn't mention that she had designed the panic room herself. Valor's safety was her responsibility, and the weight of that obligation sat heavily on her shoulders. She hadn't wanted to confront him with the brutal truth of his situation, but it was undeniable. Regardless of his magical capabilities, the elf was woefully unprepared to defend himself against modern threats.

"I am thankful for your worry for my safety, Sarah," he said, taking her hand in his, kindness in his face.

A shiver tripped up her spine, and goosebumps rose on her arms, but she didn't pull away. She felt calm again, despite knowing he was a total stranger and not even a human one. Valor had the strangest relaxing effect on her. There was something about his presence that felt fundamentally safe and familiar in a way that defied logic. She'd spent her entire life being cautious around people, maintaining professional distance even with longtime colleagues, yet somehow, this prince felt like a friend faster than anyone else who had ever come into her life.

A small cynical part of her wondered if this was a defense

mechanism for him. In these circumstances, it would be a useful trait to make people like you and feel safe around you.

Valor peered up at the unusually clear sky. Sarah's gaze followed his. Despite the city lights, a few stars remained visible.

"The future looks brighter than ever. We thought all hope was lost, and now there is hope again," he said.

Is he talking to me or to himself? she thought.

"We have a path forward. We will accomplish our quest soon," he added.

"I hope so," Sarah said truthfully.

But to be honest, she wasn't sure at all.

CHAPTER
EIGHT

Even after she'd calmed down, Brenda couldn't stop the tears from falling.

They'd given her something to settle her nerves. She'd refused at first, but after sobbing non-stop for the first two hours of the flight to London, she'd finally agreed.

I was supposed to be on that flight. I'm supposed to be dead now. The thoughts repeated over and over in a loop.

Not long after taking the pills, a strange numbness began to creep through her body like slow-moving fog. It started in her fingertips and toes then spread inward until even her thoughts felt muffled and distant. Her limbs grew heavy as lead, and she sank deeper into the plush leather seat as if gravity had doubled its pull on her. The sharp edges of her panic began to blur and soften, her racing heartbeat gradually slowing to a steady, drowsy rhythm.

It felt like someone had draped a heavy blanket over her mind and body, wrapping her in artificial calm. The tears still slid down her cheeks, but even her panic felt distant now, happening to someone else. After a while, the tears slowed and then stopped, but she sat motionless, staring blankly at the basket of fruit and cheese on the table in front of her as if she couldn't quite remember what those objects were for.

The big man who had dragged her through the airport took a seat across from her. The controlled professional from the terminal was gone. His silver hair was disheveled now, no longer the neat military style she remembered. His eyes, which had been sharp and alert during their escape, were now red-rimmed and hollow. Deep lines seemed to have carved themselves into his weathered face in just the few hours since she'd first seen him. Whatever had happened since their escape had broken something fundamental in this strong man.

"Brenda, my name is Richard. You spoke with my colleague Sarah on the phone yesterday," he said gently. His eyes followed the fresh rush of tears on her cheeks. "I'm sure you have a lot of questions," he said in an almost sympathetic tone. "I know this is a lot to take in, but I want you to know we have your best interests at heart. We're here to keep you safe."

Brenda sniffed but said nothing, her mind cycling through contradictory thoughts. On the one hand, she had no reason to believe this man. He was a complete stranger who had abducted her from the terminal. On the other hand, he had saved her from certain death. His demeanor had never been cruel or threatening, and something in his gentle tone made her feel like he genuinely didn't want to harm her. Then again, what the hell did she know? The man had literally kidnapped her. Her ability to make good life decisions was clearly questionable at best, considering she'd trusted a phone call from a complete stranger and ended up on this fucking private plane on her way to... to... who knew where.

He leaned forward slightly. "There's a lot I can't tell you yet, I am sorry, but please, ask anything. I'll answer what I can."

"Can I go home, please?" she whispered in a soft, small voice.

"I'm sorry," he said softly. "Not right now." He paused, clearly searching for the right words. "You're in danger. That bomb on the plane... it was meant for you."

Her eyes widened with disbelief.

The bomb was intended for me?

"They probably think you're dead now," he went on. "If you go home, they'll know you survived, and they'll come after you again."

"Who are *they*?" she asked.

"An organization called Kildare," Richard said. "I'm afraid there's not much I can tell you about them right now."

Brenda's throat tightened, and she pressed her hands together to keep them from shaking. "Why would they do that?" she whispered.

"I can't tell you that either," Richard said quietly, "but... your parents weren't as crazy as you thought when they told you you were special."

She shook her head and turned away, closing her eyes and drawing in a trembling breath. She said nothing for a long while.

Her parents. That was a whole category of trauma by itself.

They'd been old when she was born after years of failed treatments. The medical expenses had left them poor, exhausted, and overly protective. Paranoid, really.

They'd wrapped her in layers of rules instead of love. No biking to school. No staying over at friends' houses. No eating out. If she so much as sneezed, she was kept home. They were always watching. Always warning.

You're not like the other kids, they said. *You're special.*

And when she asked how she was special?

You'll find out when you're eighteen.

Yeah, right.

The pressure in their house had been unbearable, crushing all three of them in different ways. It drove her mother to drink a lot. Most nights, Brenda would find empty whiskey bottles hidden behind books or tucked into closets, and her mother's words would grow slurred and mean as the evening wore on.

Her father, quiet and withdrawn, drowned himself in work rather than alcohol, pulling endless shifts as an emergency surgeon and coming home exhausted and distant. Truth be told, young Brenda had grown up in a completely fucked-up household where she'd spent every day trying not to drown herself, watching her parents sink deeper into their own ways of coping while she struggled to keep her head above water.

But giving up wasn't an option for Brenda. While some people choose to become victims of their household trauma or end up becoming younger versions of their broken parents, Brenda had felt something fierce and stubborn rise up inside her, an urge to survive and overcome that grew stronger with every hidden whiskey bottle, every paranoid rule, every night spent listening to her parents' muffled arguments through thin walls. Instead of breaking her spirit, the dysfunction had forged her resolve to carve out a completely different life. She would not drink herself into oblivion like her mother, she would not disappear into work like her father, and she sure as hell wouldn't spend her life afraid of shadows and secrets.

She did not wait for her eighteenth birthday. She left when she was sixteen. Took her passport and the emergency money they kept in the drawer. She didn't just leave the house. She left *Julia*. Her old name. Her mother's name.

Her stomach twisted as a horrible thought struck her, and her eyes snapped open. She studied Richard, eyes sharp now. "The woman... the one who took my jacket. She took my place on the plane?"

"Yes," Richard said. His voice was hoarse and low. "She took your place."

"Why?" she asked, dreading the answer.

"You're... very important," Richard said. "She knew the sacrifice she was making. We were prepared for this as much as anyone can be." He sounded like he was speaking to himself more than to her.

"She was important to you," Brenda said. Her chest tightened, and her world tilted.

"Yes," he said, his voice barely above a whisper. "Very important."

Brenda remembered the way the woman had kissed Richard before running. Not a casual kiss. Not staged. Familiar. Intimate.

Ever since she was a kid, Brenda had possessed an uncanny ability to connect dots that others missed. She always knew how mystery novels would end by the third chapter and could predict which couples in her social circle were headed for breakups long before anyone else saw the signs.

There was a tiny voice in her head that whispered these intuitions to her, and over the years she'd learned to trust that quiet certainty. It was the same voice that had told her to leave home at sixteen, the same instinct that had guided her through countless small decisions. And right now, that voice was telling her something she didn't want to believe about the woman who had taken her place.

The nausea rose in her throat. The pills were pulling her under now. The world grew syrupy, thick and slow. Like swimming through honey. Or maybe mud.

"I like honey better than mud," she muttered to herself, or thought she did.

Richard gave her a puzzled look.

"I'm sorry your wife is dead," she added. "I'm so, so sorry your wife is dead, Richard."

He froze. "How did you know she was my wife?" he asked, his voice cracking.

"Bla da ga va za," she slurred.

Then, her eyes slid closed, and darkness surrounded her. Through the fog of medicated sleep, she felt the plane jolt and heard the distant thud of landing gear touching down, followed by the bright intrusion of overhead lights being switched on. Muffled voices drifted around her like sounds heard underwater, speaking in hushed, urgent tones she couldn't quite decipher.

Gentle hands lifted her from the airplane seat and placed her on something firmer. A stretcher? Maybe. Then, she was moving again, the sensation of being carried blending with the rumble of a car engine and the soft vibration of travel. Lastly, careful hands settled her into what felt like the softest bed she'd ever known, and her mind finally let her sink deeper into sleep.

When she opened her eyes again, she was sitting upright in bed in a fancy-looking white room.

She vaguely remembered leaving the plane. Didn't remember arriving here. She scanned her surroundings, blinking.

What the hell is going on?

CHAPTER NINE

Sarah sat in the small, dimly lit control room, surrounded by multiple screens that cast an eerie glow across her face. The monitors displayed black-and-white feeds from cameras throughout the house and yard, hallways, entrances, and the garden where Valor had practiced his magic.

Her fingers rested on a keyboard that gave her complete control over the cameras, microphones, and what appeared on each monitor. The screens closest to her were dedicated to different angles of Brenda's room, creating an uncomfortably intimate surveillance setup. The room felt like one of those security rooms in banks, where screens automatically switched from one angle to another in rotating cycles, except here she was watching Brenda as she processed what had happened instead of monitoring for thieves.

Richard stood behind Sarah, his eyes still red and puffy.

"She doesn't know a thing," Sarah said quietly. "It's unbelievable, boss."

"Don't call me *boss*, Sarah. You know it pisses me off." Richard's voice cut sharp.

Sarah cringed. She knew he hated that title. He always said being the oldest didn't make him the authority. "We're all in this together," he used to tell her in his fatherly voice.

But she didn't apologize. That would only make him more irritated.

Her heart went out to him. He'd brought the Witness back, but he'd lost his wife. Sarah had tried to comfort him and had told him how sorry she was, but he hadn't wanted to talk. "It is what it is," he'd kept saying. "Let's continue with the mission."

Sarah scrutinized him now, taking in the way grief had transformed him in just a matter of hours. Age had sneaked up on Richard overnight. His eyes seemed broken and hollow, and the lines on his face had deepened into permanent creases of sorrow. She had known Richard and his family her entire life, long before she'd taken any official role in the Brotherhood, but for the first time, he reminded her of his elderly father in those final months before he died. The strong, military bearing that had always defined him had crumbled, leaving behind a man who looked far older than his years. He was still staring at Brenda on the screen, saying nothing, as if watching her could somehow fill the void his wife's sacrifice had left behind.

"Brenda isn't stupid. She'll figure her role out," he said at last, "but her parents didn't prepare her for this at all. She's not even aware of the concept of the Reappearance. I'm not worried about her intelligence. I worry about her emotional maturity."

"Well, it's going to be a crash course for both of them," Sarah said. "Valor seems kind of young, right? I wouldn't put him at more than eighteen." She frowned. "This all feels so different from how I imagined it."

"You're not the only one. All the previous ones who came through looked much older. The last one had to be at least twenty-five," Richard said grimly. "Maybe they ran out of adult royalty members and had to start using teens. Maybe they figured out young elves are more resilient and can survive the Travel. You must remember, Sarah, that elves age differently than us. Valor could be a hundred for all we know."

"It's so strange seeing one alive," Sarah said softly. "At first, he seems almost human... until you notice the small things. He's more... wild. Like petting a cat only to realize it's a lion."

Sarah couldn't put her finger on exactly what made it so obvious he wasn't human, but there was an intensity about Valor that seemed to vibrate just beneath his skin. Was it those catlike eyes that seemed to see straight through to her soul? His voice that somehow resonated in her chest when he spoke? Or maybe it was his strange combination of ancient wisdom and childlike trust, like a friend's Lab that immediately accepts you as family after the first gentle touch. Valor also had a royal, commanding confidence that could not be ignored. There was something both comforting and unsettling about how easily he offered his trust, as if he operated by completely different rules than any human she'd ever known.

"More like petting a horse and finding out it's a unicorn," Richard replied.

She gave a dry smile. "Be careful what you wish for, Richard."

They sat in silence, watching Brenda on the screen. She was standing by the window, looking out toward the gardens.

Sarah found herself running her fingers through her hair, a habit she'd had since childhood when she was nervous. They both knew these were the most important days of their lives. Bringing magical creatures back from extinction was the Brotherhood's ultimate mission, a goal its members had been preparing for for generations. Now, it was finally happening in their lifetime, yet the strangest part was how normal the control room looked while hosting the impossible.

Sarah kept expecting Mission Impossible-style dramatic

music to play, something to mark that they were living through the most important moment in Brotherhood history. Instead, it was just her and Richard watching grainy black-and-white monitors while an elf prince walked around upstairs and Brenda examined her new surroundings.

Generations of preparation have led to this utterly ordinary morning.

“Any news from headquarters?” Richard asked.

“Our guy says they killed the one responsible for the failed assassination attempt on Brenda,” Sarah said.

“Does that mean they know she’s alive?” Richard asked, tension creeping into his voice.

“Our source says no. They’re not sure. They were upset they couldn’t confirm it was her.”

“Damn right they couldn’t,” Richard muttered through clenched teeth. “I still can’t believe they killed someone from their own organization over that. I guess these are desperate times.”

Just like the Brotherhood, Kildare was an ancient and secretive organization but one tasked with preventing the Reappearance of magic. God knows why. Over the years, it had proven extremely difficult for the Brotherhood to penetrate the Kildare organization, the intelligence gathered sparse and inconsistent at best. After many failures and suspected leaks, the Brotherhood's intelligence team protected their few assets carefully and shared information strictly on a need-to-know basis. Even Sarah and Richard only received fragments of what their source was actually reporting. What they did know painted a picture of an organization just as dedicated to stopping magic as the Brotherhood was to restoring it. Sarah wondered, as she had many times, why on earth would they want to do away with magic?

Sarah's attention snapped back to Richard when he cleared his throat.

"Right," she said, looking back to the screen to avoid meeting his eyes. "Our source thinks we have two days before we need to move."

Richard's expression turned deeply concerned. "That's not much time. We can't move *him* yet, not without sedating him first. We need more time."

They had developed a careful two-week acclimatization protocol for exactly this situation, gradually introducing Valor to the modern world, teaching him about technology, briefing him on current science, geopolitical developments, and many other topics. More importantly, they needed time to learn from him what the next steps for the Reappearance actually were and then help him execute his quest to achieve these.

"We might not have that luxury," Sarah replied. She kept her voice calm. Richard had been on edge for days now, and showing her own nerves wouldn't help. "We'll have to work with what we have, Richard."

He didn't answer.

She hesitated before she added, "The sooner we introduce Valor to her, the better."

On screen, Brenda had begun going through the drawer of clothing they had prearranged for her in the room. She started to change her clothes.

Richard turned his gaze away. "I'll let Valor know she's ready for their first meeting."

"Just remember, he knows her as the Witness. Or Julia." Sarah didn't look away. Brenda was beautiful. It was hard not to watch. "I'll go and pick her up in five minutes," she added.

"Got it," Richard said and left the room.

Sarah continued watching the screen. Brenda was now fully

dressed, picking a few personal items and putting them in her pockets, and then glancing at the mirror straight at the camera.

Brenda was undeniably attractive and exactly Sarah's type. In a different life, Sarah might have approached her at a bar and struck up a conversation over drinks.

She shook that thought from her mind immediately. This was definitely not the time or the place for such distractions. Maybe when all of this was over, there might be space for normal human connections again, but not now.

Not today.

Sarah's finger slid slowly across the screen until it touched Brenda's image. "You don't know what's waiting for you, do you?" she whispered. "You have no idea... but you're about to find out. Fast."

She stood up and left the control room. It was time for the next step.

Time to meet the Witness and introduce her to her future.

CHAPTER TEN

The knock on the door didn't startle Brenda. She'd been expecting someone eventually. A woman stepped inside, compact and professional-looking with short auburn hair.

Brenda met her gaze directly despite the lingering effects of whatever they'd drugged her with. She'd woken up determined to get answers rather than wallow in self-pity. Yes, she'd been kidnapped and drugged, but she'd survived worse than pushy strangers with questionable methods. She looked at the woman with frank assessment, ready to deal with whatever came next.

"Who are you?" Brenda asked, her voice serious, cutting straight to the point.

"I'm Sarah. We spoke over the phone," Sarah said, her voice gentler than Brenda expected.

"Where are we?" Brenda asked.

"We're in London, near Richmond Park if you're familiar with the area," Sarah replied matter-of-factly. She opened her mouth as if to continue, but Brenda interrupted.

"There's no job offer, is there? Tell me why I'm here... please." Brenda was pleased her voice sounded calm.

"Not exactly the job we discussed," Sarah said. "There *is* a job offer, but it's not in research. It's in teaching, and it's quite... unique." Sarah paused, as if letting Brenda absorb that. Then, she walked across the room to the small dining table against the wall. "Please, take a seat. This will take a while to explain."

The room around them spoke of quiet luxury that was a stark contrast to Brenda's cramped New York apartment—cream-colored walls, polished hardwood floors, and furniture that looked elegant, if understated. Tall windows let in soft London daylight, flooding the space with natural light she rarely saw through her small, cracked window back home. The space felt more like an upscale hotel suite than a holding cell. A small dining table with a bottle of wine and two glasses sat against one wall, two chairs next to it.

"We've all had a long week. I'll answer any questions I can. I'm sure you have many." Sarah's tone seemed deliberately even, almost soothing. "Shall we start with some context as to why you're here?" she asked, pouring wine into both glasses, nodding toward the glass, as if pausing for Brenda to make the next move.

Brenda hesitated, weighing her options. The wine, despite the early hour, looked tempting, and honestly, after the last twenty-four hours, she could use it. She studied Sarah as she made her decision. The woman looked like the kind of person who got things done, the no-bullshit type Brenda had always aspired to be. She was older than Brenda but not by much, and her clothes were all black in a way that looked good but suggested function over fashion—tactical pants, fitted top, and practical boots. She resembled one of those special ops characters from movies, except this was real life.

Slowly, Brenda crossed the room and sat down, accepting

that playing along might get her more information. She took a sip of the wine and examined Sarah without speaking, waiting for her to start.

“That’s better,” Sarah said. “Let’s start from the beginning. I work for an organization called BRHD. It’s a very old company, with deep roots in science, defense, agriculture, and other fields. It has many branches, one of which is secret. The mission of the entire company is to fund and protect that secret branch.”

She paused, meeting Brenda’s gaze.

“This has been going on for over six hundred years. Most of our ten thousand employees don’t even know that branch exists. Its name is the Brotherhood Reception Committee.” She held Brenda’s eyes. “My family helped found BRHD in the 15th century... alongside *your* family.”

Brenda didn’t say anything, but she set down her glass. Despite her shock, she almost laughed out loud. Her parents were a part of some ancient, secret organization? The idea was so absurd it was almost funny.

"You've got the wrong family," she said flatly. "Trust me, my parents couldn't organize a birthday party, let alone participate in some secret society. They are way too dysfunctional for that level of responsibility."

“You were meant to work here, too. It’s a family business, if you understand what I’m saying,” Sarah countered. “Your entire family line has worked with BRHD for generations.”

“But I didn’t,” Brenda said slowly. “Neither did my parents.”

“I don’t know why they left the fold. It’s not as though we didn’t *try* to convince them to stay,” Sarah said with a hint of irritation.

Brenda wasn't surprised at all that her parents had left "the fold," whatever that meant. She would have been more shocked if they'd managed to stay in any kind of organized group for longer than five minutes. Her parents couldn't even maintain a supermarket membership without forgetting to renew it or losing the card. The idea of them successfully participating in some ancient secret society was laughable. Of course they'd left, probably in dramatic fashion, burning bridges and making enemies along the way.

"Honestly, it's not a shocker," Brenda said. She did not want to dwell on her fucked-up family, so she moved on. "But what does it have to do with me? What is this 'secret branch'? Is it connected to why I'm here?"

"Getting straight to the point. I like that," Sarah said, giving her a small nod of approval. "Yes, it's exactly why you're here. We're executing the mission of the Brotherhood Reception Committee. In fact, that's the entire purpose of the BRHD," Sarah said while running her hand over her hair. She paused, taking a breath.

They sat for a moment in silence, each waiting for the other to speak.

Brenda broke first. "Which is?"

Sarah studied her, as if weighing whether she was ready for the truth. Then, she sighed. "You studied anthropology, right?"

Brenda blinked. "Yes... what does that have to do with anything?"

"Did you study myths? Greek, medieval German, Nordic, English myths?"

"A little. Why? What do myths have to do with this?"

"What if I told you some of those myths weren't myths at all but distant memories of a real world long forgotten?" Sarah smiled faintly at the look of disbelief on Brenda's face. "Feels like I'm offering you the red pill, right? Shall I continue?"

Brenda nodded slowly.

"Well," Sarah said. "Many of the myths from the 1500s and 1600s are true. Twisted over time, yes, added to, embellished, but the core of them is real." She leaned in slightly. "Six hundred years ago, the world was very different. Humans lived alongside magical creatures. Elves, fairies, dwarfs... magical creatures that vanished from this world and were forgotten apart from in children's stories and folk tales."

Brenda observed Sarah take a sip and swirl the red wine in the glass, the rich burgundy liquid creating small whirlpools. She seemed to be letting her words hang in the air between them, waiting for them to sink in.

"The secret role of BRHD, through its secret branch, the Brotherhood Reception Committee, is to welcome those magical creatures back when they return. To protect them. To help them survive in the modern world."

They both sat in silence for a long while, but this was not a friendly intimate silence. It was an awkward, tense one.

"You mean... Dwarfs? Elves? Unicorns? Are they all real?" Brenda finally asked. This lady was surely fucking with her.

"Yes," Sarah said simply, "and we have the first one in the next room."

"A unicorn?" Brenda asked, half-smiling in spite of herself.

"No. An elf," Sarah said, her voice serious. "Your job is to educate this elf about the modern world and slowly reintroduce him to human society."

Brenda stared. "You've got to be shitting me."

"I shit you not," Sarah said, matching her tone. "We have archaeological evidence of fairies, unicorns, dwarfs, elves, evidence dating thousands of years, all the way to six hundred years ago. Most of it has been dismissed by the scientific community as hoaxes or fakes, but it's real. The BRHD kept scientific evidence that humans lived in a mixed society alongside these magical creatures for centuries."

"And there's an elf... in the next room," Brenda said, still disbelieving.

"Yes, In fact, it's high time you met him. I'm sure you have a lot of questions and doubts, but we'll have plenty of time to answer them all. Don't worry." Sarah glanced sympathetically at Brenda who gave her a skeptical side look. "Shall we counter your first assumption, which is that I am completely insane, and go meet the elf?" she asked.

"Yes, that would be a good start. Let's do that," said Brenda. Her palms were sweaty. Everything was so surreal. It felt like she took the red pill without knowing she did. She brushed her hands nervously on her pants.

"I hope the clothes we arranged for you fit you well?" Sarah asked, evaluating Brenda from top to bottom.

Brenda glanced down, remembering the cabinet full of clothes that surprisingly fit her perfectly. "Yes. They fit really well," she said, smoothing her hands over the fabric of her new hiking pants. "Thank you, I guess."

"No worries at all." Sarah was cheerful again as she rose to her feet. "Let's go introduce you to your first elf."

Those were words Brenda had never thought she would hear in her life.

CHAPTER ELEVEN

Following Sarah out of the room, Brenda asked herself: *Why am I going along with this?*

Why wasn't she just telling this lady to fuck off and leave to go home or go to the police? Why would she want anything to do with an elf, as if such a thing actually existed?

But for a reason she couldn't explain, she was compelled to discover if the ridiculous story was true. Like some invisible pull was guiding her, she felt like she *had* to follow Sarah. Like it or not, she'd already taken the red pill, and the rabbit hole had already opened. She had to see it through.

And so she did.

They entered what looked like a premium guest quarters, though something about it felt carefully orchestrated rather than naturally luxurious. A wide bed was positioned against one wall. The small dining area nearby looked more decorative than functional. French doors opened to a patio and the expansive green grounds beyond, flooding the space with natural light through several large windows.

To the left, Brenda noticed a shower area behind a sleek

glass wall. On the opposite side, a compact kitchenette was tucked efficiently into the corner. Unlike a hotel, there was nothing electronic in the room—no lamps, no microwave, no mini bar, no oven, not even a coffee maker. Just basic cabinets and a sink.

In the center of the room stood a tall figure, facing her direction. To Brenda, he looked like an athletic college undergrad. He wore tan fitted trousers and a dark green tunic.

"You must be Jul—Brenda," he corrected himself mid-sentence. She noticed he spoke with a very light accent Brenda couldn't place.

He bowed slightly from the waist. His face was long, his hair pulled back into a ponytail. His ears were unmistakably pointed, but his eyes were the real kicker. They were genuinely catlike, not the fake contacts she'd seen at Halloween parties, but actual feline eyes with vertical pupils that dilated and contracted as he looked at her. The irises were a deep blue-green that seemed to shift in the light, and there was an intelligence behind them that felt both ancient and startlingly young. This wasn't a costume or clever makeup. This was something entirely other than human.

Fuck me, he's an elf, Brenda thought. *Or this is some kind of elaborate joke.*

She frowned, her natural skepticism flaring, but something inside her whispered that her eyes weren't lying.

He extended a hand with a polite, graceful tilt of his head. "I am Valor. It is a great honor to meet you."

She froze. *Okay. Deep breath. This is happening. How do you greet an elf? Do you shake hands? Bow? Offer a leaf? God, what even counts as respectful here?*

Going with the only thing that felt vaguely diplomatic, she gave a stiff, awkward bow. "Nice to meet you, Valor," she said, cringing inwardly.

He took her hand gently. "I trust your journey was safe?" he asked. "You arrived so quickly, especially considering you cannot cast travel spells. Are boats quite swift these days?"

Brenda shot a glance at Sarah. *He doesn't know?* her eyes asked.

Sarah returned the look and slightly shook her head. *No. Don't bring it up.*

Brenda turned back to Valor, who still held her hand. "I had a safe journey, Valor. Thank you for asking," she said carefully, "and yes, there are many fast ways to travel these days."

He nodded, clearly pleased with her answer, and he squeezed her hand. His dark, catlike eyes were both strange and fascinating.

She had stumbled over her earlier words slightly, tumbling through the new reality she now struggled to grasp. Maybe this might all be real.

"That is wonderful! I am so eager to learn about it. Will you teach me?" He still held her hand, his eyes bright with curiosity.

A loud crash sounded from somewhere in the far corner of the house.

Sarah quickly excused herself and exited through a door hidden by the paneling, leaving them alone in the large bedroom.

Brenda felt instantly awkward, nearly embarrassed by the intensity in Valor's gaze. She wasn't ready to be alone with Valor, not yet, and he was still holding her hand, still waiting for her answer. His eyes moved over her face, taking her in. His enthusiasm was infectious. Still...

"I don't know about a long-term teaching job," she said hesitantly, lightly tugging on her hand, encouraging him to release her—without success. She glanced at their clasped fingers. "But I'll answer your questions as long as you promise to answer mine. Up until five minutes ago, I would've laughed at the idea of real elves. I thought you were mythical creatures."

"Laughter is very good for your being," Valor said earnestly, as if giving medical advice. "You should laugh about everything, mythical or not. And yes, I will answer all your questions. I have so many things to teach you as well."

"Where are you from, Valor?" Brenda asked. *Where on earth did they find you?* She thought about her study of hidden tribes in the Amazon.

"The question is not 'where.' The question is 'when,'" he said with a smile.

That was an annoying answer, but before she could say anything, the door slammed open. Sarah burst in, blood dripping from her left arm. In her right hand, she clutched a handgun. Her tight grip steadied the barrel even though there was fear in her eyes.

Brenda gasped.

"To the panic room!" Sarah yelled, shoving both Valor and Brenda toward the bathroom and bundling them into the shower.

"What's happened?" asked Valor, confused.

"Press the red button!" Sarah shouted, pointing toward the wall above the water faucets. There was a button marked with a red "P."

Brenda obeyed without hesitation.

The shower door slammed shut. Metal bars shot out from the walls, locking into the thick glass. Through the bars, Brenda saw the faraway door open, and a small object rolled next to Sarah. There was a blinding flash of white light and a deafening bang. Brenda lost her balance, her ears ringing, the world spinning.

Just outside the panic room, on the other side of the glass, Sarah staggered to her feet, one hand pressed to her ear, blood trickling from her nose. She mouthed something, and her face twisted in frustration.

Brenda screamed for Sarah to get inside the safebox, but Sarah darted away from the panic room.

Through the dwindling smoke, figures emerged. Before Sarah could react, one of them stopped, raised a gun, and shot Sarah in the head.

Sarah was thrown backward and collapsed instantly, crashing against the translucent glass doors of the safebox. Her body slid down, smearing blood all over the separation between them. Her body came to rest with her face pressed grotesquely against the glass, like a child peering through a toy store window.

Sarah's eyes were wide open, flat and lifeless, staring into some distant abyss beyond Brenda. The same eyes that had been sharp and calculating just minutes ago were now empty, reflecting nothing.

Brenda's stomach lurched violently, bile rising in her throat. This wasn't an action movie. This wasn't something she could pause or look away from. Sarah was dead, really dead, her blood pooling on the floor.

Brenda's hands began to shake uncontrollably as her body finally caught up with what her mind was struggling to process. Time slowed to a crawl, and Brenda's thoughts turned foggy.

I'm in shock, she told herself, still staring at Sarah's lifeless body.

Valor's hands moved to her shoulders, and he forced her to turn away from the image of death already seared in her mind. Gently, he took her chin and lifted her gaze to meet his. His face was calm, his strange eyes serious.

The world spun, and her knees threatened to give way.

"Brenda, Sarah is dead, and we will be, too, if we do not act quickly." His voice remained steady, almost detached, like he was explaining a math problem. "I cannot fight them, and they *will* get through this... panic room eventually."

She understood his words, but they made no sense. What the hell was happening?

"I COULD POSSIBLY TAKE us away from here to another location known to me... but there is no other location known to me in this world."

Bullets slammed into the glass, pinging and cracking it slightly with each impact.

"But *you* can help," Valor said urgently. "If you can think of a place—somewhere far from here, somewhere you remember well—I may be able to take us there. A childhood place. Somewhere you felt safe. The stronger the memory, the better."

She didn't answer.

"Brenda?" Valor pressed.

"I... I can't think of anywhere right now," Brenda stammered. Panic flooded her. She glanced over her shoulder, and her eyes locked on Sarah's shattered skull. She couldn't look away.

"Brenda." Valor's voice rang, not from his mouth but from inside her mind. *"I am not asking. You need to do this, or we will die."*

A woman dressed in a military uniform with red hair and a fresh cut on her cheek stepped into view. She smiled coldly then carefully attached a small device to the wall of the panic room. She flipped a switch.

The countdown began. *Seven.*

The redhead woman turned and ran, glancing back once.

Brenda stared at the ticking digits. Every second dragged.

Six.

"Brenda." Valor's voice echoed in her head again, calm and

resolute as he stepped into her field of vision, almost blocking Sarah from her view. *"The future of all things depends on you now."*

Talk about putting on the pressure on the first date, a tiny voice in her mind said.

"You should laugh about everything, mythical or not..." he had told her earlier.

She took a breath, finally looked away from Sarah's lifeless body, and locked eyes with Valor.

"A safe place from my childhood," she said softly.

Three.

The countdown ticked, slow and thunderous.

Two.

It's too late, she thought. *Just when things start to get interesting, they kill me.*

She focused on the one place she remembered feeling safe. Time slowed to nothing.

She saw the light.

She felt the heat.

Then, everything turned dark.

And very cold.

CHAPTER TWELVE

"You did well... You did *really* well." Valor's voice echoed in Brenda's mind.

The experience had been jarring but strangely mundane at the same time. It felt like her mind had simply dissolved in one place and reformed somewhere else entirely. No sensation of movement, no transition, just off and then on again.

It reminded Brenda of when she'd been put under anesthesia for her wisdom tooth surgery years ago. One moment, she had been counting backward from ten. The next, she had woken up with no memory of the time in between. Except now, instead of a dental chair, she'd awakened standing in a completely different place.

As her vision cleared, the shapes around her came into focus. They were standing in a small clearing near the top of a hill, surrounded by trees whose dark silhouettes stretched up into the star-filled sky. The clean scent of pine needles filled her lungs, comforting yet so different from the exhaust and concrete of New York. The air was chilly but not uncomfortably cold, with a fresh, dry quality. Everything around them was thick and quiet, as if the world had gone still for a moment, waiting. There was something familiar about this place that tugged at the edges of her memory, something she couldn't quite put her finger on, like a word balanced on the tip of her tongue.

Down below, a wide valley stretched out, scattered with lights. Some flickered from houses. Others glowed steadily from tall buildings. Roads cut through the dark, and the faint orange haze of a city hovered beyond at the edge of the horizon.

The elf waited next to her, gazing out at the view. It was a dark, moonless night, and she could only make out his silhouette against the distant glow of the valley below.

"Are you well, Jul—Brenda?" Valor asked.

The fog in her mind refused to clear as quickly as her vision. "Probably," she mumbled, still dazed. "But where are we?"

"I have no idea, but it's wonderful! This is the longest distance I've ever Teleported. I could feel it. I have never traveled this far in my life," he mused. "And it's a forest! You couldn't have found a better place." Joy vibrated in his voice, elation tinged with sadness. "It hurt to be away from the trees for so long."

"I remember this place..." she said slowly. "We're in California. My parents once took me camping here. You told me to think of a place from my childhood where I felt safe. I have no idea why I picked... or even remembered this place."

He turned toward her, and though she couldn't make out his expression in the shadows, she knew he had to be beaming. "All young animals, including humans, have a unique awareness of what is safe and what is not," he said. "You didn't pick this place. Your inner child did. That's why I asked you to think of somewhere you felt safe as a child."

Brenda's thoughts sharpened. "Holy shit. You teleported us here! What happened? Who *are* you? What the fuck is going on?" The realization was crashing in now. This was a rabbit hole she wasn't sure she was ready for.

"Do not worry," Valor said soothingly. "All your questions will be answered in time, but for now, we need to make a shelter." A gentle blue light outlined his silhouette, and he smiled.

Suddenly, the word "Charm" appeared in her vision like text on an augmented reality screen, floating half-transparent between them. Her panic started to drain away. Oddly, she didn't care about the answers anymore.

Intuitively, she realized what he was doing—using magic to force her into a calmer state. She'd always despised when people told her to "just relax" or "calm down," but having someone magically manipulate her emotions was worse.

"Do *not* fucking Charm me!" she snapped with a strength she didn't know she had.

His eyes widened. "You can detect magic... and quite accurately... Of course. I'm sorry. I won't do it again. Please, ask your questions," he offered.

Men's faces always look the same when they are trying to apologize.

She let it go.

"Why are we staying here tonight? Shouldn't we call the police or something? Tell them what happened? Sarah's dead, and we have to tell someone." Calmer now, she still had trouble believing what had happened in the last hours.

He considered her, his pleased expression fading into a grimace. "I think we may have a traitor in the Brotherhood. I don't know who this 'police' is, but I don't think we can trust anyone outside ourselves anymore. The Brotherhood has served its purpose. From now on, we must continue the quest alone."

"And do what, exactly, Valor? I have no fucking idea what it is you're trying to do. What is this quest? Who volunteered me, and why?"

She studied him. He reminded her of the little, lost puppy she'd fed outside of her shitty apartment building once.

"I need to bring my family and the rest of the elvish people here. If I don't, they'll all die," he said in a soft voice

"How is that my problem?" she demanded.

He took a deep breath. "You, Brenda, have a unique ability to help me. It's something passed down through the women in your bloodline. You are... special," he said.

She wanted to scream. She *hated* that word.

She wanted to tell him to fuck off, that she wasn't special, and that he sounded just like her crazy parents. The Pulp Fiction scene with Samuel L. Jackson snapped into her mind. *Say special one more time, I dare you!* she thought.

But deep down, she knew he was right. She *did* feel a connection to Valor, a bond that didn't make any sense. It wasn't a crush or infatuation like she'd known before. It felt more like the kind of love she had long imagined between siblings. Valor infuriated her and delighted her at the same time, and her soul... Well, it deeply *yearned* to help him.

The images of Sarah's death still haunted Brenda's mind, but she had to admit that going to the police was completely out of the question. Trying to explain to a California police officer that they'd just witnessed a murder in London would be a fast track to a padded room.

"Officer, an elf magically teleported me here after I watched armed soldiers kill my kidnapper." Yeah, that would go over well. Up until an hour ago, she wouldn't have believed the story herself, and honestly, she still wasn't entirely convinced she wasn't having some kind of elaborate psychotic break rather than experiencing actual reality.

She let out a hard breath, the weight of the day pressing down hard. Her shoulders sagged. "Okay, Valor. No more questions tonight. We'll talk more tomorrow."

Valor gave a small nod, and his gaze returned to the lights below. "There are so many lights... Why do they need so many campfires?" he asked, sounding genuinely concerned. "Are they expecting an attack?"

"What?" She frowned as she worked out what he meant. "Oh. Those aren't campfires. That's a city, a big village where lots of people live," she explained. "We have other ways to light our homes now. Most of them don't involve fire."

"I've heard of cities but never seen one," he said. "It seems so large. How many people live there?"

"Around half a million," she guessed. Taking out her phone to check felt wrong just then.

"So many people... So this is what it came to," he murmured, mostly to himself, his voice laced with sadness.

She didn't know what he meant by that, and she didn't ask.

A sudden gust of wind made her shiver.

"You must be cold," he said, noticing her discomfort. "Let's go into the woods, and I'll make shelter."

He took her hand and led the way. She followed without complaint, feeling oddly safe with him, trusting him to guide her through the dark. Every podcast, every true crime show she'd binged in the last five years should have been enough to make her run the other way, but she knew Valor wouldn't do anything to hurt her. How she knew that... Well, it had to have something to do with her connection to him.

They walked on until Valor found a flat patch of ground he seemed happy with. He released her hand and pulled a small object from his pocket. It glowed faintly. He whispered something, and the glow brightened just enough to light his face, his hands, and the clearing. The object was a sphere the size of a large marble, attached to a black box no bigger than a matchbox.

He whispered again, and the black box expanded into a staff

in his hand in a liquidlike movement. The marble had grown to the size of Valor's fist.

Brenda's eyes widened. The light came from a glowing green liquid inside the orb.

Then, without warning, he began to dance, circling the clearing in front of her.

It was one of the most beautiful things Brenda had ever witnessed. His movements were precise and fluid, like water cascading from a fountain. The glowing globe at the end of the staff flowed with him, and sweeping arcs of light painted the air like long-exposure photographs. Threads of soft green light stretched from tree to tree as if he were building a home out of the missing moonlight and his life force.

The air around them grew warmer. In moments, a glowing tent pole-like structure surrounded them. Valor kept dancing swiftly, decisively, elegantly, drawing two nestlike bed frames and a partition wall inside. In less than five minutes, it was done.

He planted the staff with a final graceful motion and stood still, swaying. He scanned the structure, his expression focused, an artist judging his work. He raised his staff again and hit the ground in front of him with it, whispering something she couldn't catch.

Nothing happened.

He frowned. Then, gritting his teeth, he raised the staff again and said aloud, "Vennori."

For a moment, still nothing changed, but then, there was movement.

Brenda gasped as the plants around them began to stir with an almost audible rustling. Grass wove itself into beds, forming soft pallets on the frames. Trees and shrubs leaned in to form the walls. The shell he had sketched with light was filled in with living nature. The air smelled of fresh earth being turned.

They stepped out through a curtain of vines, flowers blooming around the tent's edges. The inner glow had dimmed to nothing.

"And *that* is how you build a palace in the woods," said Valor softly. "'Build with nature and heart in mind, and you'll always have a home,' so the saying goes."

Brenda had no idea where his saying had come from, but exhaustion clouded her mind again, and she let it go.

"We can sleep safely here tonight. Bugs and animals will respect our space, and the wards will make any intruder want to walk away," he said confidently. "Take the left bed. It's an elvish design. Four hours will feel like a full night."

She climbed into the bed and settled into the lush vegetation. "Where are you going?" she asked, nearly asleep already.

"I'm going to walk for a while. Then I'll come back. I've been away from the forest for too long," he said. He smiled at her, and she felt safe.

"Night," she murmured.

"Good night, Brenda."

CHAPTER THIRTEEN

"Damn it! Damn it! Damn it!" Mary's voice echoed through the destroyed room as she ripped off her tactical gloves and hurled them to the floor with vicious force.

Her rage demanded a target, and she drove her bare fist into the nearest wall, leaving a bloody smear across the lavish wallpaper. The pain felt good, deserved even.

She took a deep breath, forcing her fury back under control, then retrieved her gloves and smoothed her red hair back into its regulation position.

The bloody elf and the Witness had vanished into thin air. She'd managed to clear the room just before the charge she'd placed on the panic room wall detonated, shattering the bulletproof glass in a thunderous explosion. The blast should have killed anything still alive. There was nowhere to hide, nowhere to run.

By the time she had strode back inside, the luxurious room had been transformed into a war zone. All the windows had been shattered, leaving jagged glass teeth hanging from twisted frames and glittering fragments scattered across the hardwood floors like confetti. The panic room wall was a gaping hole surrounded by chunks of concrete and twisted metal. The woman's mutilated body lay crumpled where she'd fallen, covered in glass shards and surrounded by a dark pool of blood that had spread across the expensive flooring. The strange, sharp scent of pine still lingered in the air, completely out of place in the destroyed room. There wasn't a single trace of the elf or the Witness.

"Graaa!" she snarled.

A heavily built soldier ran in, dressed in black-ops gear with his vest pockets full of ammo for his M4 automatic weapon. Three grenades hung from his belt. His black mask had been removed, revealing a rugged face and a comms headset tucked in one ear.

"Perimeter's clear, Commander. Five dead on their side," he said crisply, pointing to the woman's body. "That bitch took out Andy when he breached the first-floor corridor. She clipped Brad in the leg, too, but he'll walk. Other than that, we're good."

"And yet we failed," Mary spat.

I'd have traded all of you for a clean shot at the elf, she thought.

"The police will be here in twelve minutes. No bodies left behind. Not even that bitch," she ordered, her voice filled with contempt. "Bleach everything. I'll be in the study for the next nine minutes. No one comes in. No matter what."

The soldier nodded and started barking orders into his comms.

Mary entered the study and shut the door behind her with deliberate finality. She dropped to the floor and opened her backpack with urgent but practiced movements. From a protective red velvet pouch, she carefully extracted a small ceramic bowl, handling it with the reverence of a sacred object. A surgical knife came from a black leather kit, its blade catching the light as she withdrew it with precise, graceful motions. Despite her haste, every movement carried the ritualistic elegance of a Japanese tea ceremony, each gesture deliberate, respectful, and performed exactly as she'd been taught. She placed both items on the ground in front of her with careful symmetry.

Roy is going to lose his shit, she thought. He'd scream and maybe kill someone, but he wouldn't lay a finger on her. He knew better.

She was *made.*

She was a member of Bellum Sacrum.

Roy was just a hired gun, a mercenary the Kildare Corporation paid to run things. Operational heads were expendable. They could be fired or just set on fire. Roy could drop dead tomorrow, and James Webber, that dried-up old prune, would take over before Roy's blood cooled. No one would care.

But not Bellum Sacrum members. They were sacred. Almost irreplaceable.

She pulled out a stopwatch, set it for five minutes, and started the countdown. After placing the timer on the floor to her right, she picked up the knife and, without hesitation, drew it across the palm of her left hand. The surgical blade was so sharp it sliced through her skin like butter, parting flesh with almost no resistance. She didn't flinch, didn't even blink. The pain was familiar, expected, even welcomed. Her eyes followed the stream of blood as it welled up from the clean cut and dripped steadily from her fingers into the waiting bowl below, the dark red liquid pooling with quiet determination.

Unlike the despicable Roy, Mary was a true believer. A daughter of true believers. The Bellum Sacrum wasn't just an elite faction within the Kildare Corporation. It was a religion. Pure. Ruthless. True. No more than ten members existed at a time. One had to die for another to take their place.

And that might just happen today, she thought, stabbing her other palm. Blood now flowed from both hands, dripping off of her skin and collecting steadily in the bowl.

"Kador, guide me. Kador, show me the way. Kador, give me the strength to pass the test of blood," she chanted softly.

Kador was the prophet. Their founder. A visionary who saw truth in the world and recognized the evil within himself. A man who outshone all other prophets with the scale of his sacrifice.

Three minutes left.

Her head was starting to swim. The bowl filled slowly.

The Bellum Sacrum's core belief was simple. There is only one God. Islam, Judaism, Christianity... they all had pieces of the truth, but none understood what truly mattered.

Bellum Sacrum existed for one holy purpose—to annihilate magic. Paganism. Nature worship. All magical powers and creatures. They were all a threat to humanity.

Two minutes.

Her vision blurred as the room began to tilt and sway around her, and her hand cramped painfully as it continued to drip blood into the bowl. The ceramic seemed to be filling faster now, as if her body was eager to purge itself of weakness. She remembered the old military saying her father had taught her. "Pain is weakness leaving the body."

Her flesh might've been failing, but with each drop of blood that fell, her soul was being forged stronger, purified, made worthy of the sacred mission she carried. The agony was a gift, proof that she was willing to sacrifice everything for the holy war. Kador's war.

Kador had been the untold prophet. He had founded the Bellum Sacrum and gained the respect of all the other religions.

He saw his path a month before he issued his final decree and ended his life. Other prophets sacrificed for God as an act of virtue. Kador sacrificed himself because he *was* the enemy. The most powerful wizard of his time. He destroyed magic and, by that, slaughtered the magical beings, including himself, casting his damned soul into Hell, where it belonged.

The ultimate sacrifice.

One more minute.

For a long second, she thought the stopwatch had gotten stuck and wasn't progressing, but then she realized it was her mind playing tricks on her.

Do not focus on the stopwatch. Bring your mind back to the Bellum Sacrum.

For centuries, the great religions supported the Bellum Sacrum. They knew the organization's existence was necessary, but eventually, the other religions grew soft and worried about public image. They outlawed the Bellum Sacrum and erased Kador's name from their histories.

But the Bellum Sacrum continued its holy work, tirelessly eliminating any trace that magic had ever existed. They burned ancient texts, destroyed artifacts, and incinerated every bone or relic that proved the existence of non-human intelligent life. When complete destruction proved impossible, they planted alternative explanations, seeding extraterrestrial conspiracy theories to explain away the remnants they couldn't destroy.

Ten more seconds remained on the stopwatch. Every second seemed like an hour in her mind.

The world was spinning now. She could barely keep her eyes open.

Kador's last decree burned in her mind. *Never stop the holy war, Bellum Sacrum. One day, magic will return, and humanity will crumble without you. Prepare humanity to face its mortal enemy, or perish. Fight all agents of magic. Show no mercy. Never stop the holy war.*

After delivering his final words, Kador unleashed his power and purged the world. All magical creatures started to die, including him. The evil within could not be redeemed. No, it had to be destroyed.

And now Mary was purging *her* failure. Bleeding out her weakness. Maybe making the world a little better. Maybe dying.

But not today.

The alarm sounded.

The ceremony was over, and she was still breathing. Barely. The world swirled around her, and her vision darkened at the edges as consciousness threatened to slip away. A few more seconds, she knew with crystal clarity, and she would have lost consciousness entirely. Her soldiers would never have broken direct orders not to enter the room, no matter what.

She moved quickly before consciousness slipped away. Salt on the wounds brought pain, which snapped her mind back into focus. She wrapped her hands in Army-grade bandages, grabbed a bottle of orange juice with additives from her pack, and chugged it.

She tried to stand up, but her legs betrayed her. What should have been a simple movement became a monumental effort as her body fought against the blood loss. The bowl felt impossibly heavy in her trembling hands, and she nearly dropped it as she swayed, watching the dark liquid slosh dangerously close to the rim. This was the closest to death she had ever been, she realized with a mixture of awe and satisfaction. Each previous ceremony had been an offering, but this one had been a true test of faith. Her body had nearly given everything to prove her devotion, and the knowledge filled her with a perverse sense of grit.

In the bathroom off the study, she cleaned the bowl and

blade, packed everything away, and walked out of the house without looking back. She slid into the back seat of a black car waiting at the curb, just as a wail of sirens echoed in the distance.

She had lived to fight another day.

Her holy mission for the Bellum Sacrum continued.

CHAPTER FOURTEEN

The stupid door lock wouldn't let him in.

Was the first digit a six or a nine? Chris squinted at his note where he'd written the code, but his own handwriting was as illegible as usual.

68781, he typed again.

Red beep again.

Chris aimed a frustrated kick at the door, immediately regretting it as pain shot through his toe. He hopped on one foot, biting back a curse and glancing around to make sure no one had witnessed his moment of brilliance. Why did everything always have to be so unnecessarily complicated?

There was a click as locks disengaged, and the door flew open in a sharp jerk that startled him.

Richard stood behind it, his eyes darting nervously toward the stairwell like he expected armed soldiers to come charging up at any moment.

Damn, the man looked like hell. The stress, lack of sleep, and the loss of his wife had aged him at least ten years in the past few days. His usually perfect military posture had collapsed into a hunched, defensive stance, and there were dark circles under his eyes that made him look like he'd been punched.

Chris considered making some sympathetic comment about how rough Richard looked, but honestly, he had more important things to worry about than playing grief counselor to the old bastard.

"Are they with you?" Richard asked, frantic.

"No, it's just me. I wasn't at the house," Chris said, a little hurt that Richard didn't greet him more respectfully.

Richard's face dropped. "Oh. Just you then... Get in here."

"Thanks, mate," Chris said, sarcasm heavy in his voice. "Really appreciate how much you care. I came here the moment I heard about the attack."

"Here" was one of the Brotherhood's secondary safehouses in London, or, rather, a safe *apartment*. This place was to be used only if the main house was compromised. Then and only then, each member of the Brotherhood Reception Committee was supposed to report here as quickly as possible, preferably with the Witness and the elf prince. The Brotherhood had detailed contingency plans for protecting and evacuating these safe houses—multiple escape routes, secure communication protocols, emergency supplies, and more.

The apartment was sparse and functional. Basic IKEA furniture was arranged with institutional precision—a couch, glass table, and matching chairs that looked like they belonged in a hotel catalog. The smell of cleaning chemicals and artificial air freshener hung in the air, the scent of a place that was maintained rather than lived in. White fluorescent lights hummed overhead. Boxes labeled "WATER" and "MREs" were stacked in the corner, along with other emergency supplies. It looked like the bachelor pad of someone with no aesthetic ambition.

A six-pack of beer, with two missing, sat on the table. Chris grabbed one without asking permission, cracked it open, and dropped onto the couch.

Richard relocked the door behind them before grabbing what looked like his third beer.

"Do you know what happened?" Chris asked, his voice grim.

"Nothing," Richard said flatly. "Just spoke to my contact in the police. We know nothing. Camera footage's gone. The house was probably sterilized—no blood, no signs of a fight. The neighbors reported gunshots, explosions, and screaming, but by the time the cops arrived, and it took them forever, they found nothing."

He took a long drink and stared at the blank wall with the hollow gaze of a man who'd lost everything that mattered. The confident leader who'd once commanded respect had been replaced by a broken man staring at institutional beige paint and probably only seeing the wreckage of everything he'd worked for.

Richard took a deep breath as if to focus himself. "There are three possibilities," he stated, counting them with his fingers. "One, they're all dead. That means we failed completely. Two, they were taken alive, which is basically the same thing because we've no clue where they are. Three, they managed to escape. That's the least likely, and even if they did, it's not like Sarah would go dark. She'd have made contact by now."

He glanced sideways at Chris. "And let's face it, if I were them, I'd keep my distance from us, too. It's not like we did our bloody jobs and protected them." His voice was bitter. "I wouldn't trust us."

Chris slipped on his go-to confused look, that carefully practiced expression of mild bewilderment he used whenever he wanted to avoid contributing anything meaningful. Richard must have mistaken his silence for disagreement.

"Why should the elf trust us now?" Richard continued.

“Somebody has clearly betrayed us and given up our location to Kildare. A house that was supposed to be a safe haven for at least two weeks has been compromised in less than two days. Someone with access to our most sensitive information has sold us out, and until we figure out who, the Brotherhood is more dangerous to Valor and Brenda than protective.”

Chris kept his face blank. “I’m heading out to brief my father tonight. He’s not going to be happy.”

“Who cares what *he* thinks?” Richard spat. “People *died* for this, good people, and it was for nothing. Screw your dad.”

Chris gave a faint smile. "Don't worry. I won't mention what you just said in my report."

His father had no tolerance for insubordination or for most things, really, including his own son. Chris rarely spoke to the old man, a situation he greatly preferred over the alternative. Their conversations usually consisted of his father listing Chris's various failures and disappointments, delivered in that cold, clipped tone that made it clear he regretted ever having children. The less contact they had, the better for everyone involved.

Richard shot him a murderous look. “I went to get my wife’s death certificate today. Heard about the attack in the back of a cab. Came here hoping, *praying*, they’d made it out and came here.” Richard faced Chris, his jaw clenched. “Where the fuck were you?”

It wasn't exactly an accusation, but Chris recognized the dangerous edge in Richard's voice and knew this wasn't the time to be flippant. Richard was usually a gentle giant, patient, understanding, even protective of the people around him, but when it came to team safety or mission accomplishment, he could turn cold, professional, and downright intimidating in a heartbeat. Chris had witnessed that transformation before and had seen Richard's military training take over when someone had put the operation at risk. The last thing Chris needed right now was to become the target of that heated anger.

So, he didn't flinch. "Sarah sent me to get more of those stupid nuts and berries for Valor," he said. "By the time I got back, the police were already there. There was nothing I could do, so I came straight here."

They sat in uncomfortable silence, the only sounds the steady *tick-tock* of the wall clock and the occasional rumble of cars passing outside the narrow window.

"Yeah, I figured," Richard finally said, his face drawn. "There's nothing either of us could've done."

"Exactly," Chris said a little too loudly.

"And there's nothing we *can* do now," Richard added, his voice low, "except wait and hope they find a way to contact us... if they're alive. If they still need help."

They drank in silence, staring at the empty space between them.

Chris gave Richard a small nod and finished his beer.

Poor fool, Chris thought, watching Richard blankly. *Sacrificed his wife for nothing.*

CHAPTER FIFTEEN

The next day, Brenda woke up feeling fresh as rain, which genuinely surprised her. She should have been exhausted, traumatized, barely functional after everything that had happened. Instead, she felt like she'd had the best sleep of her life. It was as if all the madness of the last few days had somehow faded with a good night's rest and didn't seem quite so jarring in retrospect.

It reminded her of conversations she'd had with her college roommate, Milica, a tall, funny Serbian girl who had a completely different perspective on life and dealing with personal trauma than Brenda. Coming from a war-torn country, Milica believed that trauma and mayhem were just integral parts of living.

"You experience a near-death car bombing in your street in the morning and go to practice basketball with friends at night," she'd said in her deep Serbian accent. "Life does not wait for you to 'process things.' Life does not wait for anything, really. Life is the madness that happens while you are planning other things. Deal with it, move on, and don't forget to enjoy it a little."

Brenda had never fully understood her friend's point of view until this moment.

She sat up slowly and registered two wooden bowls on the floor beside her bed, one half full of berries, the other with water. Valor sat cross-legged next to them, watching her with those catlike eyes.

"Good morning, Brenda!" he said brightly. "How are you feeling?"

"Okay, I guess... considering yesterday."

"Yes, I think we need to talk more about that. I know you have many questions, but too many answers at once might give you a stomachache," he said, smiling shyly, like it was an old joke he was sure she'd get.

He's so strange, Brenda thought. How could he seem like a man one second and a child the next?

"You may ask three questions," he said, "and I will give you three answers."

"Are you really an elf?" she blurted, without even thinking.

"Yes," he replied, raising one finger to mark it.

"Where did you come from?"

"A forest in a place humans call Germania," he said, raising a second finger.

Brenda frowned. "This isn't a game, and that doesn't satisfy my curiosity at all."

"Maybe you're not asking the right questions," he said, quirking an eyebrow.

"What happened last night?" she asked.

Valor sighed. "I don't know the answer to that, unfortunately. I am as lost and as baffled as you." He raised a hand. "So you get an extra question."

"Why are you here?"

"That is a much better question." He looked pleased, which annoyed Brenda slightly. "I was sent here by my father, King Valor the Third. I'm here to bring magic, and my people, back to the world, to this time." He peered at her and waited.

They sat in silence for a moment. She studied him with unease.

"Magic was expelled from this world a very long time ago, even by elf standards," he said eventually, studying his palms. "A lot has changed, and I need your help to figure it all out." His next words were barely a whisper. "Will you help me?"

Her silence drew on, the weight of his question hanging between them. Brenda could feel Valor seeking her acknowledgment, her commitment to his cause, but she wasn't ready to give it. She wasn't ready to fully accept that this was reality and not some kind of elaborate mental breakdown she was experiencing. Part of her still needed someone she could trust, someone objective and familiar, to look her in the eye and confirm she wasn't completely losing her mind. The problem was, her list of people she could trust in the world, let alone in California, was painfully short.

"I don't know, Valor," she said honestly. "I need a lot of answers first."

"Let's eat, and then I will answer three more questions." His expression turned even more gentle. "I'm sorry I joked about the stomachache, but truly, there's a lot to process. It will take us days to go through it all."

Brenda was about to argue, but voices and laughter outside the tent made her freeze. "Shit," she whispered, suddenly alert. "They can't see you. They'll freak out if they see an elf!"

"Don't worry. People tend to see what they want to see and ignore what doesn't fit their reality," Valor said.

He mumbled something softly under his breath, and Brenda watched in fascination as his features began to shift with subtle, fluid movements. The transformation was gradual but unmistakable. His chin became rounder and less angular. His sharp cheekbones softened and became less pronounced, and the distinctly pointed tips of his ears seemed to melt into more humanlike curves. The biggest change was in his eyes, which shifted from those catlike orbs with vertical pupils to normal blue human eyes with round pupils and visible whites. Brenda could still easily recognize him as Valor, but he looked far less obviously inhuman, just an unusually attractive guy with striking features rather than an elf.

A tiny voice in her head whispered that he was using Minor Disguise, the knowledge appearing in her mind like text she couldn't quite read but somehow understood. She decided to keep that to herself and possibly consult a mental health professional at a later stage.

He pointed at the vine curtain, and she exited the tent. Valor stepped out after her.

Three students, a girl and two boys, all in crimson Stanford T-shirts were hiking through the woods about thirty yards away. They waved at Brenda and Valor then kept walking.

"I have an idea. They might help us get unstranded." Brenda waved and started after them.

"I didn't know we were stranded," Valor mumbled but followed her.

"Hi, guys!" Brenda called out. "My car got stuck. Can you help us out with a ride to the city?"

Valor gasped but kept walking after her. "Did you say *car*?" he asked.

She ignored him. *This is not the right time for lengthy explanations.*

"Oh, man, sorry about your car," one of the boys said.

Valor snorted with uncontrollable laughter.

They all looked at him.

"Is he okay?" the boy asked.

"He's just a little strange, that's all," Brenda said with a casual wave, giving Valor a sideways, *shut up* glare. "Can we hitch a ride with you down to the university?" she asked, flashing her best *please* smile at the group.

"Sure! Our car's old and not very big, but it should fit all of us hopefully," the boy said. His voice was warm and friendly. "I'm Daniel. This is my girlfriend, Violet, and my brother, Jonathan."

Brenda smiled warmly. Daniel and Jonathan definitely looked like brothers, both muscular and carrying themselves with the easy confidence of athletes, probably wrestlers or martial arts enthusiasts based on their build and the way they moved. Violet radiated the happy, worry-free energy that seemed so common in sunny California, all bright smiles and casual optimism. Two or three years ago, Brenda had been in the same carefree place in life that these three occupied now; her biggest concerns were her grades and which party was hottest that weekend.

They shook hands with Brenda and gave Valor a polite wave. He didn't reach out to shake their hands.

Daniel and Violet led the way down the hiking path, chatting loudly about last night's party. Jonathan walked beside Brenda, while Valor trailed behind, absorbed in the flowers and butterflies. He made no attempt to join the conversation.

From time to time, Brenda glanced back at him. It was hard to read him. One moment, he was crisp and intelligent, the next laughing like a lunatic, and now... totally spaced out.

Is he really who he says he is? Is this an elaborate hoax? Had he drugged me and flown me to California? But why? Why me?

She couldn't think of a reason anyone would go to all this trouble just to mess with her, and the events of last night, which she was trying not to think about, had felt horribly real. Then,

Valor had made their shelter with magic... She shook her head, nearly overwhelmed again and unwilling to try to process anything more.

When they reached the edge of the parking lot, Daniel pulled water bottles from his backpack and handed them out. "Hot day. Might as well hydrate before we get in the oven that is our car. No AC. Sorry!"

Valor laughed again, too forceful this time, and the others studied him curiously.

Daniel offered him a bottle.

Valor took it gingerly and examined it like it was alien tech. "It is translucent," he said to Brenda, as if he was explaining a wonder.

Daniel and Violet exchanged a glance but politely said nothing.

Valor studied the cap, glancing sideways at how the others opened theirs. He fumbled with it until Brenda reached out and twisted it open for him.

He beamed. "This is a clever contraption."

Now it was Jonathan's turn to chuckle. "This guy's a trip."

Soon, they reached the car.

Jonathan called "Shotgun!" and dove into the front seat.

"Jonny, Violet gets the front seat!" Daniel frowned.

Violet gave Daniel's hand a squeeze. "Don't worry. I'll sit in the back with them. I really don't mind," she said with a smile.

"Fine," Daniel said begrudgingly.

The car was small, old, and scorching in the sun like a metal oven. Valor stared at it with reverent awe, as if he was looking at a technological marvel rather than a beat-up Honda Civic, but he said nothing as he attempted to fold his tall frame into the cramped back seat next to Brenda. It was almost comical watching the long-limbed elf try to arrange himself in the middle seat, his shoulders hunched and cramped as he gave apologetic smiles to everyone around him. His elbows kept bumping into Brenda and Violet, and his knees were pressed almost to his chest, but he bore the discomfort with patient grace, seemingly more fascinated by this metal contraption than bothered by the tight fit.

Daniel turned the key, and the engine sputtered.

"Where are the horses?" Valor whispered. "You forgot the horses," he said louder this time.

"It's not *that* old." Violet laughed. "Hey, Daniel, Valor thinks your car needs horses!"

Daniel pumped the gas pedal and muttered something under his breath. Finally, the engine roared to life, and they started moving.

"There are no horses..." Valor whispered, visibly stunned.

"Very funny," Daniel said. "It's old, but it's saving your ass."

Valor's eyes widened. He turned to Brenda and made a quick, strange gesture, touching his mouth then her ear and then her lips and his ear.

That's not weird at all, Brenda thought.

"Is this contraption, this horseless cart, called a *car*?" he asked.

The sounds in the car were muffled, like she'd slipped on noise-canceling headphones, and she realized no one else could hear him. "Yes. Why are you acting so weird?" she whispered.

His laugh was loud and pure. This time, it was one of the most beautiful sounds she'd ever heard.

"*Car* means excrement in Elvish," he explained. "I think the common word for it now is *shit*. I use magic to understand the human language, but when a word is unknown to me, it translates literally."

"Oh." She didn't know what else to say.

He blushed. "I couldn't figure out why you were telling Daniel your shit was stuck and asking him to help with it."

Brenda burst out laughing. "I thought you'd gone insane."

"How does this chariot work without horses?" he asked.

"Humans have made a lot of advances. We don't need animals for transport anymore. There's an engine in the front. It burns a substance called gasoline to make it go."

"So humans have developed gnomish machinery... but without perpetual motion," Valor mused.

Brenda made a mental note to unpack *that* cryptic sentence later.

Valor made another movement between them, and the invisible noise-canceling headphones disappeared.

Soon, they reached University Avenue in Palo Alto. Brenda decided she didn't want to drag Valor all the way to Stanford's campus, so she asked Daniel to drop them off at the curb.

She thanked them and pulled Valor out of the car. Daniel, Jonathan, and Violet waved goodbye and drove off toward Stanford, probably laughing while they rehashed the oddball strangers they'd picked up on the hill overlooking the city.

How simple and carefree their lives are, she thought. *How did mine get so complicated?*

CHAPTER SIXTEEN

Rosy hated the world, and the world hated her right back.

She sat on the couch in her shit trailer, where the air hung thick with cigarette smoke and the sour smell of old alcohol. Empty bottles cluttered the counters. Unwashed dishes filled the sink to overflowing, and somewhere, a faucet dripped with the steady rhythm of water.

Rosy was watching TV through her one good eye. It was a boring rerun of a soap opera she was sure she'd seen twice already, but that was okay. Anything to help her forget the pain in her stomach and in her mouth.

He kept coming home drunk and hitting her. She was smart enough to know it wasn't her fault and there was nothing she could do better to make him stop. He was a drunken fool, just like her dad. And just like her dad, he either hit her or tried to get into her pants.

The bruises on her face were fresh and sore, making it hurt just to turn her head, open her mouth, or even take a deep breath. She had plenty of experience with pain over the years, but this beating ranked at the top of her personal chart of misery. God help her, she didn't know if she could take another night like that.

I won't.

Today was going to be especially bad. They were out of money, which meant she was out of booze. She needed a drink before he got home so the beating would hurt less. This was the first time in five years she'd been sober at four in the afternoon. Her hands shook, and her head was already starting to ache.

"Rosssyyyy!" came the slurred shout from outside. A truck door slammed. "Rosy, you fat bitch! I hope for your sake you didn't forget the beer!" he yelled as he banged through the door.

Hearing his voice while sober was unbearable.

Rosy scowled. She knew the drill.

"Billy, you fat fuck!" she snapped back. "Bring home some money, you lazy idiot, and maybe there'll be beer and smokes. There ain't nothing here!"

Sometimes that line got him to drive to Walmart.

Today wasn't one of those lucky days.

Rosy was a large woman who could handle herself in any bar fight, tall and strong enough to intimidate most people, but Billy was still bigger and meaner, with the kind of muscle that came from years of hard labor. Even at her size, she didn't stand a chance.

He stormed in and backhanded her hard across the mouth. She tasted blood. It hurt so much more without the alcohol.

His fist smashed into her bad eye. It was puffy from the last beating, and she still couldn't open it all the way. Not that it mattered because another blow came down on her ear, and her other eye blurred.

This might be the day he finishes me.

As if reading her mind, he growled, "Say goodbye to life, you stupid bitch." He smiled viciously. His fist smashed into her cheek, and something cracked. "I'm going to end you."

She remembered that sound. It was the same one from when she had been five, when her father had beaten her real bad. That day hadn't been all bad. Her mom had taken her to the hospital, and they had gotten ice cream on the way back to the house they'd been living in. She never called it her home.

Today, there would be no ice cream.

The punches kept coming to her stomach, chest, face. Her world spun, and her teeth shattered. Something snapped, her nose probably. Then, something else broke.

Her mind.

A strange fever filled her aching gut then surged warmer throughout her chest, down her arms, and burned like fire in her fingers. The heat felt like pure rage, but it wasn't painful, more like the last desperate punch you throw with everything you have left before you collapse. It roared like a scream of defiance. For one split second, she didn't feel helpless anymore.

She raised her bloodied arm and screamed, "*Valashi!*"

The man's head burst into flame, and he shrieked in agony.

Rosy gaped at him, her mind struggling to process what her damaged eyes showed her. The stench of Billy's burning hair and flesh flooded the trailer, making her gag even as she stared in disbelief. Fire spread from his scalp to his shirt collar then crawled across his shoulders with unnatural purpose. She was shocked, but the furious heat still coursed through her veins, unspent and demanding more destruction. She wasn't about to let him hit her anymore.

"Rosy!" he cried out in anger and pain, raising his hand again.

"*Valtor!*" she shrieked, not understanding what she was saying.

Billy's head and shoulders exploded into a cloud of pink

vapor. His body stood upright for a second longer then dropped like a sack of meat.

What just happened? What did I do?

Her face felt wet with his blood. She tried to spit out the tiny parts of him that had gotten into her mouth.

She thought she heard herself cry out, but she wasn't sure. Her thoughts were slow, her vision cloudy. Black spots danced at the edges of her sight. She glanced down. There was blood everywhere. Sweat and tears and bright, red blood dripped from her chin.

She heard movement and looked up, barely. Through the fog, she saw her neighbor standing with a hunting rifle, staring at her in shock.

"Fuckem," she slurred through broken teeth.

Then, the world tilted and went dark.

SHE WOKE UP IN A CELL.

It was dark, cooler than the usual humid heat. She recognized the place. She'd been in this cell as a teenager. The pigs used to throw her in here until her dad would come to collect her. Just like the good old days. It looked clean but smelled of piss.

Her whole body ached.

Nathan Tucker strolled in. "Damn, Rosy, you really got yourself up a shit creek this time," he said. "Joe said he saw you blow Billy's head off. He's on the TV talkin' about witchcraft or some shit." He gave her a long, suspicious look.

She looked right back at him.

Nothing more than a miserable deputy sheriff, excited to have something more serious than another drunk driver to deal with. What a loser.

"Fuck Joe. Fuck Billy, and fuck you, Nathan," Rosy muttered. Her head throbbed. She'd hated Nathan since he was six and had tried to pinch her butt at camp.

"I'm real sure there ain't no such thing as witchcraft," Nathan said with a half-smile. "Almost as sure as I am you ain't gonna be free again in this lifetime."

Rosy ignored him, and he left.

The hours passed slowly.

It was dark out by the time Nathan came back, dragging someone else in cuffs. The woman was drunk and filthy, and Rosy silently prayed he'd toss her in the farthest cell.

No such luck.

Nathan uncuffed the woman and shoved her straight into Rosy's cell. The woman stumbled then collapsed onto the floor, but Rosy didn't get up from her seat. The world hadn't given her any handouts.

"My bitches' cell," Nathan sneered then stalked off.

"Hauggghh..." the woman groaned then vomited violently.

Rosy curled her lip in disgust. "What the hell?"

"I'm sorry," the woman said. "My boyfriend threw me out of the car in a fuckin' gas station." She spat, wiped her mouth, and looked up. Her face was bruised, her hands wrapped in dirty bandages. Her eyes were as red as her hair. "I know you! I saw your picture on TV. You're Rosy Underwood! You blew your husband's head clean off, right? You're famous."

"I'm Rosy," she said, "but I ain't done nothing. The son of a bitch blew his own head off."

"Yeah, right. Torched himself and then blew his own head off. Sure." The woman chuckled.

After a long moment, Rosy chuckled as well.

"I'm Mary," the woman said, raising one hand and wiping her mouth with the other.

Rosy felt a flicker of sympathy, and she reached out. The

woman was beaten to hell and drunk as a skunk. "Let me help you."

Mary grabbed her hand. "Thanks."

In one fluid motion, she stood, yanked Rosy off her seat, twisted her arm behind her back, and slit her throat with a shaving razor.

Rosy stumbled to her knees. She grabbed at the deep gash in her neck. Hot blood gushed between her fingers. She slid to the floor, her eyes wide with shock.

Mary waited, watching until Rosy stopped twitching. Then she calmly wiped the razor on Rosy's shirt. "Guard! The witch is vomiting blood!" she yelled, hiding the knife in her pocket. "Come quick!"

Rosy's eyes were frozen open, glassy with death, but her mind hadn't quite left her body. *The bitch murdered me. Murdered me. Murdered me.* The words echoed in her head, keeping time with her slowing heartbeat.

Two minutes later, Nathan showed up, buckling his belt as he walked down the corridor.

Mary stepped back, pretending like she hadn't done it.

Rosy couldn't even blink, and the stench of blood filled her mind.

"What the f—" Nathan yelled, flinging the cell door open. He kneeled by Rosy's body before he turned to Mary. "What the he—"

Mary slit his throat in one clean motion. "Sorry," she whispered. "Nothing personal. I just need to go."

He gurgled and fell, his dead weight landing on Rosy's chest.

It didn't hurt Rosy, though. Nothing hurt anymore.

Mary stepped over them, stopped at the sink, and cleaned herself up. Then, she strolled out of the jailhouse, calm and composed. She looked like a woman satisfied with her night's work.

Back in the cell, as the last bit of consciousness was fading away, Rosy felt the warmth once more.

And the wound on her throat began to close.

CHAPTER SEVENTEEN

It took Brenda a hot second to realize Valor had marched into the middle of University Avenue. Now he was standing in the center of the road like a deer in headlights, about to get hit by a bus.

Brenda suddenly understood how overwhelming this must be for him. His pupils were huge and dilated, his gaze shifting constantly as he tried to process the cacophony of traffic, music, and dozens of overlapping conversations. His breathing was rapid and shallow from the sensory overload. What seemed like normal city noise to her was probably hitting him like a wall of chaos.

“So many people,” he rasped.

Brenda rushed out and tugged at his sleeve, trying to pull him out of harm’s way. “Are you okay?”

He didn’t speak.

“Valor? Are you okay?” she repeated, touching him softly on the cheek.

His eyes focused on hers, but he didn’t move. “Yes, yes,” he said, his eyes wide. "The crazy lights and noise of the street are unlike anything I've experienced before."

She studied him, worried. *What the hell do I do with an elf in the middle of a breakdown?*

"I have never been to a human establishment before, much less a city," he continued. "I was the youngest of my brothers and was not allowed to leave the Elvish lands." His pupils were so big they seemed to fill his eyes.

"Let's get you off the street," Brenda said. "I know a good coffee shop just two blocks away."

He held her arm and allowed her to lead him. He stared at the people who passed, seemed startled by two dogs barking at each other, but was soon distracted by the street musicians on the sidewalk. It took them ten minutes to walk the two blocks to the shop.

They passed through the crowded outdoor seating area where laptop-wielding customers filled every table then walked into Coppa Cafe. The place was a bustling Silicon Valley institution where entrepreneurs and investors met over expensive lattes to discuss their latest brilliant ideas for changing the world. It was also a popular gathering spot for students, and Brenda had spent countless days here during her undergrad years, nursing a single coffee for hours while using the free WiFi to finish her papers. Thankfully, today, the line was short.

Brenda put her hand on Valor's to calm him down. "We'll get some food and figure out what to do next."

"Food would be delightful. Thank you, Brenda." He smiled weakly, still glancing around in wonder and confusion.

"What can I do for you today?" the man behind the counter asked. He had tattoos on his neck and arms, a long beard, and large earrings. He wore an upside-down name tag with the name *Tim* on it.

"Coffee and a BLT sandwich, please," Brenda said.

“Fruits and nuts, please,” said Valor, copying Brenda’s tone.

“Umm, you mean granola? Are you gluten-free?” Tim asked.

“Who is Gluten? What’s granola?” Valor asked.

“Are you fucking with me?” said Tim. “It's been a long morning, man, and the line is still growing.”

Valor looked at the man curiously, his head tilted sideways. “Fucking with you...?”

“He’ll have the granola!” Brenda interrupted, shoving the fifty-dollar bill she had hidden in her back pocket into Tim’s hands.

“One coffee, one BLT sandwich, and one granola,” Tim repeated the order, giving them a look that said he felt they were a total waste of his time. “That’ll be $41.25.” He gave Brenda a number.

She looked for a table. “Okay, we’re almost out of money,” Brenda said when they sat down, holding the five dollars and change that were left after a modest tip.

"Can I have a look at this 'money'?" Valor asked. She gave him the five-dollar bill, which he held in both hands as he examined it. "Strange... Why is cotton so valuable these days?" He frowned, clearly puzzled.

“What do you mean?” asked Brenda, confused.

“This!” He held the bill out in front of him. “This is made of cotton.”

“No, I think it’s paper,” she said, “and the material is not relevant. The paper notes are worth more than the coins, for example. This is what we use to pay for things in our world.”

“This is a strange world,” Valor murmured. He examined the bill carefully. After smelling it, he nodded and looked at her. “This is definitely cotton.”

“Here is your coffee, BLT, and granola.” Tim deposited everything on their table. “Do you want almond milk with it?”

Valor seemed befuddled. “How can you milk almonds?”

"You could have just said no, you know? Right? No need to be a smart-ass," Tim muttered and left.

Valor took a handful of the granola and sniffed it. He threw it in his mouth and let out an ecstatic sound of delight.

"What now?" Brenda groaned.

"Thus es amausing!" he said with his mouth full, his eyes glowing with excitement as he chewed.

"Glad you like it," Brenda said, pulling the BLT in front of her.

"So delicious!" he said to the couple at the table next to him, who tried to politely ignore him.

With his mouth full and noisily crunching his food, Valor returned to examining the five-dollar bill and started humming to himself.

Brenda stopped listening as a figure passing outside the cafe caught her eye. "Oh, my God, it's Doctor Greenfield! That's my old teacher from the university," she said, excited. "Valor, please wait here. I'll grab him. He'll know what to do."

Brenda ran out of the cafe and rushed out along the sidewalk to catch the professor.

"Doctor Greenfield!" she called.

He turned with a friendly smile. "Brenda, my dear! It's been so long. Your parents didn't mention you were coming to town," he said, his eyes warm. "Tell me, how are you?"

The simple question almost broke her completely. Tears threatened at the corners of her eyes, and she didn't know why those three innocent words triggered such a response, but she rushed to her former mentor and hugged him fiercely, burying her head in his familiar tweed jacket. Dr. Jacob Greenfield was roughly her parents' age, but he'd been more of a father figure to her than either of her actual parents had ever managed to be.

He'd been one of the very few family friends she could remember, always present at holiday gatherings and always kind to her, but she hadn't really gotten to know him until he had become her professor at the university. Unlike her parents, Jacob had understood why she'd left home at sixteen and had never once berated her for it. He'd been supportive through her struggles with money, grades, and figuring out who she wanted to be. He'd always been on her side, even when she wasn't sure she was on her own side.

Standing there in his comforting presence, she finally felt safe enough to be totally honest with herself.

"Oh, Jacob, I think I'm losing my mind!" she said, her words muffled by his coat. "I'm going to tell you about my last two days, but you have to promise not to think I am insane." She sniffed back another gush of tears. "Or if you do, please tell me and tell me what to do."

She gave him a quick summary of what had happened, starting with the out-of-the-blue phone call.

His face turned ashen, the expression in his eyes changing from friendly and amused to worried and bewildered. When she finished her story, there was an awkwardly long silence.

"This sounds... quite delusional, Brenda," Jacob said. "I don't think you're crazy, but you might be under the influence of drugs. That would explain some of the story you're telling me."

Brenda looked at him. For what seemed like the first time since she'd known Jacob, he seemed deadly serious.

"Do you want to meet the elf?" she asked. "You can tell me if I'm delusional after you meet him yourself!"

"He's here?" Jacob asked, his eyes wide in surprise.

"Yes, he's inside the cafe. Come, let me introduce you two," she said, grasping the professor's hand.

Valor busied himself with his sweetened granola. The sugary food made him feel strange, but in a good way. Everything seemed more intense, especially the light and the sounds, and he had a strong desire to jump up and down. He fought the urge as a little voice in his head told him that it would draw too much attention, but he definitely felt jittery.

Brenda came back in, towing her friend behind her. Her eyes were strangely red and puffy. "Valor, I want to introduce you to a good friend of mine, Doctor Greenfield."

The man she'd called doctor looked old, but most humans looked old to Valor. The man could have been no more than ninety years and still looked old. Humans were odd that way.

"It is a pleasure to meet you, Doctor. My name is Valor. Do you want some granola? It is fantastic!" said Valor with a friendly voice.

"Please call me Jacob," the man said, taking a seat at the small table. "Brenda, I've told you a million times not to call me Doctor."

"Which just makes me want to call you Doctor even more," Brenda said with a mischievous tone, and she settled in the seat between them.

Apparently, this was a joke, but Valor didn't get it.

"Why should I call you Jacob if your name is Doctor?" Valor asked.

"Ha, no. My name is Jacob Greenfield. My title is doctor," the old man said.

Valor remained perplexed. "Sarah told me titles are gone these days because everyone is equal," he said.

"Doctor is not a title of nobility," Brenda explained. "It is a title of study or academic proficiency."

"This, I understand. He is like a master!" Valor felt delighted that he finally understood. "And what did you master, Jacob?"

"Psychology. The study of behavior and mind," Jacob said.

This confused Valor, but Jacob pivoted the conversation. “Do you have a title, Valor?”

“Yes,” Valor said, “I am a prince.” His face darkened suddenly. “Actually, with the passing of my elder brothers, I have recently been named Crown Prince.” His voice had dropped to nearly a whisper.

The doctor eyed him, as if trying to figure him out. Valor smiled at him kindly despite the man’s appraisal. He was Brenda’s friend, after all.

“Clearly, he’s a delusional young adult,” the doctor remarked, as if to himself.

Valor did not understand what he meant.

“Brenda tells me you are not human. I would love to know more about that,” Jacob probed.

Valor ignored the question altogether, as it was clearly rhetorical. However, something else bothered him. “Why are titles obsolete? Why do you people think you are all equal? This is a very silly notion.”

“Don’t you think we are equal?” asked Brenda, a hint of anger in her voice.

“Clearly not!” Valor said, smiling. “Let's take you and Jacob for example. You are very much not equal. You are clearly different. You are a young woman, and he is an elderly man.”

“Does that make him worth more?” she asked. Her eyes were surprisingly angry.

“Or less?” Jacob chuckled.

“What does worth have to do with it?” asked Valor. “Worth and equality are two different things. An apple and a pear can be worth the same but are obviously not equal. On the other hand, an apple to a starving man can be worth a fortune, while it can be worth nothing to a man with a full stomach, yet these apples are equal.”

“Clearly intelligent,” commented Jacob sideways to Brenda.

Brenda sighed. It was obvious she felt frustrated by the lack of common points of reference. However, Valor knew this was part of their journey.

"Tell me about magic, Valor," Jacob said.

Jacob looked at him as if figuring out whether Valor was totally insane or bluntly lying. Valor's parents had prepared him for people treating him with disbelief and suspicion. He decided that a forthright approach would be best.

"Magic is very hard to explain in human words, and some of my wording might be incomprehensible to you," said Valor in a serious voice, "but let me try."

Jacob leaned forward in his chair.

Valor took a deep breath, remembering his education. "Magic is a form of energy. It is a meta-energy that can influence how other types of energy, whether it is in the form of matter or of time or raw energy, behaves and interacts," he said carefully.

"Go on," Jacob said.

"In the same way you can project energy by throwing a ball at a wall for example, magical creatures can use their magical energy to influence themselves and their surroundings. In this, magic is also a life force, and without it, magical creatures cannot survive," he explained.

Brenda remained quiet, listening as intently as Jacob was.

"There are many types of magical creatures, and even some humans can manipulate magic," finished Valor.

"You mean like unicorns and such?" Brenda asked, half amused.

What an odd thing to say. Unicorns of all creatures.

"Unicorns are notoriously..." He frowned, looking for the right word, but the translation from elvish was hard. "Assholes," he finally said, happy he found the right word. "But yes, unicorns are amongst the magical creatures of the world."

“Can you show me a use of magic?” asked Jacob, sounding slightly worried now.

“Yes, let me show you what I was about to do with this ‘money,’” Valor said, showing them both the five-dollar bill he still had in his hand. “Brenda said that this piece of cotton is worth a lot and can be used for many things, including but not limited to getting more granola, which I would very much like to have. It would make sense then to create more of these cotton sheets, correct?”

Without waiting for an answer, he continued, “Now, I need to use simple magic to transform one form of cotton to another, and I need some ink to make the markings.” He stood up, walked to the counter, and grabbed a few pens and a handful of cotton napkins.

Tim gave him a fake smile, and Valor smiled genuinely back and returned to the table.

“Okay,” he said, much like an eager teacher in a science class. “We have all we need right here. Now it is just a simple Transformation spell,” he explained.

He drew shapes with his fingers and chanted under his breath. It was as if an invisible money-printing machine was spitting bills out beneath his hand while digesting the napkins and emptying the pens’ ink. After a few seconds, he held about fifty five-dollar bills in his hand. He smiled proudly at Jacob and Brenda.

“Oh,” said Jacob softly. “Holy shit.”

“This was a very simple Transformation spell. I had all the materials I needed and was able to examine the desirable outcome for a long while. There are many, many other ways to use magic,” Valor finished. He smiled sheepishly. “And now we can buy a whole lot more granola.”

Brenda paled. “I’m... feeling a little sick. I’m going to the restroom," she said. She stood up and walked slowly away from the table.

"Holy shit," Jacob repeated. "What do I do now? This is going to change science as we know it. I must get you into a lab and record this!"

Valor looked up at Jacob and tilted his head. His gaze narrowed, and his expression turned grim. "No, I am sorry. I have a quest to finish," he said flatly.

"What do you mean 'no'? This is the biggest discovery since electricity. You must share this with the scientific world," insisted Jacob, his tone dismissive.

Jacob was quickly changing from a friend to an actual risk to Valor's quest.

"Listen to me very carefully," Valor said in a commanding voice. Valor's pupils expanded to nearly fill his catlike eyes as he looked directly at Jacob. "You are going to calm Brenda down. You will tell her that she is a part of something wonderful and exciting and that she should expect to learn a lot from it... On your way home, doubt will start to grow inside you. There is no way this can be true. You will think how could it be true? And of course, you will lose your credibility if you bring this forth to your friends. You will need to think about what you have seen and let the matter rest for two weeks."

Jacob nodded. "That makes perfect sense," he said softly. "Perfect sense."

Brenda came back, still white-faced. "Jacob, it must be late for you. Can I walk you outside?"

"Of course, dear," said Jacob, slightly perplexed, as if he were waking up from a dream. "Goodbye, Valor."

"It was a pleasure making your acquaintance, Doctor," said Valor with a smile, nodding at Jacob.

Brenda led Jacob outside and looked at him intently. “Do you think I’m crazy now?”

“No…” Jacob said. “I think you stumbled into a fascinating adventure, one which I cannot fully understand but cannot deny either.”

She laid her hand on his arm. “What are you saying?”

He studied her face. “You are definitely not crazy. I don’t know what the future holds for you, but it looks like an opportunity to see great wonders. A truly great opportunity.” He smiled gently. “I’m sorry I doubted you initially. As a man of science, this was a very puzzling experience, one I’ll need to think about for a long time.”

Brenda chewed her bottom lip, uncertain what Jacob meant.

He glanced toward the road with a confused look, as if trying to remember where he had wanted to go. “Good luck, my dear. Please send my regards to your parents.”

What a weird thing to say. He knows I haven't visited my parents in years.

But since he seemed so confused and lost in thoughts, she did not bring it up.

“Thank you, Jacob,” said Brenda, feeling slightly reassured but left without a clue what to do next.

The realization hit her suddenly. There was only one thing she could do. It would be awful, and she'd probably regret it immediately, but she was out of alternatives.

She sighed. “Speaking of my dad, do you mind if I use your phone?”

CHAPTER EIGHTEEN

Joe and Ted had had a wonderful day.

They'd already shot and killed two small deer and were on their way back to the truck. It was still early enough in the morning that the oppressive heat and humidity hadn't kicked in yet, making the walk through the dense green hills pleasant despite the extra weight from the deer carcasses slung over their shoulders. The constant buzz of insects filled the air, mixed with the calls of unseen birds and the rustle of small animals moving through the heavy brush. Their boots squelched softly in the muddy soil as they picked their way along the narrow hunting trail that wound between the rolling hills.

They'd been best friends since middle school when they would skip class to go on frog hunts down by the creek. Ted was a few years older than Joe and walked with a slight limp from a bad leg that gave him constant pain, but Joe had always been patient enough to match the slower pace without making a big deal about it. Both men lived for their weekend hunting trips and spent most weeknight evenings at the Trippy bar, nursing beers and talking about the ones that got away.

"So, you really saw old Rosy blow Billy's head off?" Ted asked.

"Yes, sir," Joe bragged. "She fucking seared his head and then blew it and his shoulders off clean. What a scary bitch she's always been."

"Well, now she's a dead scary witch," Ted corrected him, and they both chuckled.

They were getting close to the road when they heard a sound in the woods to the left of their path.

"Leave it be," Ted said. "We got enough game for today. Don't want to carry any more."

"Fuck that," whispered Joe. "No such thing as too much game, and that goes for women and deer! Ya hear me, Ted?"

Joe stepped into the woods, pulled his rifle from his shoulder, and signaled for Ted to follow him. They peered into the bushes, moving slowly. The sounds became very clear ahead of them, and then they saw it.

"Oh, my fuckin' Lord!" Joe said.

"God damn! That is a big beast!" Ted said.

It was a white horse, the biggest they had ever seen, maybe twice as large as the biggest horse either of them had ever laid eyes on. The horse was standing with its tail to them, head down, grazing.

Joe took a step forward, and the beast raised its head and considered them for a moment.

"What the..." Ted's mouth hung open, his eyes wide. "Do you see what I see, Joe?"

"I sure do. It's a fuckin' unicorn," Joe whispered. "I didn't know these things were for real."

"Me neither. They've got to be so freakin' rare, dude!" said Ted.

Joe slowly raised his rifle and used the sight to get a better look. There was no mistake. Adorning the horse's head was a huge, white, somewhat translucent horn. It caught the light like a diamond.

For a moment, both men just stood there in silent awe of the magnificent creature. The unicorn seemed to radiate its own soft light, making it appear almost ethereal against the muddy grass and wet undergrowth. Everything about it was impossibly clean and pure in a way that didn't belong in this damp, dirty bush.

The beast looked at them with intelligent eyes that seemed far too knowing, as if it were sizing them up for potential danger. After what felt like a long, evaluating stare, the unicorn apparently decided they weren't worth worrying about and lowered its head to continue grazing peacefully.

"It's beautiful... It'd be a fucking awesome addition to the Trippy bar. Think of its head over our favorite table. Man, I bet Andrew would give us free entry for life if we mounted it up there!" Joe whispered.

Ted aimed at the beast. "It's so big. It's almost too easy," he whispered. "Let's take it out together. One shot might not be enough."

"Yes! And that way, we can both say we killed it!" agreed Joe.

They both took aim.

"On the count of three," whispered Ted. "One... two... three. Fire!"

Joe fired before Ted said "fire," so technically, he figured he should get the credit. And a glorious kill it was.

The beast let out a haunting whine as it collapsed, the sound reverberating through the trees like a bell tolling. Both hunters felt the earth shake beneath their feet as the massive unicorn hit the ground, and birds burst from the surrounding bushes with sharp, accusatory cries. Two crimson wounds bloomed like terrible flowers against the creature's pristine white coat.

Joe and Ted walked slowly toward the unicorn. It was even bigger up close, at least six feet tall at the shoulder if it had been standing. Now, it lay on its side, trembling slightly and breathing hard. It'd be dead any minute.

It was a wonderful animal, pure white in an unnatural way. *Nothing in nature should be that clean,* Joe thought.

The horn was about three feet long and looked deadly sharp. The unicorn's breathing grew shallow, one eye blinking up at them in clear distress. Then, it stopped breathing altogether. The forest fell into eerie silence. The birds ceased chirping. Even the bugs stopped buzzing.

Blood oozed from the beast's wounds...

"Hee-ya! We fuckin' killed a unicorn!" Ted gave Joe a big high five. "How the hell are we going to take it back? Do you happen to have a chainsaw in the truck? We should take its head and..." He tilted his head, staring at Joe. "What's the matter?"

"The gunshot wounds... They're gone," Joe said softly, pointing with a trembling hand. Somehow, the wounds had disappeared, leaving the fur pristine.

Silence pressed in.

Then, the unicorn gave out a loud neigh, and suddenly, the forest came alive again—birds chirping and insects buzzing, like all of nature had been holding its breath.

The beast staggered to its feet and stood calmly next to Joe and Ted.

"What the fuck!" Joe said, panicked. "What just happened, Ted?"

"I don't know. Holy fuck!" said Ted.

The unicorn lowered its head to graze again.

Joe, mesmerized, reached out a hand to touch it. The animal

was so clean, so pure.

In the blink of an eye, the unicorn raised its head, twisted, and impaled Joe through his stomach. It lifted him high into the air like a rag doll.

“Aaaah!” Joe's scream erupted from deep in his chest as he stared down at the gleaming horn piercing straight through his belly. His hands trembled against the wound on either side, blood seeping warm between his fingers.

"Aaah!" Ted's cry cracked through the quiet forest as he stared up at Joe in horror.

Joe could feel three feet of pristine white horn piercing straight through him, and through his agony, he watched Ted's rifle slip from his grip, hitting the muddy ground with a wet thud. Ted's hands reached desperately toward him, but Joe could see terror had frozen his friend’s feet in place.

The unicorn neighed.

“Help... me...” Joe gurgled, blood leaking from his mouth.

“What the fuck! What the fuck! I don’t know what to do!” Ted screamed.

Joe could see the fear in Ted's eyes, could tell every instinct was screaming at him to run, but Ted stayed because that was what best friends did. You didn't abandon a best friend skewered on a unicorn horn.

The beast seemed unnaturally calm, showing no signs of fear or aggression despite having a full-grown man impaled on its horn. It simply studied Ted with the same intelligent, majestic stare it had given them before they'd shot it.

The unicorn lowered its head slightly.

“Get me off,” Joe whispered, his chin dripping blood.

“I’ll try!” Ted took a shaky step forward.

As fast as the first strike, the unicorn raised its head again, impaling Ted. Its horn pierced through his stomach.

"Heeaaa!!" Ted's scream exploded right above Joe's head, so close it hurt his ears.

Suddenly, Ted's full weight crashed down on Joe, pushing him farther onto the horn. Joe felt Ted's hands frantically pushing against his shoulders, his friend's desperate movements sending fresh waves of agony through Joe's pierced body. Warm blood dripped onto Joe's back. He couldn't tell if it was Ted's or his own anymore. Through his pain, Joe realized with horror that Ted was now sharing the same horn, both of them skewered like meat on a spit.

“Ugeeee,” Joe's moan came out weak and breathless.

Ted's full weight pressed down on Joe, crushing the air from his lungs. Each breath became a struggle as his friend's frantic movements sent fresh waves of pain through his entire body.

The unicorn neighed again. It looked around then moved slowly toward a nearby tree, graceful and unbothered by the weight of the two men on its horn. Their blood flowed freely but left no stain on the white coat.

The unicorn used the bark to scrape the bodies from its horn. They collapsed in a tangle of roots. Ted fell face-first into a muddy puddle and gurgled once before quickly going silent. Joe slid down, slumping against the trunk of the tree.

Joe stared up at the immaculate white animal above him. *Nothing in nature should be that clean...*

As his eyes closed, he finally figured out one last truth.

Never fuck with a unicorn.

CHAPTER NINETEEN

Brenda woke up in her childhood bed. What a strange feeling. The smells and colors of her old room were familiar to her yet jarring because she hadn't slept in that bed for years. It was comfortable and uncomfortable all jammed together.

Last night had been more than awkward.

Her father had picked them up from the cafe after she'd called him using Jacob's phone. He'd looked the same but felt even more distant than before. He had moved past Jacob with a distracted air that had surprised her, so absorbed in his own thoughts that he hadn't acknowledged the professor's greeting. Brenda had flushed with embarrassment as her father treated their friend so poorly. His nod to Valor had been polite but lukewarm.

During the drive, she had stolen glances at her father's profile, watching the same distant expression she'd grown up seeing across the dinner table. His knuckles had been white against the steering wheel, gripping it like he was holding himself together.

She hadn't seen him in five years and had expected a little more warmth from him. She should have known better than to expect care from a man who had always preferred the surgery room to conversation with his daughter.

They had driven in near silence to her parents' house near Stanford. Brenda had been shocked when her father had announced that he wasn't going to come into the house with them. He'd explained that the relationship between her mother and him was difficult right now, so he was staying at a friend's house for the time being.

"It is what it is, Juli... Brenda," her father said in a quiet but resolute voice when asked why.

Brenda hadn't been able to believe what she was hearing. Throughout her childhood, there had been many instabilities and changes, but her parents had always been resolutely unhappy *together*. Not apart.

She had tried to get him to talk about the situation, but he had been unwilling to go into any details. He'd promised things would get better, though he hadn't looked so sure.

"She's drinking again," he'd warned her when they left the car. "Give her some slack. She is going through a rough patch."

When Brenda and Valor had rung the doorbell, her mother, Julia, had answered immediately, unable to fake her surprise well enough to fool Brenda into believing she hadn't known they were coming. The older woman had given her a quick hug and had assessed her from head to toe, as if to confirm that her daughter was okay. Then Julia had turned to study Valor, and her eyes had widened.

To Brenda's utter amazement, Julia had fallen to her knees and cried, "Mok le Julia Mountain! I am so sorry, my lord. I have failed so miserably, and it was all in vain!"

Valor's expression had held no surprise, and his bearing had remained steady. "My name is Valor, son of Valor the Third," the young elf had said in a surprisingly authoritative voice. "It is nice to meet you, Julia, and you have not failed me at all," he'd added in a kinder tone. "You raised an amazing daughter as the Witness. Come, please stand up." He'd extended a hand and helped her to her feet.

Julia had sobbed, her tears glistening in the porch light.

Brenda had never seen her mother overcome by emotion. The woman had rarely cried, and it had been startling to see it then.

"It was all in vain. It was all for nothing," Julia had moaned, but she'd refused to explain more.

Brenda had been desperate to know what she meant and to tell her about the events of the last few days, but her mother had put up a wall around herself and clearly needed time to adjust to Valor's presence. The elf on her doorstep had seemed to be almost too much for her to handle.

Julia had ushered them into the house and quickly organized a bed for Valor in the living room, and he'd thanked her. The house was a mess, but it had always been like that.

Their dinner had been awkward and silent, all of them quiet and reflective rather than talkative. Valor had kept to himself and to his granola. Her mother kept drinking whiskey and mumbling to herself that it was all over. Brenda had never seen her mother so upset, and she hadn't known how to make things better. She had gone to sleep feeling sad and helpless, hugging her old pillow.

Morning came before she'd even realized she'd fallen asleep. Sunlight streamed through a crack in the blackout curtains. Quickly, Brenda got up and dressed in some of her old clothes. Her parents had left her room exactly as it was when she'd left; they hadn't touched a thing.

She washed her face, brushed her hair, and went looking for Valor and her mother. Their soft voices carried from the direction of the living room, their tone conversational, like two old friends. Brenda padded carefully down the hall and stopped out of their view, shamelessly determined to eavesdrop.

"Stop saying that! You have not failed our mission, Julia. I don't see it that way, and that is what matters. You know this to be true." It sounded like this was not the first time Valor had said these words. He sighed. "Julia, the cause is progressing. We are on our way to releasing magic into the world again." His voice turned eager and hopeful.

Brenda inched forward, hoping her movement wouldn't be noticed by either. First her mother's face came into view, then a bit farther brought Valor's into sight as well.

Her mother's eyes were red-rimmed and glassy from the tears swimming in them. Her chin quivered. She took a shuddering breath before speaking in a voice barely above a whisper. "I need to tell you what happened. I need you to judge me, my lord. Your kind words are empty without you knowing the entire truth."

He studied her soberly, his chin lifting slightly. "That is fair enough. I will hear your story and pass judgment," he said gravely, his tone deep, almost regal.

It was strange to see the young elf appearing so confident and strong in front of an older woman like her mother.

After taking another long, shaky breath, Brenda's mother began her story. "We moved from England to America when I was one. This was after a great war that killed millions around the world. By the end, my mother was one of the only survivors from her family. She had betrayed the Brotherhood by taking part in the United Kingdom's war efforts. Despite strict instructions not to interfere in human wars, my mother could not ignore her country's call. To add to her sins, she did not bear a child during those long war years. The Brotherhood was not happy with her, but what could they do? They had already lost many members to the war, including much of my mother's family.

"I didn't know it at the time, but my mother went dark and ended her affiliation with the Brotherhood when she moved to the United States. She raised me with all the knowledge of the Brotherhood but without the obligations or the community that came with it. When I was twenty-five, we had a terrible car accident. My mother died before the police arrived." She paused for a long moment, as though she replayed the sorrow of her difficult memories.

"What happened to you in this accident with the car?" Valor prompted.

She blinked and refocused on him. "I broke both my legs and an arm in three places. I required surgery to repair my arm. When I woke up from the anesthesia, a Brotherhood representative waited next to my bed as a dashing young doctor changed my bandages. That year, I married that doctor and rejoined the Brotherhood. I learned a lot about your kind and why it is important to have magic in the world again. I learned about Kador and his mortal sin against magic. I learned about our war to bring magic back, and the long wait for your kind to return safely to this land."

Brenda remembered laughing when she heard Sarah's crazy story about her parents being a part of a Brotherhood. *Not so crazy after all. How did I not know about this?*

"My membership in the Brotherhood was brief. After a few years of trying to have a baby with my husband, I was told by the Brotherhood that I needed to get pregnant, regardless of my marital status or my spouse's fertility. They pressured me to find other ways to pursue pregnancy, but these were times of freedom, and we were in love. I didn't want to carry anyone else's child. We hated the Brotherhood for what it was asking us to do, and we decided to run away and start a new life.

"We spent the next several years away from the Brotherhood. Ironically, I really wanted to carry his baby, and no matter how much we spent, we couldn't have one. My relationship with my husband became strained, and I had an illicit affair, short but fruitful. Nine months later, Brenda was born. My husband didn't know about the affair and loved the child as a father. I truly didn't know if she was his or my lover's, and I didn't really care."

My father isn't my father!

Brenda bit back her anguished gasp, her mind reeling. Everything she knew about herself and her history crumbled away. She wanted to rush out and demand the whole truth from her mother, but she forced herself to remain still so she could hear the rest of her mother's story.

"We called her Julia, in accordance with the Brotherhood's rules. We no longer belonged to the Brotherhood, but we still believed in the cause. We wanted to wait until she was old enough to understand to tell her about her role in the future of the world. We wanted to give her a normal life. We were wrong, and we delayed until it was too late.

"Brenda was strong-minded and didn't want to be called Julia, like me, her mother. She was a clever and rebellious teenager, and she didn't want anything to do with us. Somehow, she sensed and hated the secrets we kept hidden from her, I think, and resented us for keeping them. The unspoken words poisoned the relationship. A year and a half before college, she packed up and left home, and this is the first time she's come back. My husband wanted to reach out to the Brotherhood, to tell them we had a new Witness and ask them to protect her. He was a bigger believer than I was, until he found out she wasn't his..." Her voice trailed away.

"Go on," Valor said firmly.

Julia nodded. "He went to the Brotherhood, despite my

objections, to tell them we had a child. They ran a test and told him he was sterile and therefore a liar. They thought he wanted money. They didn't know he was a true believer... and a fool." Julia wiped fresh tears from her cheeks, but her sobbing had subsided. "He left me that day, and I have spent the last five years alone."

Valor's gaze narrowed, and a long, hard silence fell.

Brenda leaned against the wall. Her knees threatened to buckle under the weight of the shock. Her heart pounded, and her breath came in shallow gulps. She wanted to scream, but more than that, she wanted to hear Valor's judgment. It felt like the moments before a jury proclaimed its verdict.

Finally, Valor spoke. "You have left the Brotherhood for love. You have given a child to a man who was not your husband. You have stopped believing, and you have lost your husband and your child." His voice was serious and regal.

Brenda held her breath.

"I have failed," Julia murmured.

"Elvish ways are very different from humans," Valor continued as though Julia hadn't spoken. "Your lives are so short and eventful. You are like the flames of a forest fire to us—hot, furious, and fleeting. You have almost broken the chain and doomed us all to failure, but you have not done so. I judge by action, not intent, and by action, you have raised a wonderful child. The Witness lives because of you."

Julia's eyes once again filled with tears, and they rolled down her cheeks in fat drops.

"You have made dangerous choices in your life but paid a great price for them," Valor said. "As I said, elvish morals are different from human ones, but if I were to judge you, I would say that you have more than paid for your choices." Valor took Julia's hand in his and smiled kindly.

Julia bowed her head, weeping softly.

Brenda didn't know what to feel. She'd always had a complicated relationship with her mother and her father who wasn't her biological father at all.

The recent days had changed her perception of reality and crushed what she'd thought she'd known to be true.

Her world continued collapsing around her. Valor's arrival had taken every part of her life and shaken it, rearranging it into something she hardly recognized, yet strangely, it all made sense. With that realization, a calm spread through her. Somehow, she'd always known, and the weight of the unvoiced, long-kept family secret lifted from her. She felt a glowing warmth, and the tiny voice in her head uttered the name of her real father.

The puzzle pieces clicked together with startling clarity. His special attention, his unwavering presence in their chaotic household, the way he'd always seemed to understand her better than anyone else... Everything had a reason now. No wonder her father had been so harsh with him when they had met. The interaction must have been a painful reminder of his own failure.

She squared her shoulders and marched into the room.

"Was it Jacob?" Brenda demanded, startling her mother. "Is he my real father?"

Julia's eyes widened. She sniffed. "Yes," she said softly. "How did you know?"

Brenda didn't answer. Having this conversation wasn't something she had in her right now. Instead of answering, she walked straight out of the house and let the door slam behind her.

CHAPTER TWENTY

Chris Senior, the current chairman of the Brotherhood and CEO of BRHD Inc., peered from his third-floor office down at the street to see Chris and Richard enter the Brotherhood headquarters. He had called them to Zurich for some well-deserved ass-chewing. None of the search teams in London had come up with any results. The reigning assumption was that Valor and Brenda had been captured or killed, and Chris Senior was not happy.

The headquarters sat unremarkably among the banking district's stone facades, a three-story building that wore respectability like expensive camouflage. Traditional European architecture in pale gray stone suggested old money, while spotless windows reflected nothing but the overcast sky. Inside, the lobby's marble floors stretched beneath soft fluorescent lights, and minimalist furniture offered no comfort to visitors. Chris Senior, like his predecessors, did not like the limelight. No need for attention or pesky visitors.

He heard them walk down the hallway toward his office. His assistant, Mia Meier, always wore heels that made enough noise to raise the dead. She had a frown that never left her face, making all guests feel unwelcomed. She was perfect for her job.

Mia knocked on the door and did not wait for him to answer. His schedule was clear. She owned his calendar and knew every appointment. She let the two poor bastards in.

Chris Senior took in their disheveled appearance with clear disapproval. His son's clothes looked like he'd been sleeping in them for a week, wrinkled and stained. Richard appeared uncharacteristically unshaved, his usual military precision gone. Both men looked jet-lagged despite the relatively short flight from London.

He did not wait for them to sit. "You only had one job..." he said, threading a threatening tone through his words. "I want to know how this happened."

Richard's expression turned grim. "Sir, Kildare is a well-funded and well-run organization... just as we are. It's a deeply religious group, so infiltrating it has proven difficult throughout the years. We've not been successful in penetrating their leadership or developing a strong intelligence network inside their organization. Foolishly, we thought we were as impenetrable as they are, but they seem to know far more about what we're doing than we know about them."

"Stop," Chris Senior said loudly. "I really don't care about your excuses."

Frankly, Chris Senior didn't care much about "the mission" or the fucking elves. His own father had been a true believer but hadn't paid nearly enough attention to the business. As a result, his old man had nearly run BRHD into the ground.

Well, not on his watch. Chris Senior was an excellent businessman. Under his leadership, BRHD had flourished and had become one of the top research organizations in the world. He enforced all of BRHD Inc's patents and had increased the company's revenue a hundredfold.

No, Chris Senior had not believed in elves until last week. He thought they were a childish tale, a stupid thing to believe in. The only reason he continued to fund the Brotherhood was because of a stipulation in the founding documents of BRHD Inc. When he had become CEO, the company's legal department had made it very clear that the Brotherhood's budget was ring-fenced, and that if he ever tried to cancel it, he would be fired, and the board would happily appoint a replacement. God knew there were plenty of people waiting for him to fuck up. He hadn't made many friends with his aggressive, if effective, business strategies.

Chris Senior had spent decades systematically reducing the Brotherhood's ridiculous operational budget to the absolute minimum required by the charter. Every dollar not spent on the "fairytale mission" was another dollar of profit for BRHD's real business. He'd cut their staff from dozens to just a handful and eliminated any extra funding that his father had considered essential.

Putting his idiot son in charge of any part of the Brotherhood was as close as he could get to killing the organization. The boy was from his first marriage, before he'd learned the hard truth that beauty didn't compensate for a lack of brains or personality. He'd gotten rid of the wife, but the son had to stay and keep the name. That was another stipulation in the Brotherhood's charter.

And now, this recent development has become a royal pain in the ass. Supposedly, the elves were back, and the enemy's organization had successfully attacked their secret stronghold, kidnapping or killing this elf. It was clear that his son had been completely unable to deal with the situation.

What scared Chris Senior the most was that his lawyers had never clarified what would happen if the Brotherhood failed in its ultimate mission.

Chris Senior had never asked. He didn't want to know.

He stood and leaned on the conference table. “Gentlemen, in the entire history of the Brotherhood there has never been a surviving Traveler, and it will probably never happen again.” He was using the assertive voice he usually reserved for board meetings. “You've completely fucked this up and might have ruined the mission of the Brotherhood forever,” he continued, glaring at his son, who lowered his head in shame.

He let the silence stretch, another boardroom tactic.

Chris Senior loved using silence to examine people. Discomfort revealed a lot about a man's character. Richard took the silence in stride, sitting perfectly still as if nothing Chris Senior could say would be worse than his internal guilt. His son fidgeted with some dirt on his pants, unable to handle the pressure of quiet scrutiny.

“Luckily for you, I am not so incompetent,” he said. *Or so naive*, he thought. “With a small bribe, I secured the police report, including the CCTV footage.”

Both men's eyebrows climbed their foreheads as they shared a look of shock. *Good.*

Idiots.

“The reports and footage confirm that Sarah is dead, along with a few other members of the Brotherhood's security team and two members of the enemy's assault team.”

He looked at Richard as he spoke, knowing Sarah had been Richard's friend. The man seemed beaten. Richard's face remained stony but very exhausted, his two-day stubble aging his already pale features.

“And?” Richard pressed.

Chris Senior nodded. “They do not, however, mention or suggest the presence of anyone resembling Valor or Brenda. The footage shows all the surviving members of the assault team leaving through the front door two minutes before the police arrived. They weren't carrying anyone."

The two men straightened in their chairs.

Now that he had their attention, Chris Senior added, "More importantly, my contacts in the U.S. say that surveillance indicates Kildare's headquarters has been fully staffed for the last forty-eight hours. Private special-ops mercenary teams were sent to London and are still patrolling the streets."

Richard's face started to brighten, and his posture straightened slightly, while his son's expression remained predictably blank.

Chris Senior drummed his thumbs on the elongated wooden table. "This leads me to believe that Valor and Brenda are still on the run. If the stories are true, the elf is a powerful creature and may be able to protect himself and possibly Brenda. In short, she's the only one he really needs for the mission to move forward," he said, summarizing for his son who hadn't shown the faintest sign of comprehension.

"What are we supposed to do now?" his son whined. "They could be anywhere."

"They may be in China for all I care. You just need to find them," he barked, pleased when both men wilted in their seats.

"Yes, sir," Richard muttered.

"The Brotherhood's charter is clear—ensure the survival of any elf who makes it through the Travel and aid them in their mission and their magic," Chris Senior reminded them.

"Yes, sir."

Finally, his son had actually joined the discussion.

Chris Senior returned to his desk chair. "Now, go find them. Valor doesn't know anyone in this world, but Brenda does," he said. "Go through all of her contacts, friends, coworkers, boyfriends, family. Those are your best leads."

Both men nodded and stood.

Chris Senior watched them leave without any of them saying another word.

God help us, he thought. *God help us if they fail, and God help us if they succeed...*

The truth was, Chris Senior only cared about stock prices, keeping the board happy, and keeping the lawyers at bay. He had saved his company from devastation, and that was his legacy and his priority, not some fairytale quest. He would play along with this nonsense as long as it aligned with his interests, but the moment it threatened BRHD's bottom line, the elves could go to hell.

If they failed, Chris Senior promised himself that he would bury the story and continue running BRHD Inc. like a normal corporation, as if the other mission had never existed at all.

CHAPTER TWENTY-ONE

Hoping to avoid her mother, Brenda returned to the house very late. She tucked the day's purchases under her arm and opened the door to the dim light of the television in the living room. With a sigh, she came in, bracing for the uncomfortable conversation ahead.

But instead of her mother sitting in front of the TV, Valor waited. The young elf was slumped couch-potato style on the sofa, his eyes fixed on the screen. A half-eaten bag of yesterday's granola lay in his lap. He was watching the third installment of *Planet of the Apes, War for the Planet of the Apes.*

Relieved her mother wasn't around, Brenda smiled and flopped onto the sofa next to the elf prince. He handed her the bag of granola, smiling. There was a comfortable silence between them. The movie was about to end with the avalanche burying all the bad humans, leaving the apes to rule the world.

"This is very biblical," said Valor, pointing toward the screen. "Rather similar to the story of the Israelites and the opening of the sea."

"I never thought of that," said Brenda. "Of course! Caesar is so like Moses by the end."

They sat quietly, as Caesar led his tribe to the promised land but could not enter it.

"Your mother taught me how to use the TV and explained about movies. It is fascinating really! It's like a super realistic play. It looks real, but it is all fiction. Even the monkeys are not real," he said in a delighted voice, visibly marveling at the wonderful invention.

"You don't say," Brenda said with mock shock as she took some more of his granola.

"She is not as bad as you think. Your mother," he said after a while, keeping his eyes on the screen.

"I never said my mother is bad," Brenda protested.

"But you were trying to avoid her today. People are pushed to extremes when it comes to love and war... Please don't judge her too harshly," he added.

"You don't know our history," Brenda said unapologetically.

"Only the ancient one," he replied with a smirk.

She studied him, puzzled. "How old are you, Valor?"

"Age is a strange matter, Brenda," Valor said pleasantly. "I have experienced one hundred eighty-five summers. I am fairly young by elvish standards." He paused. "But I traveled to this time, which is more than seven hundred summers from when I was born... I don't know if that counts."

Her jaw dropped, and her hand froze halfway to the granola bag. He was a hundred and eighty-five years old?

She stared at his young face, trying to reconcile what she was seeing with what he'd just told her. He looked no older than nineteen, but he was older than her great-great-grandfather would have been.

"But you look so young," she said plainly then immediately worried the comment might sound rude.

"I am very young in elf terms," he said, his smile warm. "Elves live to be more than a thousand years, and even when our bodies die, we merge with the trees we are buried under and continue to exist. My father is almost eleven hundred years old. That is old."

"Holy shit," concluded Brenda.

"How can a shit be holy?" he asked. "Do monks produce holy excrement?"

She didn't know how to answer that without laughing.

The humor drained from his features as his expression grew serious. In an instant, the ancient prince emerged from behind the curious child who had been delighting in human customs.

"We really need to leave tomorrow," he told her. "We do not have much time. There is a limited window of time to finish our quest. My people's lives are at stake."

Brenda was happy to leave. "Let's go early in the morning before my mother wakes up," she said, showing him the package. "I bought a phone and some clothes for you while I was out. I have my old clothes here, so I'll pack a few to take with us."

He nodded, smiling like a child given a new toy. "Thank you, Brenda! So will you help me in this quest?"

She nodded her head, her mouth twisting in a lopsided smile. He was a study in contrasts, this childlike, ancient elf with granola scattered all over his clothes and the sofa.

"Yes, you idiot. I guess I was born to help you," she answered.

She hadn't realized she'd come to that conclusion until the moment she said it.

His eyes had a hint of surprise, like he was expecting something else, but he smiled warmly and said nothing. She liked his silence.

"We need to find the most remote place in this country, and

we will be safe there," he said after a while. "My people will need a peaceful place, just like in the end of the movie. Far from any human center." He pointed to the screen again to make his point.

Brenda recalled the last scene where Caesar's apes had finally found their sanctuary away from human conflict.

She grinned. "It's time for me to show you some magic."

"Magic?" Valor asked, interest in his voice.

Boy, he is a one-trick pony. She rolled her eyes.

"You'll see." She retrieved her mother's laptop, opened it, and typed into the search bar "most remote forest in the United States."

Valor's eyes widened.

A list popped up. The first item was Barrow, Alaska.

"Alaska is too far to drive. Besides, it's freezing most of the year," she added with a shiver.

The next one was Redstone Springs, Arizona, in the Grand Canyon.

She tapped the name on the screen. "That's more like it! It'll take us about twelve hours of driving, assuming we can't fly to Vegas. I imagine you didn't bring your passport or driver's license, right?" she asked with a note of humor in her voice.

Valor looked at her like she was crazy. "Humans can fly?" he asked slowly. "What is a passport?"

"Yes, well, sort of. We have flying machines. I don't think it'll work, though. Getting you the right papers would be hard and take a while, and I wouldn't even know where to start doing that. Besides, I haven't had much luck with airports lately."

Brenda already felt more optimistic now that she knew she'd be leaving her childhood home before her mother woke, and her sarcasm was resurfacing.

"What do you suggest we do?" Valor asked.

"We'll need to rent a car," she mused. "I'll book it now, and we can pick it up in the morning. You should go and get some rest. We've got a long day of driving ahead of us."

While Valor dozed the instant his head hit his pillow, Brenda didn't sleep at all. Her thoughts raced as she pondered her dad, her mom, her newfound father who was her old friend, and Valor, who honestly felt like the younger brother she had never had.

Excitement and fear churned together, preventing rest. She kept thinking about how drastically her life had changed in just three days. Her head swarmed with a thousand questions she wanted to ask Valor, and it dawned on her that she was doing her "Brenda thing" again, jumping into decisions without understanding all the context and consequences. Well, at least her Serbian roommate would have been proud. She smiled.

When Brenda finally fell asleep near dawn, her dreams were haunted by Caesar the ape dying just short of the promised land.

Before they left the next morning, she placed a short note on the table next to the credit card she had probably maxed out.

So long, Mother, and thanks for ~~all the fish~~ everything.

They left the house just before dawn.

Julia woke up a few hours later and stumbled into the kitchen. She scooped the note from the table, read it, and sighed.

She walked to the messy kitchen, opened a cabinet door, moved some things aside, and pulled out a bottle of whiskey. It was the cheap kind, but that is all she had. She took a coffee mug and filled it with whiskey, the golden liquid sloshing against the ceramic.

"Good morning, my daughter!" she said bitterly, raising the mug in the air in mock salute before taking a long drink. “Fuck it,” she muttered to herself.

She grabbed her cell phone and dialed a number. Her call was answered on the first ring.

“They were here.”

A long string of expletives answered her admission, followed by an angry question.

She gave a derisive snort. “Listen, don't ask me. They just left a few hours ago. No, I don’t know where. They’re your problem now.”

She said nothing else, ended the call, and threw her cell across the room, secretly hoping it shattered into a million pieces. They could all go to hell.

She’d just given up on it all.

CHAPTER TWENTY-TWO

Brenda was not a morning person, and last night's lack of sleep certainly didn't help.

Before leaving Silicon Valley, they stopped at a gas station to fuel up and grab supplies for the long journey ahead. They walked back to the rental car from the convenience store, Brenda carrying a twelve-pack of water and a heavy bag of groceries while Valor balanced three light boxes of granola. Brenda muttered something about chivalry, slightly annoyed that the elf hadn't noticed she was hauling the heavier load and hadn't offered to help.

After they loaded the trunk, Brenda got into the driver's seat and buckled up, only to see Valor fumbling once again with the door handle.

Valet service was not in my job description. Relax. Take a deep breath.

She stepped out of the car and showed Valor how to open the door again. They practiced a few times and finally both climbed in.

It was a beautiful day, as it always was in this part of the world. The temperate weather and bright sunshine stood in stark contrast to the tension pulling at Brenda's limbs.

"What's wrong, Brenda?" he asked.

She was surprised he noticed her frustration. Most men wouldn't.

She tried to pinpoint what was bothering her. It wasn't the water, and it wasn't the damn car door, though that had really pushed her buttons. It was something else.

"I feel like I'm jumping into the deep end of a pool without knowing if there's even water in it," she said honestly. "I promised I'd help you with this quest of yours with very little context and zero preparation."

Valor nodded, but he'd kept his thoughts to himself for most of the morning, and that didn't change now.

He wasn't distant, just quietly intrigued. He kept peering out the window in a way that reminded her of a kid taking his first airplane flight. His eyes were wide, and he seemed to be talking to himself so softly that she could not make out the words. He had this weird fascination with trees, and every time they passed a large oak or eucalyptus, he pointed them out with quiet excitement. "Look at that one," he'd murmur or "Beautiful specimen." It seemed like nature captured his attention far more than the sprawling suburbs, strip malls, or highway overpasses they drove past.

They left Palo Alto and took the 101 toward LA, leaving the hills of Silicon Valley behind. Green fields of Northern California spread on both sides of the road. Once they got on Route 5, the terrain became more barren, and the elf's fascination seemed to wane.

"I am sorry you were thrown into this story without any preparation or context, Brenda," he said gravely, turning to her with his big eyes. "Perhaps I should explain more."

"That'd be great," Brenda answered.

"My father conceived and created the Brotherhood for the sole purpose of completing our quest. My mother thought it was a bad idea. 'Can we trust humans with the survival of our race?' she asked him at the time," Valor said.

Brenda hit the blinker to pass a slower car, but she didn't answer.

"My father told her that 'race is not the defining characteristic of brotherhood' and that 'true brothers are brothers to the cause.' He said, 'Vision is thicker than blood,'" Valor added, glancing out again at the passing view.

Brenda studied him out of the corner of her eye. "First things first. It's a crappy, chauvinistic name."

Valor frowned. "Oh?"

"I'm not a brother. If anything, I'm a sister, and judging by the members I've met, it should definitely be called the Sisterhood!" Her tone made Valor shrink back in his chair. She noticed his reaction and softened her voice. "Listen, hearing half-told stories isn't very useful. Tell me everything from the start. You said it yourself. I need context from the very beginning, please." She spoke in a manner that made it clear this was not a request.

This was followed by a long silence. Brenda wasn't sure if Valor was angry or scared, and she didn't care. She was in the driver's seat now, and she needed more.

He stared out the window for a long time, clearly thinking. Then, he eventually sighed and nodded. "You are right. You deserve the context. I can't tell you everything from the absolute start. History is too long, and you would probably die of old age before we finished, but I can shed light on our quest."

"Please do," Brenda said, ignoring the remark about dying of old age. Coming from anyone else, she would have interpreted it as snarky, but he sounded sincere. Given the last few days, she doubted she'd ever see old age anyway.

There was another silence while Valor seemed to gather his

thoughts. Then, he began. "I come from six hundred years ago, when this world was a very different place. Brenda, you must understand that when I was a child, this world was full of wondrous magic. There were magical creatures, wizards who wielded magic, and magical artifacts and scrolls as common as... your cars nowadays." He gestured at the trucks and cars on the road around them.

"Humans were not the only ruling race in the world. We had dwarves, gnomes, elves, powerful fairies, giants, and many others. We sometimes fought and sometimes loved, but we all lived together. That was the nature of things," he said, as if stating a well-known fact.

"Loved?" she asked. "Can magical creatures and humans mate?"

"No, of course not! We are different races and therefore incompatible." His face turned crimson red, and his eyes darted uncomfortably away from Brenda, like a teenager talking to his parents about sex.

"Okay. Go on with your story," she said, growing embarrassed she had brought the topic up.

"Well, the only race that was almost magicless was humans. Only one in ten had magical capabilities, and while all other races received their magic at birth, humans had to try to learn magic and mostly failed at it," he said sadly.

"It was a time of prosperity, and the elves, being the long-lived creatures that we are, decided to leave the mainland—what I think you call Europe today—and go and seek new lands to the west. We gathered on the island of Britannia to set sail west. From my perspective, this was two years ago." He looked out the window before turning back to her.

"I was the youngest prince with six older brothers. This was very rare, as elves usually do not have more than two children throughout their lives. My father is an elvish king, and he is an elf of great charisma and strength."

Brenda could not decrypt his smile.

"Shortly after we reached Britannia, we heard rumors of a plague that was killing the magical creatures on the mainland," he continued. "My father sent his best human friends, those without magical skills, to investigate the plague. They came back with horrible news. The plague was killing everyone with magical abilities, from human wizards to dwarfish priests and healers, and not only ruling races. Magical animals were dying by the thousands," Valor said. The morning sun illuminated his face.

"My father's human advisors tried to analyze the plague and find a cure. It was the first ever plague that targeted only magical creatures. We received reports that magical artifacts were also being rendered useless by the plague. We were at a loss."

Brenda thought she saw a tear glimmering at the corner of Valor's eye.

"Before my father closed the ports of Britannia in order to avoid the plague spreading to the island, one last messenger came through with a story of the ultimate betrayal. You see, my father was one of the strongest elvish wizards of our times, but he had only one apprentice. The apprentice's name was Kador, and he was the greatest human wizard of the time. The messenger brought a letter from Kador to my father."

Whenever Valor said the name "Kador," his body tensed and his eyes hardened. It was unsettling to see the pain and anger in Valor's eyes.

"In the letter, Kador told my father that he had come to the realization that magic would ultimately mean the end of the human race. 'The existence of magic meant that humans would always live at a disadvantage,' he wrote. He told my father that he had cast a powerful spell that would dispel magic forever, wiping out magical creatures and removing magic from the world altogether. Kador begged for my father's forgiveness, telling him he was sacrificing all of our lives, including his own, for a better future for humanity."

Valor studied her, waiting as though she would surely have something to comment on what he'd just said, but Brenda resisted his nudge. She really wanted to hear the whole story first.

Brenda shook her head. "And? Go on."

"We do not know exactly how Kador did it, but my brothers told me they thought Kador had probably expelled his magical powers, thus killing himself and sacrificing his life force in order to cast a spell above his level," he said, his voice low.

"Though Kador's admission broke my father, he did not fail to act. We created a blockade and banned ships from entering Britannia, but we knew that one way or another, the plague would hit us as well. The news from the mainland still terrified us. Humans and magical creatures were dying left and right. They called it the Black Plague. My father could not see a way out. There were stories about magical creatures that went into hiding in the mountains, other stories about faraway lands that the plague could not reach, but my father could not trust these solutions. He knew that Kador, who was his student, had the power to cast powerful spells and that by sacrificing himself, he could have strengthened the spell tenfold. But he also knew that no wizard is almighty and therefore concluded that this plague, like every spell, would weaken with time and eventually fade away."

Brenda glanced at Valor, noting the tears forming in his eyes again.

"Initially, my father did not know how long this plague

dissipation would take or the cost to our lives... Watch out!" he said loudly, pointing at the road.

Brenda's eyes snapped forward again, and she slammed on the brakes bringing the car to a screeching halt. His warning had saved them from driving into a big truck that had been rapidly slowing in front of them.

They sat in the car in the middle of the highway. Brenda's pulse pounded in her ears, and she gripped the steering wheel with both hands. Smoke from the tires slowly faded in the wind, and the silence of the desert around them crept in as all the cars on the road came to a stop.

After her initial shock dissipated, Brenda unclenched her hands from the steering wheel. Her fingers felt rigid. They'd come within seconds of a deadly wreck. Yeah, there was no way she would live long enough to see old age. She needed to burn off some of the adrenaline coursing through her. She had to get out of there.

"I'm going to see what happened," she told Valor.

The elf nodded, probably still in shock himself.

Brenda climbed out of the car. The truck blocked her view, so she walked to the edge of the road and counted the short line of cars ahead. There was a police blockade fifty yards from where they had stopped. A load of people had been taken off a bus, and an officer was checking their IDs before letting them back on one by one.

Her skin prickled, and she chewed her bottom lip. Something wasn't right.

The officer took a long time to study each of the people before letting them go, and there were two police officers behind him with what looked like automatic weapons, clips in, ready to fire. The last passenger got back on the bus after a thorough conversation with the officer checking IDs. One of the others removed a spike strip from the road, and the bus drove off. Her spidey sense, as her ex-roommate used to say, screamed at her. Something was really off.

The cars in front of the truck started creeping forward, and Brenda rushed back to their vehicle and started the engine.

"Shit, shit, shit!" she said as she jumped back in. "I don't think they're legit cops... I think they're looking for us!" She glanced at Valor. "If you have a Jedi mind trick, these-are-not-the-droids-you're-looking-for style, now would be a great time to use it."

Valor cocked his head and frowned at her. His eyebrows pinched. "What is a Jedi mind trick?"

"Valor, I have a weird feeling that these guys are looking for us," Brenda said deliberately, glaring at him. "Can you cast an illusion spell or something?"

The line of cars inched slowly closer to the barricade, one car's length at a time.

"Magic has not yet come back to the world in full force, Brenda," Valor said. "I still don't have my defensive or offensive spells. Also, most of my spells are weak and require a lot of my life force. The teleporting we did this week has taken so much out of me. The excitement has been a distraction, but I still feel sickly weak," he said apologetically.

"Then what are we going to do?" she demanded.

"I could try to cast an illusion, but it will be weak and will probably break at the first physical contact and won't stand up to much examination."

"Do it!" Brenda commanded. "We don't have a choice."

Valor startled, probably at her tone.

"Listen, I don't care if you don't think you're strong enough. You have to try," she added, nearly growling the last words.

"Very well." Valor took the small box from his pocket and muttered a few words under his breath. The box transformed into a simple two-inch rod. He murmured a few more words and waved the rod around like a conductor.

Nothing happened.

Brenda's head swiveled, studying the road in front of them, her hands clenched on the wheel. "Do something," she whispered.

The words "Advanced illusion" flickered in her mind.

She turned back to Valor. He was gone, and in his place sat a breathtaking young Black woman with natural curls framing her face and warm brown eyes. She wore a simple sundress that looked effortlessly elegant, the kind of casual beauty that made people stop and stare without understanding why.

"Oh, shit! You're good!" she said, but her voice sounded very strange, old and raspy.

She glanced in the rearview mirror and saw an elderly Asian man looking back at her. His gray hair was thinning but well-groomed, thick eyebrows framed tired dark eyes, and he wore the expression of someone who balanced budgets for a living. Completely forgettable and utterly harmless.

"How the hell did you come up with these characters?" she asked with amusement.

"Worked better than I anticipated!" Valor said in a sultry feminine voice. "They sat next to us in the café where we met Jacob." He shot her a grin. "Be careful, though. The spell is weak, and the illusion might evaporate if they touch us or inspect us carefully enough."

The large truck in front of them cleared the police barricade, and the officer who had been checking IDs signaled to them to move forward. Brenda slowly complied, stalling as long as she could.

"Will you be able to move the spike strip if we need to?" she asked quietly, watching one of the other officers place it on the road in front of their car.

"I am not sure," he said. "I have not tried Telekinesis yet. Let's hope I don't need to."

The police officer was built like a bodybuilder, his muscles straining against his uniform. Something about his smirk brought back memories of the entitled athletes from high school who thought the world owed them everything.

She rolled her window down as he approached her door. "Hello, Officer. How can I help you?" she said in her best good-citizen voice.

"License and registration, please." The officer gave her a bored look. Then, he noticed Valor in the passenger seat. The officer smiled and winked at the disguised elf. "I'll also need both of you to turn off the car, step out, and open the trunk," he added with a suggestive leer.

Brenda hid her grimace by hunting for the rental car's registration in the glove box and handed it over. She cut the engine.

They both climbed out of the car and joined the officer at the rear, leaving the car doors open.

She hoped the officer would forget to ask for her driver's license again since it wouldn't match her face much at the moment.

He didn't even look at the registration papers, keeping his eyes on Valor instead. He asked the elf to come join him a few paces away on the passenger side and told Brenda to open the trunk.

He started chatting to Valor as Brenda moved to the back of the car. She couldn't make out the conversation, but the cop seemed to be enjoying himself.

It all went wrong really fast.

The cop escorted Valor back to the passenger door. He gave a quick glance in the trunk when they passed behind the car, and he closed it. Brenda, still standing behind the car, saw the officer wink to his buddy.

Then, he slapped Valor on the ass.

The illusion faded for a split second. Instead of a curvy Black woman, the cop had his hand on the bottom of a skinny, pale elf.

The officer's eyes opened wide.

Brenda's brain screamed. *Shit!*

"Get in the car!" Brenda shouted, running for the open driver's side door.

The cop was already reaching for his gun, but Valor elbowed him aside and dove into the passenger seat.

"Move the spike strip!" Brenda screamed as she started the car and threw it into gear.

Valor pointed at the spikes, and the strip slithered like a snake off the road.

Brenda stomped the gas pedal, and the car launched forward. "What the fuck?" she screamed.

"I told you the illusion would fade the moment anyone touched us," he said. He sounded much calmer than she felt, quite entertained too.

Damn him.

Gunshots echoed behind them. The rear windshield exploded, and the front windshield filled with a spray of blood.

There was a single bloodied hole in the front windshield, a small crater dead center in front of Valor's seat, and the wind roared in through it with a loud whistle.

CHAPTER TWENTY-THREE

"There's no such thing as the tooth fairy! You're just a stupid little girl," Timmy told Jin as the whole class looked on.

Almost twenty kids snickered.

"Kick him," Lixi whispered, fluttering closer to Jin's ear. Neither of them liked Timmy.

Jin shook her head.

"You can do it. Kick him," Lixi repeated.

Jin stiffened, and she rounded on Timmy. He was a fat, horrible boy who she really didn't like. Now, he was standing too close to her, and his breath smelled like rotten apples.

Wham!

She didn't mean to kick him. Well, she kinda did but not where it really hurts boys.

He collapsed to the hallway floor like a sack of potatoes, clutched his privates, and started crying. The crowd of kids cheered and yelled. Jin didn't like that. It hurt her ears and made her stomach feel funny.

"I *have* a tooth fairy, and there's nothing you can do about it!" Jin yelled, standing over him. She bent forward and raised her hand, but Miss Pepper was too quick and grabbed her arm before she could slap him.

Miss Pepper was Jin's gym teacher, although Lixi often whispered that she doubted the woman had visited any gym lately herself. The teacher's grip was surprisingly strong for someone who spent most of PE class sitting in a folding chair.

"Jin! Go to the principal's office immediately!" Miss Pepper commanded, tugging her away from Timmy.

Jin was told to go to the principal's office quite often, especially since she'd figured out how to kick boys where it really hurt. When a different bully had cornered Jin on the playground, Lixi had been the one to let Jin in on the vulnerable spot. It had taken care of that bully too.

Even though it happened a lot, Jin was never reprimanded harshly by the principal. She knew her sweet face dulled any ire, and even her blonde ponytails often seemed sad, like the drooping ears of a scolded puppy. This time, Jin walked slowly, dragging her feet, her sneakers making a squeaky sound all the way down the corridor.

Deep down, Jin felt that today she would not get out of it so easily.

Lixi sat on her shoulder and tried to cheer her up. "You did good, girl! You rock, Jin!"

Mr. Skosh, the school's principal, looked like a grown-up fat version of little fat Timmy, and Jin hated it. His shirt was too small, the buttons stretching over his round stomach like they might pop off any second. The front of his khaki pants was spotted with ketchup stains that made Jin wrinkle her nose in disgust. He sweated a lot, and as she knocked on the open door, he was trying to straighten the last few hairs left on his head.

"What are you doing here *again*, Jin Barry?" he asked in a sharp voice.

"Miss Pepper told me to go to your office." Jin didn't want to share more than she had to. She studied her shoes as if they were the most interesting things in the world.

"And why would she ask you to come to my office?" he pressed.

"I don't know," she said.

"Is that so?"

"Uhm... I kicked Timmy, but he's okay now!"

At least, she *hoped* he was okay.

"And why would you kick Timmy, Miss Barry?" the fat man asked in a nasally voice that reminded Jin of her neighbor's old, wheezy dog barking.

"He said there are no tooth fairies and that I'm stupid if I think I saw one," she said, defiantly crossing her arms and setting her chin.

"Well... what makes you think there are tooth fairies, and why would you think denying their presence justifies kicking someone?"

"Well..." Jin mimicked his tone. "It just so happens that *I* have a tooth fairy, although she says she prefers just 'fairy.'"

"You tell him, girl!" said Lixi from her perch on Jin's shoulder.

Mr. Skosh chuckled. "Well... you are a very silly girl, Miss Barry. Of course, tooth fairies aren't real! That means you're lying, so basically, Timmy was right." He leaned across the desk toward her and smiled his sweaty smile. He smelled like an old tuna sandwich.

"I am not a liar," Jin said, her voice filled with anger. "She's here, and I can see her, and she's not happy with how you're talking to me!"

"You freaking chauvinistic douchebag!" Lixi shouted right next to Jin's ear.

But of course, Mr. Skosh couldn't hear or see Lixi.

"If she's here, why can't I see her?" he asked, raising an eyebrow. Sweat rolled down his forehead to his cheeks. At least this time he forgot the "Well..."

Jin hesitated, knowing instinctively that Mr. Skosh wouldn't like what came next. "She says that adults have a rotten heart and that they lose the ability to see fairies. Black fairies or otherwise," she added after Lixi reminded her.

Mr. Skosh frowned. "Rotten heart, you say!" he growled, taking a damp cloth from his pocket to wipe his glistening forehead. "And what else does this fairy of yours say about me?"

Lixi whispered in her ear.

Jin turned red and shook her head. "No, I'm not gonna tell him that."

"Tell me what?" Mr. Skosh demanded.

"Lixi is using bad words... and some I don't even understand," Jin said softly. She felt trapped in the hot, humid room.

"I demand you tell me exactly what she's telling you, Miss Barry!" he snapped.

"She says you shouldn't call girls silly because it's demeaning and sexist," Jin said in a quiet voice.

Lixi hopped off Jin's shoulder, flitted into view, and crossed her arms. "Keep going," Lixi said. "Tell him the rest."

Lixi was the most beautiful being in the world. Jin was sure of it. Her dark skin and translucent wings shimmered with glitter, and her curly hair bounced like a princess's. She wore a wonderful green fairy gown that flowed like leaves in the wind, but she had what Jin's mother called a potty mouth, and she often said naughty words that Jin didn't understand but knew were probably not allowed.

"She says..." Jin swallowed before she continued. "She says that having intercourse with Miss Pepper at the staff Christmas party constitutes harassment, since you're her superior... and that you should relinquish your position." Jin stumbled over the unfamiliar words and closed her eyes. Her blonde ponytails shivered slightly.

There was a long silence.

"What is intercourse?" Jin whispered to Lixi.

"Get... out... of my office!" Mr. Skosh roared, spit flying from his mouth as his fat finger jabbed toward the door. His face turned as red as a tomato. His eyes bulged until they might pop out.

Jin whimpered and backed toward the door. Lixi settled back on Jin's shoulder.

"Go home," Mr. Skosh bellowed. "Do not show your face at this school for the rest of the week! If you *ever* speak of this to anyone, you will *never* attend school again. Ever!"

Jin darted out of the office, out of the school, and started the long trek home. She was a little scared. She'd never left school in the middle of the day before, and her house was three miles away.

"Don't worry, Jin," Lixi soothed. "You can do this. I'll protect you if anything happens."

Jin nodded, her ponytails blowing in the wind. She didn't hurry, stopping to kick cans across the street and read the names on the street signs.

Lixi's dark curls bounced with every step Jin took, and the fairy's brown skin and wings glowed in the sun. "Like I said, don't you worry, girl. I'll protect you. I won't let anyone hurt you. You are strong. You got this."

They passed an electronics shop with TVs arranged in the window. The screens all showed the faces of two menacing-looking men. The caption said, *Two Men Found Dead in Local Hunting Grounds*.

Jin and Lixi both stared.

"Who do you think killed them?" Jin asked.

Lixi studied the faces. Jin had never seen her so focused. For a moment, Lixi shimmered with blue light.

“I think they fucked with the wrong unicorn,” Lixi said. “Unicorns can be real assholes.”

“Like Mr. Skosh?” asked Jin.

“Even worse,” Lixi said with an exaggerated seriousness.

Jin wrinkled her freckled nose and decided assholes sounded awful.

They continued on toward her house.

"Have you ever met a unicorn, Lixi?" Jin asked.

"I think I have," said Lixi, as if trying to reach back through distant memories. "It might have been a dream, but I'm almost sure I once helped an elvish king and a powerful human wizard find a unicorn. That was a very long time ago, back when there were elves and wizards and magic everywhere."

Jin nodded. It made sense. Her thoughts were still clouded by mean Mr. Skosh, his scowling face burned into her memory.

“And don’t worry about Mr. Skosh. He’s going to find out he has testicular cancer this weekend. He won’t be bothering you anymore.”

They walked in silence for a while.

“What is testicular cancer?” Jin asked.

CHAPTER TWENTY-FOUR

They were in a dirty, old, run-down roadside motel, the kind you only stayed in when your car broke down and you had no other choice or when you wanted to do something sketchy away from prying eyes. It was the kind that had one greasy restaurant next door serving all-day breakfast and yesterday's coffee with a neon sign that flickered between "Vacancy" and "Va ancy." The carpet felt sticky, and the air smelled of industrial disinfectant that couldn't quite mask whatever had happened in these rooms before. The parking lot had very few cars, which at least suggested that most of the rooms were empty.

Brenda sat on the bed closest to the door, her legs folded, her head in her hands. Valor lay on the other bed, his breath shallow. His wounds looked fatal, and she knew he might not survive the night.

She shouldn't have accepted the stupid job offer. She shouldn't have chosen to go along with Valor, and she shouldn't have stayed with him. No, she should've gotten the fuck out after the attack on the airplane. What had she been thinking?

Stupid! Stupid! she thought. Now she had a dying elf on her hands, and she didn't even fully understand why she was there in the first place. Nothing he'd told her had explained her presence. Why did he need her? Why was magic even so important?

"Ghuaaaa..." came a groan from the other bed as Valor tried to sit up, his face ashen. His shoulder was bleeding but not as badly as his stomach wound. It gushed each time Brenda adjusted the makeshift bandage she'd fashioned from the clothes in her suitcase.

"Lie still," she commanded.

"Brenda... what happened?" he asked in a weak, raspy voice.

"You got fucking shot. Twice, actually," she said, surprised by the lack of emotion in her own voice. It was like they were discussing the weather.

He shifted on the bed and grunted. With a confused frown, he pressed a hand to his middle. "How did we escape?"

"You pulled out your magical wand and apparently made us invisible. You couldn't have done that before we encountered the roadblock?" she snapped, her anger rising.

"It's a staff, actually. Wands are much more powerful. They hold magic inside them," he said softly. "I don't have a wand yet."

"Well, you fucking used your staff too late," she said bitterly. "They shot at us, and they hit you. Twice! That never happens to the heroes in the movies. Just our luck."

"Yes, this is rather bad." He pulled up his tunic, moved the bandage aside, and peered at the exit wound in his stomach. It was swollen, bleeding, and ugly.

Brenda couldn't hold back a rush of tears. "Yes, it does look very bad! Fantastic diagnosis, fucking doctor elf!"

He studied her for a long while, his face ghostly pale. "Thank you for caring, Brenda," he said softly. "I know you're angry, and you probably have good reason to be. I dragged you into this crazy world you weren't prepared for, and now you're in a perilous situation. I'm sorry for that."

"A lot of good your 'sorry' will do me when you're dead," Brenda said, tears now streaming down her face.

"I find it very unlikely that I'll be dead anytime soon," he said encouragingly, giving her a faint smile. "I have you to help me."

She didn't answer. She just stared at him, grief building in her chest. What could she do to help the elf? It wasn't like she was a doctor. As it was, she had turned into a glorified chauffeur.

"I won't be able to heal myself unfortunately," he added matter-of-factly. "As I said, magic hasn't returned in full force. Some types of spells are still inaccessible to me. Self-reflective magic, like healing oneself, should be easy, but I can't make it work." He paused, gesturing toward his middle. "So, I'll need your help."

She scooted to the edge of the bed, moving closer to Valor. "How did you teleport us two days ago if your self-reflective magic doesn't work?" she asked, wondering again why she even cared when Valor would be dead soon.

"Good question," he murmured, cringing with pain. "I teleported you, Brenda. That's why I asked you to think of a place. I was your luggage, so to speak."

"Okay," she said wryly, the corners of her mouth twitching into a sad smirk. "Carry on."

He did not get the joke. It was a bad one anyway.

"The same goes for the illusion magic. I transformed you, and while I stayed in the same area, I was able to extend the spell to myself. The magic affected the space you were in. Some weak spells do work, like slightly altering my appearance, but healing is a much stronger spell."

"Can't you heal an area with you in it?" she asked hopefully.

"No. Healing is sympathetic magic. It's either done on yourself or on others," he said, meeting her eyes. "But you can heal me."

This claim was followed by a long silence.

He doesn't get it, does he? He's completely delusional about my abilities.

She studied the hopeful elf, his face pale and his forehead slick with sweat and blood. He reminded her of war movies when a dying soldier asks his buddies to take him home to his family, speaking with that same desperate faith in impossible things. He had no idea how fucked up he was or how utterly powerless she was to save him. Here he was, bleeding out in a sleazy motel, still believing in fairytale magic while she sat there knowing she was about to watch him die.

"I'm sorry, Valor. I'm not a wizard," Brenda said eventually. "No humans alive today are, as far as I know."

Surely, he realized that when magic had been wiped from the world, it had been reduced to myth.

"But of course you are," he said with a wan smile. "That's why you're here with me."

She gaped at him, saying nothing, her heart pounding. Finally, she shook her head. "No, that's not true."

"Of course it is," he countered.

She didn't answer, couldn't answer, merely waited for him to continue.

"Your family line possesses dormant magical skills. It isn't uncommon for humans to have these. Trained wizards can awaken magic in those with the right heritage. Before activation, these humans don't display magical signs, and it was hoped humans would survive the plague for that reason."

Brenda scrubbed a hand over her face. "So... it's in my genes?"

Valor quirked an eyebrow. "Your ancestor was a great

wizard and a close friend of my father's. When the plague hit, she worked desperately to find a cure... but eventually, everyone understood there would be no cure and that only time would undo Kador's damage. Your foremother pledged your family line to the cause of bringing magic back. She was the first Witness at the founding of the Brotherhood."

Brenda blinked a few times but said nothing, processing the information.

Valor's eyes widened. He coughed, and blood bubbled on his lips. "You need to do it now. Try, please," he whispered, urgency sharp in his voice. "Try."

Time seemed to slow as her mind raced. *This is it.*

This was the moment of truth. She could take a leap of faith or just walk out the door and try to rebuild her life and forget this madness.

Her hands trembled. She took a deep breath, made up her mind, and lifted her chin.

"Tell me what to do," she said in a clear, steady voice.

Valor sighed. She hadn't noticed he'd been holding his breath. "There are four ways to cast a spell—by device, by action, by word, and by thought," he began. "Each spell has its own requirements. Most spells can be invoked in multiple ways depending on your proficiency. For each spell—"

"Valor," she cut in, "just tell me what to do." *Of all the times for a long lecture...*

He coughed again as he removed the bandage. He had grown even more pale, and his eyes seemed less bright. "Yes, you're right. Hold your hands over my wound and say..."

His lips moved, but she did not hear him.

She leaned closer but couldn't hear the next word. "What?" she asked. "What do you want me to say?"

He smiled weakly. "Your mind is blocking the Word from your consciousness, but you should still be able to say it. Come. Place your hands on the wound."

She grimaced at the blood but did as he asked. It felt warm and wet.

He flinched in pain, but he didn't push her away. "Now say it!" he ordered, putting his hand on her shoulder.

She closed her eyes. She didn't know what to say. *This is where it ends,* she thought. *With my failure.*

His hand began to slide off her shoulder. "Say it... Say..." His voice was wet, barely audible.

She leaned forward, trying to clear her mind, and then... she said it.

Her hands glowed only for two seconds. A soft blue light started somewhere deep in her chest, flowing like cool water through her arms and into her palms before reaching outward toward Valor's wound. The sensation felt like a violent chill moving through her body, making her shiver in the warm room. The words Minor Heal popped into her mind.

Then, energy drained from her, leeching from her chest to her arms to her hands, and it felt like she'd just run five miles. She opened her eyes.

Valor was looking at her, barely conscious. A tear trickled down his cheek. "Good," he rasped. "Again."

She considered the wound. It still looked awful. Blood still poured through her fingers. Whatever she'd done hadn't been enough.

She said the word again. The glow returned, spreading from her chest to her shoulders to her hands. The wound's edges began to close. She felt like she'd run a marathon.

Suddenly, the word became clear in her mind. She heard what she was saying. "*Medirium.*"

She said it again and again. She hadn't noticed Valor's hand had fallen away. She couldn't tell if he was breathing.

"*Medirium! Medirium! Medirium!*"

Her fingertips felt frozen. The room whirled around them...

Brenda woke up on the floor.

There was puke on the carpet beside her. Hers? Probably hers. Her clothes were soaked with cold sweat. She couldn't stand. Her legs were jelly. She pulled herself up to the bed and wiped her mouth with her sleeve. Her fingers felt numb. Weird. With dread, she turned her attention to Valor.

He was breathing.

Slowly and weakly, but he was definitely breathing. He even snored a little.

She had done it. Her mind could not believe what she was seeing.

His shirt was soaked with dried blood. The room reeked of his gore and her vomit, but his wounds were gone. Not even a scar remained.

Brenda's head was spinning. She was going to be sick again. She tried to stand up and walk to the bathroom, but her legs were unable to carry her, and she fell face first to the floor. At least the sharp pain in her nose distracted her from throwing up.

Eventually, she crawled back onto her bed. All she wanted was water. Her head throbbed like it did after a night of insane drinking, where all you wanted was to rehydrate and you swore to God you would never do it again.

Her eyes closed, but she smiled.

He was alive.

CHAPTER
TWENTY-FIVE

"We believe he's badly hurt, probably dead. We analyzed the blood on one of the bullets from the incident at the roadblock. It wasn't human blood," Mary said, glancing at the nervous waiter who hovered at the far side of the dining room.

They were back at Roy's favorite restaurant, the one he'd told her he discovered after reading it was the most expensive hot place in the city. Like the tacky man he was, he confused expensive with elegant, returning here religiously to order the same overpriced steak. Roy was the kind of person who bought whatever first-class magazines and luxury brochures told him was worth having. Mary would have preferred a good ramen place, but Roy wouldn't hear of it.

Mary raised her red wine and took a sip, observing Roy through the large glass. His face distorted behind it. Grotesque. *Just like his soul,* she thought.

"But the elf still got away, making you a useless twat," Roy said, venom thick in his voice. He carved into his tomahawk steak, slicing off huge chunks and stuffing them into his big, fat mouth.

Mary didn't bother to respond. She hated him with the special passion she reserved for people she'd once liked. In her early days with the Bellum Sacrum, Roy had seemed like an answer to a prayer, a powerful ally who could give their holy mission the resources it needed. She'd thought his brutality was righteousness, his ambition a reflection of divine purpose. For months, she'd defended him to other Bellum Sacrum members who questioned his commitment, insisting that Kador worked through imperfect vessels.

But time had revealed the ugly truth—Roy treated their sacred mission as nothing more than a career opportunity. For him, this was simply a job that happened to involve religious fanatics instead of normal employees. Every time he reduced their divine calling to management speak and every moment he treated their life's purpose as his stepping stone to greater power felt sacrilegious, and for that, she would never forgive him.

"I gave you millions of dollars in budget, countless head-count, and fucking endless access to information, and all you can tell me is we think he's hurt?" Roy shouted, spittle spraying across the pristine border of his large white plate.

"You are a pig, Roy. Stop spitting, and stop your vulgar behavior. We'll get him, and you know it. Our source delivered. That's what matters. They're on the run, and they're hurt. We've got people in every hospital in Northern California. In a matter of days, it'll all be over." Mary kept her voice cold and even. He was the CEO, yes, but he was also an outsider and a hired gun.

Roy glared at her, picked up his napkin, and wiped his lips, leaving red stains. "You're fucking fired. If you weren't connected, I'd fire you out of a cannon and into the sun!" He tossed the napkin onto the table.

The waiter arrived with a mumbled greeting, removed Roy's plate and placed a bowl of chilled fruit soup in front of him.

"I'm going to take a piss," Roy announced loudly, ignoring the offended looks from nearby tables.

Mary sat motionless, her expression stony, waiting and sipping her wine while slowly eating her white fish. After a moment of thought, the decision came, and then action. She pulled a small vial from her purse and, with sleight of hand as if flicking something off his plate, poured the contents into his soup.

Ten minutes later, Roy swaggered back. "It was actually a dump," he said, smirking at the disapproving diners. "I needed more room for the rest of the meal."

Mary rolled her eyes.

He sat down and started into the soup. "This is excellent. You should try it," he said, genuinely delighted. He sipped the soup. His loud slurping noises made Mary's eye twitch. Then, he coughed slightly.

Mary gave him a soft, almost sympathetic look. "Well, Roy," she said, leaning forward. "There's one thing you never understood."

He raised an eyebrow, chewing.

"You worked for *me*," she purred. "You were a puppet CEO, a poster child we put in front of the cameras so the media had someone to love or hate. You were the violent bulldog we put in the yard to scare the employees in *my* company."

His eyes widened in shock, and a vein bulged on his forehead.

"And now you're a rabid dog," she said, her voice still gentle, "and I need to put you down." She smiled faintly as his face turned redder, both eyes now bloodshot. "James Webber will be very happy to take your place. He's boring, but at least he's efficient."

"What..." Roy started, but his voice cracked. A vein burst in his right eye, and he winced.

"You see, the Bellum Sacrum is running the show. We always have. *We* hired you. The Kildare Corporation's entire goal is to protect and support the Bellum Sacrum. I own you." She pronounced each word slowly, deliberately.

"What have you done to me?" he gasped in realization, his hands trembling as he tried to reach for a knife, but they wouldn't obey him.

"And you have the audacity to fire me?" Her voice finally carried heat. "You little rat. You worthless shit. I'm going to find the elf. I'm going to find that witch Brenda, and I am going to end magic." Her eyes burned with religious fervor. "This is my life's mission, the worthy cause of saving humanity from total annihilation. Fire me?" She leaned closer, her voice dropping to a deadly whisper. "The only way to leave the Bellum Sacrum is '*Aut vincere aut mori.*' Victorious or dead." She leaned back and pinned him with a pitying stare. "We will be victorious, and by God, you will not live to see that day."

Roy looked terrified and confused, his blood-filled eyes blinking in panic. He spluttered, unable to form words.

"Your soul will not benefit from the Bellum Sacrum's mission," Mary continued, calm as ever. "Your final act of trying to stop us has damned you." Her voice took on the tone of a judge delivering a verdict. "I hereby sentence you to death and send your soul to Hell. Goodbye, Roy."

His mouth opened and closed, but no sound came out.

She stood, smoothed her dress, and walked serenely from the table. Roy made a feeble attempt to grab her arm, but Mary easily slipped past. She waited near the dim and luckily vacant hostess stand, quietly witnessing his demise.

Roy sat there for a few more seconds, dazed. Then, blood began to pour from his nose, and his head dropped into the lavish bowl of soup.

"Good riddance," she said. She took a mint from the hostess stand and popped it into her mouth. The food here was dreadful.

As Mary left the restaurant, a woman screamed behind her, followed by the clatter of dropped silverware and the scrape of chairs being pushed back in panic. Someone shouted to call 911, while another voice yelled for a doctor. The chaos she'd created was spreading through the dining room like ripples in a pond, but Mary's stride never faltered. She didn't look back as she marched out to the car. She never looked back.

The guards waiting by the limo didn't flinch at the sight of her exiting alone. One of them opened a rear door, and she slid inside.

“Take me to the airport,” she told the driver. *Enough of this silliness.* She was going to handle it herself.

The car door closed behind her. She leaned back into the soft leather and placed a call.

“James,” she said. “You're the new CEO of Kildare. Congratulations. I'm sure you'll manage the bureaucracy just as well as you always do.”

"Understood," James said flatly without hesitation.

James Webber would be a much better CEO. She should have gotten rid of Roy years ago. James was effective, meticulous, organized, and loyal to the cause. Unlike Roy, James didn't have a large ego. In fact, she wasn't sure he had any personal aspirations at all. He knew she was Bellum Sacrum and he was not. He would never stand in her way. She felt good about this change in leadership. Now she could take care of business her way.

She appreciated that James didn't ask what had happened

to Roy. It wasn't that he didn't care. James simply understood priorities, and he always focused on what mattered most.

Instead, he just said "How can I help?"

It was refreshing to work with someone who grasped the mission's importance without needing lengthy explanations or constant pleasing.

“Thank you. Nothing right now. I’m mobilizing all Bellum Sacrum members,” she said. “We’re going to California.”

CHAPTER TWENTY-SIX

Valor woke with a cry. He felt like he'd been pulled out of the abyss and thrown into a hell of blazing lava. His face felt so hot, and he opened his eyes, blinking rapidly. It wasn't lava at all. It was just the Californian sun shining on his face through the uncovered window.

Then, he remembered getting shot and the events of the previous night. Frantically, he reached for his stomach. His shirt stuck to his skin, and it hurt to peel it away. He knew that sensation. Dried blood. He'd felt it before.

He was surprised he wasn't dead. Knowing the damage his body had sustained combined with his irritating inability to heal himself, he'd figured his odds were slim. He was even more surprised when he discovered the smooth skin where the gunshot wound had been. Nothing. He was more than fully healed. He had no scars.

She had returned him to his previous health, as though the shooting had never happened.

It was incredible in more than one way. First, Brenda could channel his magic, or perhaps she'd used her own. He wasn't sure which, but he hoped it was the latter. Second, she had endured the toll of such magic long enough to heal him *completely*. That meant her blood hadn't suffered magical dilution. Many mixed human couples—one magical, one not—had children with weak or no magical ability.

Brenda, he suddenly thought. *She must be okay. Everything depends on her.*

He hauled himself to his feet and stepped to her bedside. He leaned over her.

She was out, breathing but unresponsive. He shook her shoulder gently, and she mumbled a few incomprehensible words. That, at least, made him a little more confident she would be all right.

Next, he registered the horrible smell in the room—blood, sweat, and vomit. He opened the window as far as it would go to let in some fresh air, but he decided to deal with the mess once Brenda was fully awake. She needed sleep, and he didn't want to risk waking her.

While cleaning the room held no appeal, cleaning himself did. He fumbled with the shower handles until he figured out how to adjust the temperature. A few "too hot!" and "too cold!" attempts later, he found the perfect balance. The warm water felt incredible against his skin. He watched the dried blood wash away in rusty streams, swirling down the drain until the water ran clear. The relief of being clean again made his whole body relax. When the water began to turn lukewarm, he shut off the spray and stepped out.

He examined his clothes. They were bloodied and riddled with bullet holes. *That won't work for venturing outside.*

"*Warashi,*" he uttered.

The fabric became spotless. The dried blood vanished, leaving the material clean and fresh. *There, that's better.*

"*Tekeni,*" he continued, focusing on the torn fabric. He

frowned when nothing happened. The holes remained, jagged reminders of the previous night's violence.

Valor wondered how long it would be before his mending spells were functioning again. Magic was increasing around him each day, but it remained a shadow of what he was used to. Some spells worked perfectly. Others failed completely, and he couldn't predict which would work.

He stepped out of the bathroom and opted for the robe hanging in the closet. It was small on his seven-foot frame and wouldn't close around his chest, but at least it was somewhat clean.

Valor opened the room's door and stepped out into the corridor outside, careful to close the door as quietly as possible. This was not a well-maintained establishment. Dingy towels waited on the shelves, and dirt clustered in the corners. Chipped paint spoke of the lack of attention or care by anyone.

Exactly what my brothers told me human establishments look like.

HE STROLLED DOWN the hall toward the lobby. Behind the front desk, a bored young woman sat, blonde, maybe twenty by his very unrefined human-age-guessing skills. Her shirt was extremely tight and read "Eat Me" in bold red letters.

She must be too poor to afford a larger shirt, he thought with compassion.

She gave him a curious look. "How can I be of service?" she asked, winking as she gave him a once-over, her gaze lingering over the half-opened robe.

"I am looking for a library," he said formally. "Do you have one in this establishment?"

She stared at him, her eyebrows raised. "Whatcha need a

library for? You a librarian or something?" she asked, smoothing her shirt and running her fingers through her slightly oily hair.

"I seek knowledge. I want to learn about many things," he said thoughtfully.

She gave him another blank look, winding a lock of hair around her finger. Then, her eyes lit up, and she smiled. "We got the Internet on the computer there. You can learn a lot of stuff on the computer."

"Can you teach me how to use this 'Internet'?" he asked.

Her jaw slackened, and her eyes widened. "You don't know how to use the Internet?"

"No," he answered.

"Where have you been living all these years?" she asked.

"In a forest," he replied.

She laughed as if he was making a joke. "All right, I'll show you some things." She leaned forward suggestively, seemingly to make sure he understood she was offering more than simple tech support.

"Thank you. You are very kind," he said sincerely, formally, withdrawing slightly to communicate his refusal of any other, more intimate service.

She frowned a bit. "Are you gay? You're handsome enough to be gay," she muttered. "Well, what the heck. I'm fucking bored. I'll show you how to use the stupid Internet."

Twenty minutes later, he was seated in a small chair at a small desk in a small room, and he was hooked, reading insatiably through Wikipedia pages and searching on Google while the woman from the front desk peered over his shoulder.

"This is incredible. So much knowledge... and anyone can access this?" he asked over his shoulder.

"Yeah, it's mostly boring, though. Most people use it for porn," she added, crossing her arms beneath her breasts and pushing them up.

"What is 'porn'?" he asked, pointedly ignoring the new attempt to seduce him.

"You gotta be fuckin' kidding me!" she replied. She snorted in disgust and dropped her arms.

He didn't comment. Instead, his eyes were already back on the screen, scanning quickly. He read something in Latin aloud and smiled fondly. It was one of the human languages he natively understood.

"You speak French? That was French, right? Everything foreign sounds French to me." She giggled. "You're a real trip."

He barely registered her comment. He was reading faster now, scrolling and clicking rapidly. His typing, which had started slow, was now lightning fast.

"Don't break it!" she scolded.

He ignored her. His eyes didn't blink. He moved at machine speed.

"You wanna hook up?" She seemed as bored as ever.

Before he answered, Valor Googled "hook up." He read several definitions and articles on the topic.

He turned to face her. "That is very kind of you," he said. "You are incredibly attractive, and I would love to 'hook up' at a later time, but I must finish this work first."

The line came from an article titled *How to Let a Girl Down Easy*. He hoped it would work.

She blushed a little. "Yeah, sure, I get it."

When he turned back to the screen, it seemed to flicker because he moved between pages so quickly.

"Some of the articles contradict each other," he said. "How do you know which is the truth?"

"Who cares?" she asked flatly. "It's the Internet. Everything's the truth."

Valor didn't answer and returned to scrolling.

Eventually, the woman sighed and wandered back to the front desk, probably having lost interest.

Valor stayed put, his mind augmented by Fast Learning spells. He was surprised and delighted to find that this spell was working today.

He memorized, cataloged, and cross-referenced everything, consuming thousands of pages with wide eyes.

BRENDA WOKE SLOWLY AND GROANED. Everything hurt. It reminded her of her wilder college nights. Her head throbbed, and even the light stung her eyes.

But underneath the pain and dehydration misery, something else stirred, a feeling she'd experienced only a few times in her life—when she'd finally decided to leave her parents, when she'd gotten into her number one college on full scholarship, and when she'd taken the leap and moved to New York.

Pride. Deep, glowing satisfaction.

She had used magic. Real magic.

The memory came flooding back—her hands glowing, energy flowing through her, Valor's wounds closing beneath her touch. She flexed her fingers, half expecting to see some lingering trace of power. Control was too strong a word, but she had definitely wielded magic.

The thought made her grin despite her pounding head. Whatever happened next, she'd crossed a line she could never uncross. She was no longer just Brenda Mountain, struggling anthropology graduate. She was something else.

She rolled toward Valor's bed, expecting to see him in his.

But Valor wasn't in his bed.

She scanned the room in a panic. There was no sign of him.

She staggered up, out of the bed, and checked the bathroom. The shower was damp, but his clothes were in a heap on the floor.

"Why do men always do that? Doesn't matter what age or race. They always leave their clothes on the bathroom floor," she muttered.

Where did he go?

She clumsily searched the room until she found one of the robes was missing. That meant he'd gone out in a motel bathrobe. *That can't be good.*

She grabbed the keycard and headed to the lobby. A trashy-looking girl sat behind the desk, typing into her phone.

"I'm looking for a tall man in a robe. Did you see him?" Brenda asked.

The girl looked Brenda over like she was wasting valuable social media time. "He's at the Internet booth," she said eventually, nodding toward a door labeled "Business Lounge." The door had been propped open.

Brenda found Valor sitting in front of one of the four ancient computers. He was watching four videos simultaneously, all playing at what looked like 100x speed. Every time one finished, he clicked rapidly to the next.

She stepped closer. He must have seen her reflection on the screen because, without looking away, he said, "Hi, Brenda. I hope you slept well."

"Hi, Valor. What've you been up to?" she asked, unsettled by the intensity in his eyes.

Everything about him was faster than normal—his breathing, his clicks, even the way he sat. It felt like she was observing someone in fast forward, or maybe she was stuck in slow motion since she'd stumbled out of her bed.

"Are you okay?" she asked.

He paused all four videos with a burst of clicks, stood, and stretched, his neck cracking audibly. “I know kung fu.” He winked.

CHAPTER TWENTY-SEVEN

Finally, some luck, thought Richard.

He and Chris had landed at San Jose International Airport in California, picked up a rental, and were on their way to Palo Alto. The surveillance team monitoring all current and former Brotherhood members had sent them a report. They believed Julia knew Brenda and Valor's whereabouts.

Richard played the recording on his phone for the third time, pressing the device closer to his ear and turning up the volume. Static crackled through the speaker, punctuated by what might have been voices buried under layers of interference. He caught fragments. "They were," followed by more static, then "just left." Nothing he could build a solid lead from.

He scrolled to the attached transcription, reading the intelligence officer's confident interpretation. *Julia Mountain, ex-Brotherhood member, indicated subjects departed her residence recently. High confidence in translation despite audio quality.*

Richard snorted. *High confidence in guesswork, more like it.* But Julia was Brenda's mother. If anyone would know where they'd gone, it would be her. It was a long shot, but they had no other viable leads.

"This is all we have," Richard muttered, pocketing the phone. "You play the cards you're dealt, not the cards you wish you had."

Chris slumped in the passenger seat, his arms crossed, glaring out the window at the passing California landscape. He'd been complaining since they'd landed, and Richard could feel another tirade building.

"I hate this fucking country," Chris muttered, wiping sweat from his forehead despite the air-conditioning running full blast. "Why would the elf come here? Nobody even knew about North America where he came from." He shifted uncomfortably in his seat, tugging at his shirt. "This rental car is a piece of shit. Too small, too hot. And why is everyone here smiling like idiots? It's unnatural. The coffee tastes like dishwater, and these lunatics are all driving on the wrong side of the road."

"It's the right side for this country," Richard said through gritted teeth.

"Well, it's backward and stupid," Chris shot back, crossing his arms tighter. "Everything about this place is backward and stupid."

Richard knew that after the long flight and days of stress they were both tired and cranky, and he figured that picking a fight wasn't in his best interest right now. He gripped the steering wheel harder, wishing for the hundredth time that Chris would just shut up.

They pulled to a stop in front of Julia's apartment complex in Palo Alto and climbed out of the car. The building was one of those aging stucco structures from the 1970s, probably built when the area had still been affordable for working families. Now, it looked tired and out of place among the sleek tech money developments creeping in around it. Paint peeled from the exterior walls, and the small courtyard needed attention that clearly wasn't coming.

Richard knocked on the door while Chris trailed behind, with what seemed like the same enthusiasm of a teenager on a trip to a museum.

They waited for ten minutes, knocking at regular intervals. Richard tried to peer into the apartment through the front window, but thick shades blocked his view completely. No movement, no sounds from inside. He could see a faint glow that might have been a television but couldn't tell if anyone was actually home.

As Richard reached for his lock-picking kit, mentally calculating how long it would take to get inside quietly, the door opened.

Julia stood on the other side of the threshold, teetering back and forth as she gripped the doorframe for support. Her hair hung in greasy strands around her face, and her wrinkled clothes looked like she'd slept in them. The stench hit Richard immediately—stale alcohol mixed with old sweat. Her bloodshot eyes struggled to focus on them, pupils dilated and swimming.

Richard had never met the woman before, but he recognized the signs. This wasn't just drunk. This was the kind of sustained drinking that destroyed people from the inside out. He'd seen it often enough. Julia was drinking herself into an early grave.

Despite her deteriorated state, Richard could see the uncanny resemblance between mother and daughter. Julia was like a broken-down version of Brenda—the same bone structure, the same dark hair, even similar height—but where Brenda had been sharp and alert, Julia's face was puffy and flushed, her skin blotchy from years of abuse. The woman who answered the door was a cautionary tale of what Brenda might become if life broke her down enough.

“Whaddya want?” she slurred, eyeing them with suspicion.

“Julia, my name is Richard, and this is Chris. We’re from the Brotherhood,” Richard answered, slipping his foot into the doorframe in case she tried to slam it.

She didn’t bother. Instead, her mouth turned down, and her shoulders drooped. A ragged sigh leaked from her. Then, she opened the door wide and stepped back to let them in.

“Yur tooo late. Thyre gon,” she slurred. The drunken woman didn’t bother closing the door after them. Instead, she shuffled back to the sofa in the living room that was littered with bottles in various states of emptiness. She picked one up, unscrewed the cap, and took a long drink before dropping onto the couch. “They were here. Yesterday,” she said, slightly more coherent. “You fuckers totally missed them.” She winced, or maybe she smiled. Richard couldn’t tell which.

“Did they say where they were going?” Chris asked, already annoyed.

“Nah. They came, they slept, they ate, and they were gone,” she mumbled.

“Were they hurt? Did they give you any clues to where they were heading?” Richard pressed.

“They were messing around on the computer... but they didn’t tell me anything.” Julia’s expression shifted. Something must have occurred to her, and now she looked worried. She stood and staggered over to Chris. “I’m so sorry.”

She gave him a long, strange hug. Then, without warning, she vomited on his front, over his shoulder, and down his back before collapsing against him and passing out.

"Oh fuck this! What the..." Chris sputtered, frozen in revulsion.

For a moment, Chris's face went green, and he swayed on his feet. "Oh God, it's soaked right through to my skin, I can feel it on my chest and back!" Chris groaned, looking like he might add to the mess himself, but he managed to hold it in.

Richard watched Chris standing there disgusted and dripping, and he felt a small surge of amusement. Sometimes, karma actually worked and people got exactly what they deserved. After days of Chris's constant complaining and uselessness, seeing him get a face full of reality felt like divine justice. Richard felt marginally better. *Finally, some luck. Definitely.*

He scanned the room and spotted the laptop on the kitchen table. Crossing to the computer, he was pleasantly surprised to find it wasn't password-protected. He opened the browser and checked the history.

Chris busied himself wrestling the unconscious woman onto the couch, cursing the country and everyone in existence for all of time.

When Richard straightened, he grinned. “I know where they’re going. There’s a map link, and a bunch of articles about the same place—Redstone Springs, Arizona.”

Chris peeled off his soiled jacket and dropped it onto Julia on the couch, where she slumped in a nest of bottles. He pulled out his phone and punched in the destination. “They couldn’t have picked a more remote place, could they?” he whined.

"I think that was the point," Richard replied, still scanning the browser history.

Valor and Brenda were smart. They knew they weren't safe and that people were looking for them. More importantly, they also knew the Brotherhood couldn't be trusted to protect them anymore. Finding the most remote place possible was exactly what Richard would do if he were in their position. Get as far from civilization as possible, somewhere with natural barriers and limited access. It was solid tactical thinking.

Richard closed the computer and scooped it from the table. "We need to go," he said firmly.

Chris looked down at his shirt with his arms outstretched. "How am I supposed to go anywhere wearing these clothes?"

"Find clean ones. Don't come back without some. I'll see you in the car," Richard said, already walking out.

No way he was getting stuck in a car that smelled like puke for the next day and a half. If Chris couldn't find clean clothes, Richard wouldn't let him back in.

Five minutes later, Chris climbed into the passenger seat wearing a too-tight pink shirt with a unicorn on it. The caption read, "Baby Unicorns in the Making." The shirt was clearly designed for pregnant women, with its loose cut around the belly area, and Chris's soft midsection filled it out exactly as intended. The cheerful unicorn seemed to contrast Chris's miserable expression.

Richard burst out laughing despite everything. Chris sat there looking like an overgrown man who'd raided his wife's closet, the unicorn's rainbow mane practically glittering in the afternoon sun. It was the first genuine moment of relief Richard had experienced in days.

"Fuck off. It was the only one big enough," Chris snapped.

Richard was still laughing as he started the engine, and they headed toward Arizona.

CHAPTER TWENTY-EIGHT

"What the hell was that?" Brenda asked.

"What do you mean?" Valor replied. His hand grazed the recently healed spot.

"You were in fast-motion," she said. "All the videos and your movements were like ten times normal speed." She pointed toward the computer and where Valor had been sitting.

She wasn't going to let it go this time. Valor had an incredible talent for giving her just enough information to make her want to ask more. Now she wanted answers. All of them.

He tipped his head to the side and gave her an intense look. "Magic is coming back to the world. Minor time manipulation spells just started working today. I used a spell called Fast Learner. It gives me a hundred minutes' worth of learning for every real-world minute. The spell affects things around me—books, and apparently computers—to help me study faster. I have a much better grasp of the modern world and its history now." He smiled gently, clearly waiting for the next question.

"You almost got killed. I almost got killed," she said, not raising her voice. "I need the whole story. I need you to finish the story you started in the car before we got stopped." She glared at him with a look that left no room for negotiation. "All of it."

They stood there for a long, awkward beat. Brenda was damned if she would break first.

"You're right," he said. "You were supposed to learn all of this when you turned eighteen, but your mother's decision to leave the Brotherhood changed that." He gave her another intense look. Indecision clouded his eyes.

She realized now that he wasn't fighting her. He was fighting himself.

"Well?" she prompted.

At last, he sighed. "I'll tell you everything, and then you can decide if you want to stay or go. It's your right."

A coughing sound came from the other room. They turned to see the front desk girl watching them. She raised her phone, aiming it toward them, clearly about to snap a photo.

Valor lifted his hand, palm out. "*Dormeum,*" he commanded. He beamed. "Well, that spell works today too! Magic is getting stronger."

Brenda heard Sleep Command in her mind and guessed what was about to happen.

The girl collapsed to the floor. It was like a marionette whose strings had been cut. One moment, she was standing upright, phone raised and ready to snap a photo. The next, her knees buckled, and she crumpled in a boneless heap. Her phone clattered across the linoleum, spinning to a stop near the wall. Her body folded awkwardly, one arm trapped beneath her, the other flung out at an unnatural angle.

Brenda gasped. "Valor, you can't do that!" she reprimanded him, rushing over to the girl.

"I just put her to Sleep. It works really well on the weak-minded," he called after her.

Brenda kneeled and shook the girl's shoulder. The girl groaned softly but didn't wake. Brenda gave Valor a sharp look.

He shrugged. "She'll wake up and remember nothing."

"Well, help me move her to a more comfortable position," she muttered. After they leaned her next to a cabinet against a wall, Brenda straightened. "Now let's get out of here," she said. "I'm starving. You can tell me everything over breakfast. Honestly, I'm kind of glad she's out cold. Our room is a disaster."

Valor looked sheepishly pleased.

Thirty minutes later, they sat in the greasy restaurant next door. Valor was back in his original clothes after Brenda decided that bullet holes were less likely to draw attention than walking around in a hotel bathrobe. She'd taken a quick shower while he'd changed, using the hot water to clear her head and organize her thoughts.

Now, sitting across from him in the cracked vinyl booth, Brenda had a mental list of questions ready. The diner was perfect for their conversation. Only a few other customers were scattered at distant tables, the clatter of dishes and murmur of conversation providing cover for whatever revelations were coming. She'd chosen the corner booth deliberately, positioning them where they could see the entrance but couldn't easily be overheard.

Valor was at the end of his second bowl of granola. "Ask me anything. AMA." He grinned.

Brenda rolled her eyes. "You picked up Internet slang already?"

"The human language is amazing," Valor said, his mouth half-full. "It evolves so fast. I've never seen anything like it in any other race."

“Okay, focus,” she said. “Let’s start simple. Why am I here? Why do you need me?”

“That’s not a simple question,” Valor said. “To answer it, I need to finish the story I was telling you in the car... before I got shot. May I?”

She nodded.

“As I said, my father, King Valor the Third, learned that his apprentice, the human wizard Kador, had betrayed him. Kador committed suicide by casting a massive spell that unleashed a plague designed to destroy magic itself.”

Brenda nodded and took a bite of her steak and eggs. Even with everything that had happened, the story had burned itself into her memory.

“My father knew no spell lasts forever no matter how strong the wizard is. He believed that, eventually, the plague would fade, and magic would return to the world. The question was how long would it take? And how would we survive until then?”

"Couldn't you hide somewhere?" Brenda asked around a mouthful of eggs. This wasn't the time for table manners.

Valor picked up a slice of orange and chewed slowly. “Some magical creatures could hibernate. Others went underground, but elves... we couldn’t do either. We need trees, fresh air, and nature, so we had to find another solution, and time was running out.”

Brenda felt the urge to reach across the table and touch his hand, but she stayed still, sensing that any interruption might break the fragile thread of his storytelling.

His expression turned grim. “Elves are powerful wizards. We turned to Time magic—harsh, dangerous, and nearly impossible to control. It was our only chance. We started sending elves into the future to see when the plague would end and magic could survive again.”

Brenda frowned. “Why not just go back and stop Kador?”

“Good question. Time only moves forward. The past is fixed. No one, as far as we know, can go back.”

Brenda blinked. “So you were one of the Travelers, and you just happened to land in the right year?”

“It’s more complicated than that and more unpleasant,” he said. “One elf can’t travel more than a year forward, but each jump leaves a magical residue, which the next elf can use to go a year further. Like climbing a mountain on the backs of those before you, each Traveler builds on the last.” He paused. “The residue fades quickly, usually within a week. That’s why I have to perform the Pull spell soon. If we don’t, elves will keep jumping blindly, and the plague is continuing to take casualties.”

“What’s the Pull spell?” Brenda asked, her head spinning with new information.

“Think of the mountain again. Once a Traveler finds a safe year, they can cast a spell to pull others forward to create two ends of a stable Time Gateway. I’m the first elf to land in a safe year. If I cast the Pull spell at the right time, I’ll catch the next jump and pull it here. That will open the Time Gateway for an exodus of elves and other magical creatures from the past into now.”

Brenda stared. “What happened to the others? The ones who jumped before you?”

She regretted the question the moment it left her mouth. The words hung in the air between them, and she could already guess the answer just by watching his face turn ashen. His shoulders sagged as if carrying an invisible weight.

“They died. All of them. My friends, my loved ones. The last six were my brothers.” The light had drained from his voice. “The best candidates to cast the Pull spell are royalty, and my father's calculation suggested magic would be coming back in this decade, so he sent us to accomplish the final quest." Valor's face looked like a dark cloud was hanging over it. "The Brotherhood buried each of my brothers under a tree, as is our custom," he added softly.

The waiter returned and refilled Brenda's coffee. They sat in silence for a long minute after he had gone.

"I'm sorry," she said finally.

"Elves don't die naturally. We live for over a thousand years. When it's time, we become trees or disappear into eternal meditation, but they didn't get that. They gave their lives for this moment."

Brenda exhaled. The horror of it was overwhelming, but she knew she couldn't let it crush her.

She moved to the next question. "So what is the Brotherhood? How do they fit in?"

"The Brotherhood are human families loyal to my father. They were warriors, scholars, and historians. These families had fought beside my father in many wars and worked with the elves during peacetime. They were the closest we could get to a human family. They swore to maintain a record of the past and pass their knowledge down through the generations, teaching their children and their children's children the truth about magic and passing along their roles and their names—"

"Yeah, what's up with that crap?" Brenda felt her old embarrassment flare. "Why did my mother give me her exact name? Do you know how humiliating it is when kids tease you because your parents couldn't come up with something original? The minute I turned eighteen, I changed it. Got rid of that dumb decision."

It sounded a little petty now that she was saying it out loud, but she wasn't about to back down.

Valor gave her a warm smile. "Elves use ancestral names

and roles. I am Valor, son of Valor, and heir to the throne after my father. I read about modern ideas of liberty and self-realization at the hotel," he added, seeming amused by Brenda's independent streak, "but we're talking about events that took place half a millennium ago."

Yeah, these days we like our own fucking personal names. She didn't say this out loud, sore as the topic was. It was not his problem.

"Each family in the Brotherhood was given a specific role," Valor continued. "One example is the Guardian of the Staff." He held out the small black box, his eyes sparkling. "This is the time-travel anchor which brought me here." He paused. "And it will bring the rest of my people now that Kador's curse has finally lifted."

"What is a time-travel anchor?" Brenda was examining the black object. It looked like a plain small box.

"In order to time travel safely, you need an artifact—a magical object that anchors you to a spot in the future. When the jump is performed, the time traveler will appear beside this object. Without it, they risk appearing in the middle of a wall or five thousand feet above ground," he answered.

His voice sounded enthusiastic whenever he talked about magic, like a kid talking about LEGO. While the topic was interesting, Brenda had a more important question on her mind.

"What was my family's role?" she asked, her voice quiet.

"You were our biggest bet," he said. "As I told you, your ancestor was a powerful wizard. She had eight children, seven with active magical abilities who were certain to die in the plague and one daughter with dormant powers. A dormant wizard." He peered at her, as if his words explained everything.

Brenda's gaze narrowed, her food forgotten. "What's a dormant wizard?"

"A dormant wizard is someone with magical potential that

hasn't yet manifested. Usually, they're left alone when they're young until they're old enough to understand and harness their powers, but sometimes, a traumatic experience can awaken that potential."

Brenda's thoughts flashed back to the night before. Valor bleeding out in that grimy hotel room was still painfully fresh in her mind.

Valor studied her. "To cast the Pull spell, we need two wizards. One elf. And one..."

Brenda swallowed. "Human," she whispered. "I am here to help you cast the Pull spell that opens the Time Gateway."

He nodded. "Our bet was that your family's magic would survive the plague and reach this moment, and it worked."

She shook her head slowly. "That was one hell of a gamble."

"The only one we could make," he said, somber but with a slight smile.

Brenda leaned back. She couldn't possibly fathom how much of a long shot it had been or how lucky they were.

Brenda hesitated, turning her coffee cup in her hands. Part of her didn't want to know the answer to what she was about to ask, but the question burned inside her.

"One thing you haven't told me," she said quietly.

"Yes?"

"Who the hell is trying to kill us? And why?"

His face mirrored her frustration, as if her question had voiced the same worry that had been eating at him.

"I'm not entirely sure. I assume there are people still loyal to Kador's cause. That's just my guess. I didn't have time to fully debrief with the Brotherhood when I arrived, but it stands to reason. If the Brotherhood exists to help us, then there could be others who want to hunt us down."

Brenda looked down into her coffee then back up. "So I'm a wizard, and so is my mom."

"Yes."

"If they're looking for me... they might be looking for her, too."

Valor nodded, his expression stony.

Brenda felt her stomach turn.

Is my mother in danger?

CHAPTER TWENTY-NINE

The doorbell rang again, and Julia's head rang with it.

"God, not more questions," she groaned to herself, hazily recalling the two men who had visited her earlier. They must have left. The house was empty now.

The doorbell rang again.

"All right, hold your horses!" Julia yelled, lumbering to her feet and walking unsteadily to the door.

The living room was a complete mess, and there was a foul smell in the house, but she didn't give a damn. Those idiots and their holier-than-heaven organization hadn't been invited in the first place.

She was no longer a member of the Brotherhood, and she just didn't care. Staying drunk was at the top of her list of priorities today. Anything else was too painful to tackle.

She threw the door open, nearly knocking herself off her feet. "What do you want now?"

"Hello, Julia," a woman said.

Julia's eyes widened as she tried to place the voice she

should recognize. A jolt of pain slammed through her body, and the world went dark.

Julia woke up with a screaming pain in her head and feet. Everything was upside down. She frantically searched for the reason until she realized she was in the center of her living room tied to the ceiling light fixture by her ankles. The room had been completely cleaned and organized. Several figures dressed in dark clothes stood quietly nearby. The tall, redheaded woman from Julia's doorstep stood in the middle.

Julia screamed as loudly as she could manage.

The group studied her quietly, seeming unimpressed by the noise.

"She's awake," the redheaded woman announced appraisingly.

The others smiled as they came closer. They all marched confidently, wrapped in elegant, and obviously expensive, clothes. There were six figures in all—some men, some women. They circled Julia.

"Where are your daughter and the elf?" the redhead asked.

Julia had sobered up enough to recognize that voice. It was Mary.

"Fuck you! I told you everything I know!" Julia spat.

"Go ahead, Vera." Mary nodded to a young Asian woman standing next to her.

The woman was strikingly beautiful despite the cold efficiency in her dark eyes. Vera was small and lean but moved with the controlled precision of someone who knew how to fight. She stepped forward and delivered a vicious roundhouse kick to Julia's head, the impact echoing through the room like a baseball bat hitting a piece of meat.

Darkness claimed her again.

This cycle of refusing to answer questions, losing consciousness, and waking up kept on for the rest of the morning. Julia couldn't remember a moment without pain, and the lack of alcohol had given her the shakes. The bruises on her face had swelled to the point where she could barely see. They kept asking and asking. They seemed increasingly desperate... and more violent. Her clothes were stripped off, and she was beaten all over, still hanging upside down, barely able to touch the floor. Tears, blood, and saliva dripped from her face onto the ground, and she prayed and begged for it to end.

Finally, Mary said, "I believe her." She released Julia's bloody hair, gave a resigned sigh, and made a sad *tsk-tsk-tsk* noise.

Vera, who had delivered most of the beatings, shot Mary a dark look. "You know what that means, Mary," she said in a low, dangerous tone. "You have failed. You have failed our cause. You have failed Kador. Magic will return on *your* watch. You sacrificed our lives for nothing."

Mary gave the woman a stern look. "Not yet. There is one last sacrifice I can make," she said calmly. "Rob, give me your necklace."

The room went silent, and Julia watched through swollen eyes.

Vera's eyes flew open in shock. "You can't! No, no, no. Mary, don't even think about it," she pleaded. "Don't do it."

The tall, slender man called Rob stepped forward. His handsome face scrunched in thought. He gave Mary a questioning look as he carefully removed the necklace from around his neck and held it out to her as ordered.

"You know it's useless now, Mary, right? There are critical ingredients missing for the necklace to work," Rob said, his voice deep and tender.

Mary took the necklace from him. The thick silver chain had

a small vial hanging from it. She held it in her hands and smiled warmly at Rob. "My love, I know you're worried, but we knew it might come to this."

He ducked his head and stepped back.

Mary carefully removed the stopper from the vial. She crossed to the kitchenette and began opening cabinets, pulling out dishes, and setting them aside with obvious distaste. Julia could see her moving from cupboard to cupboard, rejecting one dish after another.

"No clean bowls," Mary said with disgust.

After settling for a dirty bowl from the counter, she pulled up her sleeves, turned on the hot water, and carefully washed it. She wiped it dry.

"Julia, your house is a disgrace," she called over her shoulder. "You must do something about it when we're done with you."

Julia whimpered, hoping desperately that Mary's words meant that Julia would be alive at the end.

Mary smiled wryly at Julia. "Though when we're done with you, you won't be able to do anything at all, you blasphemous witch!"

Mary glanced up from her task, and after catching sight of her reflection in the window, she smoothed a stray strand of hair back into place.

Julia could barely make out Mary from her upside-down position. She'd been inverted for so long, and she wasn't sure how much longer she would stay conscious. Her heart was pounding.

Mary carried the bowl back into the living room and placed it on the table.

"This won't work," Rob said. "For the necklace to work, you need the blood of a wizard. Without the elf or another wizard, this is useless." He spoke softly, taking Mary's hand in both of his.

She peered up at him. "Why does the elf want the Witness?" she asked, encouraging him to think this through. "What does this abomination to God want with Brenda?" Her eyes almost glowed. "Do you remember the scripture?"

"Of course," Rob said. "'And he shall awaken the devil's magic in the Witness, and with her evil help bring forth destruction...'" he quoted.

"That's right, my love," Mary said, pulling her hand from his and touching his cheek lightly. "The Witness is a dormant wizard, a genetic mutation passed down through the generations." She turned, pointed at Julia, and smiled warmly. "Just like her mother. We have our wizard here. God's work is always blessed."

Mary opened her duffle bag and took out a book and a small black device. She opened the book to a page with a large rune printed on it.

Crouching down, she showed the page to Julia and said, "Please read this."

Julia peered at it through her swollen eyelids. She couldn't even see the book clearly, let alone read it, but she wanted to help. She would do anything Mary said, anything to make the nightmare stop.

"I can't see it!" she cried.

The next thing she registered was a bucket of ice-cold water thrown in her face. The shock pulled her back to full consciousness, and she desperately tried to breathe.

"What? What? What do you want me to do? I'll do it. I'll do it!" she spluttered.

"Read this!" Mary commanded.

Julia could see the shape of a rune printed on the page held before her. "What do you mean? Read what? This is a drawing," Julia wailed.

Mary held out the black object from her bag and used it to give Julia an electric shock that made her lose control of her bladder. "Read it!" Mary screamed.

The bucket of ice water kept Julia from slipping into unconsciousness as Mary shocked her again and again, growing increasingly angry at her inability to comply.

Hours later, Mary stepped back and went over to her bag again. "Well, this is frustrating," she said more calmly. Turning back, she held up a wicked-looking knife and jammed it into Julia's knee.

Julia screamed again, choking on blood and tears.

"You have the book upside down," Vera finally interjected. "Maybe that's the problem."

Mary looked at the book then at Julia hanging upside down. "Brilliant, Vera," she stated.

The other woman smiled like a child pleased with the rare compliment. "No problem."

Mary crouched down again and held the book out upside down. "Read it," she said again, her voice soft and menacing.

Through blurred eyes, her mind fogged with pain and terror, Julia focused on the drawings again. They looked like runes. As she stared, the ancient symbols began to shimmer and glow with an inner light, their sharp edges softening and reshaping themselves into letters she recognized. The words burned themselves into her consciousness, searing meaning directly into her brain. And then, the strangest thing happened. She could read it!

She didn't understand how, but she knew it was an offensive magic spell. The runes shone bright in her mind, breaking through the tears and blood clouding her vision. She could see the shape clearly through the mist of confusion. She knew she had one chance, so she took it.

"*Karasula brigadum!*" Julia screamed, raising one arm and pointing a finger at the black-clad figure beside her.

It was like fire had formed in the center of Julia's chest then rushed through her body like molten metal through her veins. The energy scorched its way down her arm, burning hotter as it reached her hand. Her palm felt like it was being branded from the inside, and when the power finally erupted from her fingertips, the pain was so intense she thought her fingers might explode.

A small ball of fire flared from her fingertips and flew straight toward Vera's head. It scorched its way through the woman's forehead and out the top of her skull, leaving a clean hole. Vera collapsed to the floor, her eyes wide with surprise. The smell of burning flesh and sulfur filled the room.

The others stared in shock at the body convulsing on the floor. When the twitching finally stopped, they all turned to Julia.

A small whimper came from Julia's mouth. She pointed vaguely at Rob. "*Karasu*... haaaaa!"

She could not finish the spell because Mary jammed the taser into her neck. It was so painful Julia could not breathe.

Mary took her time with the taser, making sure Julia was out.

When Julia awoke again, her mouth was covered with duct tape, but she was feeling much better and much stronger. Her mind raced with ideas about how to escape. She looked around wildly, gathering her energy.

Mary took the bowl she had found in the kitchen and placed it on the floor under Julia's head.

"Goodbye, witch," Mary said cruelly, lifting the knife she

had stuck in Julia's knee and slitting Julia's throat in one swift motion.

Blood gushed from the wound, splattering all over the floor, splashing the only clean bowl in her home.

Julia screamed, but the tape held the sound in, and her world collapsed into darkness.

THE MEMBERS of the Bellum Sacrum stood, watching as blood flowed down into the bowl. Within moments, Julia was dead.

Mary picked up the bowl and placed it on the table. The remaining members of the Bellum Sacrum stood in silence and awe.

"You're really going to do it, my dear?" Rob asked.

"Yes." Mary poured the gray powder from the vial into the bowl of blood. "God, forgive me for what I am about to do," she whispered.

Her companions watched with glistening eyes.

As the powder mixed with the blood, it turned into a transparent liquid, clear and welcoming as water. Mary raised the bowl to her lips and drank deeply, tilting her head back to drain every drop.

The liquid tasted like fresh mountain spring water, cool and invigorating. Energy coursed through her body like electricity, making her feel more alive than she had in years. She felt good! She felt strong! Power flowed through her veins, and she could sense something ancient and powerful awakening within her.

In the reflection at the bottom of the empty stainless steel bowl, she could see her eyes had turned from dark to light blue and seemed to shine with their own inner light.

"Awaken! *Balakosom!*" she called out, the words flowing out of her with a mind of their own.

The room grew cold, and the scent of roses and fresh grass filled the air. A figure appeared in front of them, translucent and shimmering like a hologram from an old science-fiction movie. The man was genuinely handsome, tall and broad-shouldered, with a posture that radiated confidence and authority. He wore a pure-white gown.

He looked kindly at Mary. "Child," he said, smiling and raising both hands to her.

She took his hands in hers and fell to her knees like the rest of them. "Kador!"

"Rise, my children," Kador said. "Mary, I know how hard this must have been for you, knowing that practicing this magic has taken your soul." He beamed down at her like a loving father and pulled her to her feet. "You did the right thing, my child. You brought me back to a time when humanity must once again battle the devil's work." He looked around, his face somber. "The fact that you brought me here means that magic is back."

"Indeed, Kador. Everything you warned us about has come to pass. The elves are back!" Mary said, her eyes wet.

"How long has it been?" He sounded old all of a sudden.

"A little more than six hundred years," she replied, willing her knees to stop shaking.

"Has humanity flourished?" he asked.

"Yes, Kador! There are more humans than ever before. We are strong and have conquered all the lands of the world. Nothing can withstand us, on land or at sea!" she recited eagerly. "It is just as you predicted!"

"Good!" he said. "Good, good! Then, there is hope yet. This will be humanity's greatest test. This will be your greatest test." He contemplated each member of the Bellum Sacrum in turn. "My time here is short," he said, looking even older than he had a moment ago.

Mary kneeled once more.

Kador placed his fingertips on her forehead and said, "*Gomekdum*!" A glow passed from his hand to her head, and she felt the blue light fill her entire body. "Child, I am not as strong as I was in life, but my powers are yours." He gazed into her eyes. "Finish the holy task I started!" he commanded. "You now carry a piece of me within you. When you finish your work, you must die by the hand of your peers." He looked at the others again, and they nodded gravely. "After that, we will both be gone. Forever."

"Yes, Kador," they all murmured.

"Save humanity. Win my war!" He faded slowly.

"Yes, Kador," Mary answered in reverence.

The room fell silent.

Dora, a beautiful young Black member of the Bellum Sacrum, wept softly. "We are blessed..."

Mary straightened and caught a glimpse of herself in a mirror by the entrance. She looked different with her white-blue eyes glowing with light of their own. Everything about her radiated power. She looked almost holy.

"I know where to go. I know where the elf is taking her. We don't have much time." She turned to her companions.

"Let's go win this war!"

CHAPTER THIRTY

The line rang on and on. Fifteen... Sixteen... Seventeen...

Shit.

Her mother wasn't answering, and Brenda was really annoyed. She returned the phone to the bartender behind the counter of the bar in the restaurant, and she made her way back to sit with Valor in a dimly lit booth. She'd thrown away her phone that morning in the motel trash. After the incident with the "police," she hadn't wanted to be tracked.

"No answer?" Valor asked.

"No." Brenda frowned. "She is most probably passed out drunk on the sofa and not hearing the phone. That's my memory of her for most of my childhood," she added bitterly.

"We can go back, Brenda," Valor said, as if reading her mind, "but the day after tomorrow is our only window of opportunity to open the gateway for my people. Besides, I do not think it would be safe."

"I think you're right," she said softly. "Are you sure you don't know who these people after us are?"

"No... but we expected Kador to be smart and predict that

his magic spell would not last forever. He had allies too. I am sure he built an organization to ensure his work would be carried on long after his death."

"Damn it. I hate that we don't even know who we're dealing with!" She studied his face, then pinched the bridge of her nose. "Can't you use your magic to do something to them? To check on my mother? To get us to our destination? Why are we driving, anyway?"

His lips pinched, and unhappiness swam in his eyes. "I know you are worried and frustrated. I am as well. My magic is still not working as it's supposed to." The corners of his mouth turned down. "By my best guess, I am at a tenth of my power. If I had my full magical strength, everything you're asking for would be simple, but magic is still returning gradually to the world. It's getting better but is still exceptionally volatile. It seems today my healing and defensive spells are stronger, but none of my offensive or spatial magic works well at all." He looked at her again. "I am hopeful. Every day, I sense more and more magic around us."

Brenda hesitated, twisting her napkin between her fingers. What she was about to say felt uncomfortably intimate, like admitting she could read his thoughts, but he'd been honest with her, and she owed him the same.

"Valor, I think I can sense magic too." She kept her voice low, glancing around to make sure no one could overhear. "Every time you cast a spell, I get this mental image or a whisper with the name of the spell. It's super weird, but I think I know which spells you use and when they work."

She watched his face expectantly, hoping for surprise, maybe even admiration. Instead, Valor simply nodded as if she'd told him the weather forecast.

"Of course you do," he said matter-of-factly. "All magical creatures can sense magic, particularly when it's cast around them. You seem to have an innate skill called Detect Magic that lets you pinpoint exactly which spells were cast. It's useful but not an uncommon skill."

Not an uncommon skill. Thanks for completely dismissing my only magical ability, mister elf. She looked down to hide her childish frown and stabbed at her eggs with unnecessary force.

Valor, oblivious to her irritation, continued cheerfully, "Having this skill also lets you detect magical creatures at great distances." He gestured toward the window as if magical creatures might be strolling down the street.

"How?" she asked, truly interested in exploring her new skill.

He studied her, his expression thoughtful, as if evaluating whether she was ready for an important truth. "Close your eyes, put your hands on your eyelids, and press hard."

She followed his instructions.

"Do you see little lights emerging in the dark of your vision, like stars in the night sky?" he asked.

She snorted. "I used to do that as a child, and all my friends did. If this is your magic, it's total bullshit!"

He took a long breath. "Thankfully, I just read an article on the Internet about the value of staying calm," he said, his voice amused. "Now say *VirVes*," he instructed her.

The word vibrated through her being. The dots in her vision grew into a map of shining points of light. Then, after a few seconds, the map faded.

"Holy shit! *VirVes!*" she said, keeping the pressure on her eyes.

Her vision became fixed and much clearer, now a totally black space with thousands of stars floating in it. Most of the stars were white pinpricks, but far away, she could see some spots of white, blue, red, and brown. She herself was encapsulated in a red, shining glow.

"What is this?" she gasped.

"You've just cast a Wide Detection spell," he said proudly. "You can now detect magical creatures and spellcasting at an extremely large range. The colors represent types of magic. White is air magic. Most magical animals and fairies glow white. Brown is earth magic. Earth-based magical creatures like dwarves glow brown. Blue is water magic, also known as life magic. Many forest creatures, including elves, glow blue. Yellow is fire, usually associated with human wizards."

She could see a large scarlet star far away. As she focused on it, it grew bigger than most of the other specks, tens of times bigger, shining like a dark red sun in the sky.

"What are the dark dots?" she asked.

"What?" Valor's voice shifted quickly from warm to worried.

Brenda kept her eyes closed.

He murmured, "*VirVes.*"

Again, the word vibrated through her bones. She would have to ask him about that, she thought.

In her vision, Valor appeared beside her. She pointed toward the large, dark red spot in the distance.

"That is not good at all..." he said, his tone grave. It was strange hearing his voice from across the table while his image appeared next to her in the dark space behind her eyelids. He spun in a circle, scanning their surroundings, and then, he blinked out of existence.

Brenda opened her eyes to find Valor out of the booth and stuffing her things into her backpack as the black clouds and colored dots slowly disappeared from her vision.

He extended his hand to her. "Come, we have to go now," he said urgently.

They headed back to the motel and slipped around to the rental car parked in the small lot. The car looked terrible, riddled with bullet holes, blood on the passenger seat and windshield, and shattered glass across the back seat where the rear window had been blown out.

"Shit, we'll be stopped by the actual police if we drive in this thing," she said.

"Let's see if I can do anything about it." Valor gestured to the car and said, "*Cambiaris*."

Again, Brenda felt the vibrations. The words Alter Object popped in her vision. The car changed before her eyes. The color shifted from red to gray, and the blood and holes vanished. Even the license plate changed. The change reminded Brenda of the liquid metal transition from the *Terminator II* movie.

She looked at Valor, astonished.

He shrugged, looking sheepish. "I read an article about what type of cars the police consider suspicious. I thought the change might be useful. They won't notice us now, will they?"

Brenda held her hands up. "Your guess is as good as mine, but they're less likely to notice us without the bullet holes. That much is true."

After they climbed into the car, Valor said, "Let us continue to Redstone Springs. We must hurry. We do not have much time."

Brenda didn't like the worry in Valor's voice. His anxiety was contagious. Until now, Valor had carried himself with quiet confidence that everything would work out, but the way his hands gripped the door handle too tightly and his eyes kept darting around suggested he wasn't sure anymore.

Old doubts crept back. Why was she on this mad journey with this young elf? Whatever was worrying him at such a deep level was now worrying her too.

Brenda clutched the car keys. She looked at the windshield, which until a few minutes ago had a bullet hole in it and blood on it.

"I need to think," she whispered.

"Brenda?"

"I need to think!" she snapped.

"Is everything okay?"

She took a deep breath and pushed her hand through her hair. "No, everything is not okay," she said, trying to keep her voice as calm as she could. "You got shot. You almost died. My mother might be in danger." Her voice broke, and she swallowed. "And now there's apparently another magical creature out there that makes you freak out, so what do we do? We are going to fucking Redstone Springs!"

"Yes, Redstone Springs," he answered.

She pinched the bridge of her nose before bringing her hands to the steering wheel. "Redstone Springs! Why the hell aren't we going to the police? Why aren't we going to the press?"

Why am I doing this? She kept that question to herself.

Valor's face turned ashen, and his eyes darkened. "You are right. We are probably in danger, but do you think the police or the press would believe us? And even if they did, wouldn't they just arrest me? I have no rights in this land. I saw seven movies where aliens were quarantined, killed, and dissected. I do not think humans will understand or accept magic. At best, they'll arrest us, and then we'll have very little hope of preventing another assassination attempt... like yesterday's. I'll be dead. You'll probably be dead. All hope will be lost."

"Thank you for mansplaining it," Brenda said in a dry tone.

It took him a moment to remember the reference, and his gaze narrowed. "I'm not a man. Maybe the term should be *elfs-plaining* it," he said in an equally flat tone.

At that, Brenda burst into laughter, and he joined in after a few seconds. Eventually, their laughter faded, and they both lapsed into silence.

"Why is all of this happening to me?" she whispered, finally coming to the question she did not want to ask. “Why me? It’s already cost me so much. Why am I doing this, Valor?” she looked out the window, then down at her hands, and finally at him.

"Happening to you?" he asked, anger and passion mixing in his voice. "Brenda, you are not an innocent bystander here. These things do not happen to you. You are the key to changing the world. The Witness is an English mistranslation of the original Elvish word *Va-ashentis.* The Agent or the Catalyst. You are the first human wizard in more than six hundred years. Magic is in your blood. You are a magical creature. We are your people. Brenda, you are the Catalyst, not the Witness. You have the power to change everything, not just observe it."

I have the power to change everything. The words hit her hard.

His expression turned serene, and his eyes were no longer dark with anger. “Brenda, you are helping to turn back the clock on something much, much bigger than the recent wars and atrocities in the world. If you do not act, millions of beings, not just elves, will perish and vanish from the world forever.”

“Nothing will be the same anymore after this, will it?” she asked.

All of a sudden, his face took on a youthful bearing as the corners of his mouth twitched. “The world might not be the same, that’s true. Humans will have other intelligent beings to deal with. Based on the movies I’ve seen, I think it won’t be easy for a while, but what’s the alternative? To do nothing? To let all these intelligent beings die? Is that a future you’re willing to support?” His eyes shone, radiating the purpose burning inside him.

“Fuck! Fuck, fuck, and shit!” she said, banging her hands against the steering wheel. Not looking at him, she said what her heart told her. “No, I can’t let it happen. I fucking have to do what I can to help you... Goddamn it!”

"You are quite profane," he commented.

"Fuck you," she replied.

"All right then," Valor said after a long moment. "Thank you for helping me, Brenda. We will be forever in your debt."

She shifted in her seat, taking in his childlike features, his strange long face, and his intelligent, beautiful eyes. This was the most intense and meaningful experience of her entire life. She believed it.

"You're welcome," she said softly.

Truth be told, she wanted to thank him. Something fundamental was shifting in her perspective on life. For years, she'd felt that life was unfair to her, that she was always reacting to whatever the world threw at her. Her Serbian roommate, Milica, had taught her an important lesson, that Brenda wasn't a victim of circumstances and that life moves on, so don't let the world hurt you too much. But Valor had given her something different. He had given her agency. He'd made her realize that she was about to change reality, not the other way around. She was the change, and maybe it was time for the world to worry about her instead.

They waited for a few more moments in silence. Valor remained completely still until Brenda sighed. Then, she started the engine, turned the car on, and pulled out of the lot.

"To Redstone Springs we go." She heard him humming quietly. She glanced at him and saw that he was smiling like a kid on the way to a toy store. His joy was contagious and she found herself smiling.

After they passed the city limits signs and the diminishing population of the outskirts, the road stretched out before them, promising a long and boring journey. Valor kept quiet and focused on the passing view.

"Why were you so worried about the dark red sun in the Detect Magic spell?" Brenda ventured.

Valor sighed. "The dark red sun, as you call it, is a clear indicator that there is a powerful magical creature. Dark red means necromancy—spells associated with death. Raising the dead, talking to the dead, healing yourself by killing others... These are just a few examples of necromancy spells."

"Death?" Brenda gasped.

Valor nodded. "While no spell is evil by itself, necromancy spells are never used by creatures of good such as elves and fairies. There is a terrible price that must be paid every time one is cast. Creatures are awakened each time a necromancy spell is used."

A chill crawled up Brenda's spine. "What kind of creatures?" she asked quietly.

"Undead creatures," Valor replied darkly. "Like vampires."

"Vampires?" she hissed. "Vampires are real too?"

Valor's only answer was silence.

CHAPTER
THIRTY-ONE

"Ivan! This is the party of the year!" Tanya was in a jubilant mood, and Ivan seemed quite appreciative of how close her lithe body came to his as she leaned over to shout in his ear, just loud enough to be heard over the loud music.

His gaze dropped to her torso, and she let him admire her.

Tanya knew she was stunning. There was no other way to say it. Her ballet-trained body wrapped in a beautiful almost-translucent white dress, her young and beautiful face, her long, shining hair, and her amazing scent all had purpose, and Ivan basked in the sight of her provocative body, his latest catch. She was definitely the best in a long line of party girls trying their luck at breaking into his life.

Tanya understood the game. They both knew why she was being so friendly. She would have been way out of his league if he weren't so rich. While Tanya was exquisite, Ivan was the definition of plain, with a flat face, greasy blond hair, and emotionless eyes that seemed dead most of the time. But in Moscow these days, he was way out of hers. She wasn't the daughter of an oligarch, and that meant she had no real long-term shot at forever. The best she could hope for was a few weeks in Ivan's sunshine, maybe a trip to the Caribbean, before he dumped her and moved on to the next. There were a lot of stunning girls in Moscow, and Tanya was one of many.

The party was, indeed, a great party.

Ivan only hosted incredible parties. All the important families were represented. His rich friends were having fun with gorgeous girls, solid music, and lots of drugs. The DJ had been brought in from New York. The music was electronic and loud, just how Tanya liked it. It was a rare warm night, so the pool was open, and it was already full of half-naked gorgeous bodies.

Ivan's parents owned the mansion, but they were off on some vacation. They didn't care if their son trashed the place, as long as the help cleaned it up properly afterward, and Ivan had told Tanya that he always made sure they did.

She was always in awe of that. For Ivan, money was never a problem. His parents didn't care how much he spent on these parties. Ivan told her they didn't care about most things in his life.

"All the right people are here," Tanya said with an excited voice, her white dress fluttering as she danced.

Ivan surveyed the room with disgust. "They're all decoration, baby oligarchs and opportunistic influencers. They live their boring lives on social media, and their friendships are based on who has the most power this month. It's all fucking boring and depressing," Ivan said with rare honesty.

Tanya squeezed his hand and leaned in close again. "Let's go somewhere private?" she asked with a naughty smile. A little expensive excitement in her life wouldn't be boring at all.

Ivan called out to anyone who could hear to enjoy the party then grabbed Tanya's hand and led her through the crowd. "I know the perfect place," he told her. "We can get wasted."

She licked her lips suggestively.

Ivan led her downstairs. The basement was a theater room. Several couples were in various stages of having sex on the collection of large sofas. A skinny blonde teenager lay on the floor next to a low table, its mirrored surface covered in lines of white powder.

"Fucking amateurs," Ivan muttered, stepping over the girl's unconscious body.

He grabbed a small bag of the stuff from the table and pulled Tanya toward the rear of the house into a large, dark study behind the media room. A thousand books lined the walls, and a heavy reading desk dominated the center of the room. This area was off-limits to the other party guests. He didn't need to tell anyone to get out. They all knew the rules.

Reading any of the documents on that table could be detrimental at the least, fatal at the most. Moscow was a place where people could disappear if they knew too much about the wrong person's business.

Ivan glanced back into the theater to make sure no one had followed them or was watching them from the doorway. The library was dark, and everyone was busy, each with their own pursuits. The coast was clear.

He walked to the library wall and pulled the top edge of a large, dark red leather-bound book toward him. Clicks and whirs sounded. A moment later, a hidden door opened in the corner of the room, revealing a dimly lit, stone staircase leading to an ancient-looking basement.

"Exciting!" Tanya exclaimed as they descended. She followed him without hesitation.

The door closed softly behind them.

The cellar was dark and even more poorly lit. It smelled of old wood and all the darker secrets Ivan's family kept. She had no idea how this room had been used for the last few years. The thought made him smile.

After pulling a dusty bottle from a narrow wall shelf, Ivan walked over to the tall tasting table beside it. He opened the bottle and placed a couple of glasses on the wooden surface.

Tanya's perfect face beamed up at him. She remained putty in his hands, eagerly accepting whatever he offered and forming herself to his desires. How many had he seduced... Ivan took a deep breath, anticipating what always came next.

He poured the red wine and handed her a glass. "It's about a hundred dollars a sip, so appreciate it," he told her.

Tanya's pupils dilated as she took the glass with an excited intake of breath. She sipped the wine reverently, leaving a smear of red on her upper lip. She licked it away as Ivan watched. After a few more glasses and a few lines of coke, they started to make out.

Ivan liked it rough. She'd certainly heard that, and Tanya didn't mind.

At first.

When he bit down on her lip too hard, she gasped and pulled away. Blood started dripping from her mouth, and her eyes widened in pain and surprise. She wiped at the drops of blood on the front of the dress.

"Motherfuc—" she began.

He hit her hard on the side of the head. Maybe with the bottle. Maybe with his hand. She didn't know, but the world started spinning, and she staggered slowly backward until she reached the stone wall of the cellar.

There was a terrible scratching sound behind her. Behind her? In the wall? She was confused, her head ringing.

Ivan advanced toward her, his own pupils dilated, his expression cruel, but he, too, had heard the scratching and paused, visibly puzzled.

Then came a crumbling sound and a terrible, low, deep-voiced scream. A wrinkled hand broke through the wall beside Tanya's head. Frayed fabric draped the bony arm, and a golden ring adorned each finger, each ring inset with a large ruby.

Tanya screamed, the sound echoing in the room. Ivan fell backward, horror etched across his face. Stumbling, he scrambled from all fours to his feet, clearly determined to run up the stairs and leave her behind.

"No!" she tried to shriek, but it came out as a garbled whimper.

Terror curdled the wine in her belly and rooted her feet to the ground. If she didn't move, maybe the creature with that horrible hand wouldn't realize she was there.

Ivan almost reached the first step.

One of the rubies of the gnarled hand turned glowing red, bright in the darkness of the cellar.

Ivan lifted his leg to start up the stairs.

"Stop!" roared the figure from behind the wall.

The light in the ruby flared, and Ivan froze mid-step.

Another hand smashed through, reaching out on the other side of Tanya. She shook, but she couldn't move either. Whether from the command or her own fright, she couldn't be sure.

The figure slowly tore through the stone and stepped into the cellar. It looked ancient and reeked of dust and death.

Turning slowly, the figure considered her, and Tanya saw the skeletal expression for what it was.

True love.

Her fear drained from her, and she sighed.

"Come, my dear," the ancient figure said, the voice distinctly male.

Without a hesitation, Tanya fell into his embrace. Delight coursed through her as he placed his lips on her neck. He wanted *her*.

"I am yours," she whispered, inviting him.

He bit, and he drank.

Her eyes rolled back in her head, and she shivered with pure ecstasy.

IVAN WAS FROZEN, forced to watch Tanya and the filthy old creature. His leg was raised but stuck mid-step. His eyes burned, but he couldn't blink. He could only observe as his girlfriend was fondled by an old man who bit her neck and drank deeply. Blood streamed down her shoulder, soaking her white dress. The new cascade of blood covered the drops Ivan had caused.

Disgusting. Ivan wanted to scream. He wanted to cry. His weight bore down on one leg, and it began to shake. It finally gave out, and he fell like a dead log, unable even to break his fall. His head slammed the floor, and everything blinked for long seconds or maybe minutes or maybe hours. He couldn't tell. His eyes remained fixed on the ceiling, his body paralyzed by the command, issued by an ancient, skeletal man with an authority Ivan didn't understand.

Two figures entered his line of sight. The man looked much younger now, maybe in his forties. Vitality oozed from the stranger, and his clothes were no longer rags. None of it made sense.

Tanya's eyes glowed red as she peered down at Ivan. The bruises on her lip and ear were darkening. Her skin had gone from sun-kissed to porcelain, and Ivan could almost make out the veins beneath.

They both studied him as though he'd been served on a platter, and Tanya smiled cruelly.

Ivan wanted to whimper, but he couldn't move his lips.

TANYA CLUTCHED her new love's hand. Too rough. Too dry. Her love required more sustenance. Surprisingly, Ivan was still waiting on the floor.

"Stand up," her lover told Ivan, his voice younger now.

Ivan's body responded. He climbed quickly to his feet, wobbling, and still looking dazed.

The man cast an affectionate glance at Tanya. "What is your name, my dear?"

"I am Tanya, my beloved," she replied with a catlike purr.

"You can call me Boris. Tell me, Tanya, how do you feel about this young man?"

"I hate him. He hurt me," she spat, her voice full of venom. She glared at Ivan.

A puddle of moisture spread out from beneath Ivan's lower half, seeping across the stone floor, the sharp scent of ammonia filling the air.

Tanya smiled. "Oh, he cannot run."

"As I commanded," Boris answered. "He is frozen until I command otherwise."

Tanya examined the wet floor. "He's afraid."

"Of course," Boris said calmly. "Now tear off his left arm."

Tanya stepped toward Ivan, and Ivan's eyes widened as she wrapped her hands around his forearm and put her foot against his armpit. Then, she yanked.

A muffled wail escaped through Ivan's frozen lips, but she did not stop.

It took time. Tanya was stronger than she looked but still small. After several minutes, she stepped back, panting. In her hand was the bloody stump of Ivan's left arm, torn from the socket.

"Drink the blood," Boris commanded.

Tanya raised the stump and licked Ivan's blood from it. Leaning close to Ivan, she drank from the stream of blood flowing from the wound. The break was not clean at all, and Ivan would soon bleed to death. She dropped to her knees and pressed her face into the wound.

Ivan drifted in and out of consciousness. He seemed desperate to escape, but each time, Boris called Ivan back with a commanding voice.

"I will keep him alive for you as long as you want," Boris said.

"Oh, thank you, my love," Tanya purred as she worked her tongue to consume every last drop of blood from the wound she'd made.

"Are you still angry with this man?" Boris asked eventually.

"A little," Tanya said, Ivan's blood dribbling down her chin as she sat back.

"Hit his face with his arm. It's quite funny if you think about it." Boris's voice was encouraging, warm, friendly, and it made her feel safe.

Tanya had never really had the chance to hit a man back. This was not how things usually played out for girls like her. It felt refreshing to finally not be on the receiving end of violence. As she struck Ivan with his own severed hand, she remembered all the abusive men in her life, the ones who had hurt her, used her, and made her feel small and powerless. This was quite the therapeutic experience.

Ivan's face was a mess of red and blue when she finished, and he was pale from blood loss. If not for the commands from Boris, Tanya believed Ivan would have died already.

"Are you feeling better now, my dear?" Boris asked.

"Much better." Tanya smiled. Smears of clotted blood adorned her dress.

"Good! You are very special to me, Tanya. You are my love, my queen. You have great powers, and I will grant you the world, but first, let's create our first zombie slave." He nodded toward Ivan. "Die," he said.

Tanya was surprised when she felt Ivan's heart stop. She clasped her hands over her chest. "Is he our slave now?"

"Not yet. You must bite his neck, my dear, before his blood runs cold and solidifies in his veins. If you leave him some blood, he will turn into a vampire, but if you drink all the way, he will become your zombie slave," Boris explained.

She drank all the way.

Soon, the three of them climbed the stairs and rejoined the party. Tanya and Ivan were much better now. She held Ivan's right hand, and his severed left arm was slung over her shoulder. They smiled at each other fondly.

When they reached the basement, Boris looked around, pleased. "Not much has changed in the last six hundred years. Humans still like to fuck and drink. They're still easy prey," he said to Tanya.

She smiled and gestured to a ménage on one of the couches. "Quite true, my love. They make easy targets."

"Yes, I'll have my army ready in no time," Boris said, "and we will conquer the world."

CHAPTER THIRTY-TWO

Brenda and Valor crossed over from California to Arizona toward Redstone Springs. She was running out of questions to ask while she had Valor trapped in the rental. Route 40 seemed to go on forever, with the monotonous desert view on both sides of the road. Her head was starting to hurt from the long drive, the heat in the car, and the effort of trying to process all the new information she had absorbed in the past few hours.

Brenda's entire view of the world had continued to morph in the hours since they'd left the motel. As she listened to Valor's tales of wonders and truths, she had to embrace fairytales as residual proof of the time of magic. When it returned, the world was going to change over the next few years.

All the tiny stars she had seen when she had performed the Magic Detection spell, he had explained, were magical creatures slowly awakening from their enforced dormancy after hundreds of years. The world had once been full of them. Now, they were coming back.

Brenda wondered, not for the first time, how humanity

would deal with these magical beings. She didn't have great hope for a peaceful future. History repeated itself too often.

It was also clear that this wasn't going to be an entirely positive change. Some of the magical creatures were dangerous, even evil. There seemed to be an ever-shifting balance between benevolent and malevolent magical powers with different creatures fighting on both sides.

"So, elves are benevolent?" she asked after Valor explained this delicate balance. "That's kind of a one-sided and condescending point of view. I'm sure many people and nations have believed themselves to be benevolent while doing horrible things."

Valor smiled. "The road to Hell is paved with good intentions."

She was surprised by his quote, but she made no comment.

"I think, Brenda, that like always, it is a matter of definition and perspective," he said. "When I say 'benevolent,' I mean putting creating life and cherishing life above all. What I call 'malevolent' are creatures that place destruction and the pursuit of power above all. It is a spectrum, of course, with humans showing the most variation in their preferences and beliefs. Most other creatures are quite predictably either benevolent or malevolent with only minor fluctuations in their alignment. I am not sure why humans are the only ones with such variation, but it has always fascinated me." Valor was looking out the passenger window again, watching the endless Arizona desert slide by. "I have even seen a single person flip from one end of the spectrum to the other... You are strange and unpredictable creatures."

"Sounds about right," she muttered. "Ask any woman about a man's behavior the morning after, and they'll tell you the exact same thing."

"The morning after what?" Valor asked. He still stared at the view, his mind clearly elsewhere, so Brenda decided not to take the opportunity to explain the birds and the bees and changed the subject instead.

"What were wars like in your time?" she asked.

"Elves do not usually get involved in human politics or the conflicts of other short-lived species. We only make war when evil creatures are swarming the lands and the elves are asked to help defeat them," he said.

Valor had already told her about his family—his brothers, who had died in the time travel; his father, who was old even by elven standards; and his mother, the younger sister of the king's first wife, who had been killed in a war.

She put on the blinker to pass another slow truck overloaded with junk that looked like it'd come from a storage shed. "So no big wars?"

"There were always skirmishes, but not a single major war in my lifetime. Unless you count this attempt to destroy all magical creatures in the world an act of war." He smiled sadly. "It would have been easier if there had been a tangible enemy instead of this plague. We were dying without any way to fight back."

"Did you think you were going to die when you performed the time travel?" Brenda asked.

"I was sure I was going to die. All my predecessors had, my brothers and friends. We know when one of us dies. It's such a rare occurrence that it reverberates across our entire species. I felt each of my brothers' lives come to an end."

They were quiet for a long while after that. The only noise was the sound of the highway beneath the tires and the occasional gust of wind against the vehicle.

Brenda had also spoken about her own life, telling Valor about her parents and her schooling. It all sounded blandly boring to her own ears, but Valor listened carefully and asked questions that made it clear he was paying attention.

"You're not a typical man, you know," she said with a smirk. "You listen and actually care what other people have to say."

"I'm not a man at all, Brenda." He looked at her with those dark, catlike eyes. "Do not forget that. We elves may look humanlike, but we are very different. It is a mistake to expect us to act like you."

As the hours passed, Brenda grew closer to Valor. His story had captured her, and the fact that her family line was involved —she was, in fact, the key to everything—made her feel like it was also *her* story. She wasn't meant to be just a bystander in her own life. She was one of the heroes. It was surreal. The new reality gave her agency and meaning. This was her purpose, her destiny.

There was one topic Valor consistently dodged during the drive. Whenever Brenda asked about magic itself, he would smile and say that when they reached their destination, he would teach her all she needed to know.

They turned off the paved road, heading into Redstone Springs. The car trembled on the rough track, and they rolled the windows up to block the dust kicked up by the wheels. The sun was setting, and the beautiful mountains were clothed in a reddish glow. They passed a handful of single-story houses. One had a belltower like an old Spanish mission.

Brenda felt a stab of anxiety, afraid someone might notice them since theirs was the only strange car on the road.

As if reading her mind, Valor smiled. "They will all be leaving tomorrow morning. Don't worry about it."

That made her even more worried. What was he planning? She remembered his earlier comment. *We elves may look human-*

like, but we are very different. Was he planning something she would regret facilitating?

They stopped where the in-vehicle map software told them to and stepped out of the car. It felt like it was going to be a cold night. The moon wasn't out yet. The air was crisp and clean, and she could hear water falling somewhere nearby, though she couldn't see the source in the growing dark.

Valor spun in a slow circle. "It's so beautiful here! This is perfect. Thank you for finding this place. It will be a great starting point for my people." His voice was cheerful, but she couldn't see his expression in the dark, only his eyes glowing faintly.

"How can you see?" she asked, her voice shaking slightly from the cold.

"Ha, I forgot that humans cannot see in the dark. You're one of the only intelligent species that can't. Very unfortunate. Don't worry. You'll see this splendor in the morning. Let's get started."

"Get started?" she echoed, uncertain what he meant.

Valor walked around to the driver's side of the car and took her hand, guiding her gently through the darkness. He kept a slow pace, careful not to let her trip. His hand warmed hers and made her feel safer than she had before.

After a few minutes, the moon came out, and she began to make out the shapes of boulders, bushes, and short trees along the way.

They reached a clearing. The sound of water was louder there.

Valor eased her down on the ground and asked her to watch. "It will be important for tomorrow's lesson," he explained.

That's unhelpfully cryptic. But she let it go.

He stood in front of her, tall and still. The moon lit his

silhouette faintly. Brenda couldn't see his glowing eyes anymore. She guessed he had closed them.

Then, he took something from his pocket. There was a soft *whoosh* as it grew into a staff nearly as tall as he was and started to glow.

He began a martial art tai chi-like dance, graceful and precise, like the one he'd performed when they had first appeared in the hills of Silicon Valley. The staff became an extension of his body. All Brenda could see was its movement, the outline of his form, and now and then a flash of his glowing eyes.

Then, he started to chant, and Brenda instinctively held her breath, entranced. On some level, she almost understood what he was saying. She didn't know the words, but she grasped the meaning. It was like watching a National Geographic special and understanding, without language, what a mother tiger feels when she chuffs to her cubs.

Valor was creating a home, a safe, warm place. He warned others of the power here, offering hospitality to those who came with good intentions and promising wrath and destruction to those who arrived uninvited.

Each phrase of his chant was paired with a flowing movement, and each movement created a glowing rune in the air. They flowed from the tip of his staff and hovered suspended in space. More and more appeared, forming a faintly glowing sphere around them.

He moved faster now, his body elegant and fluid. He invited the ground to be fertile, warned pests to stay away, and added a rune for protection, another for good weather, and on and on. Sweat shimmered on his skin, lit by the hovering symbols.

Finally, he slammed the staff into the ground, and the runes flared and grew more solid. The runes linked to form a dome around them like an igloo. Their dim light reflected on the rocks inside but not outside the dome. It cast its glow inward only. The dome was small, about ten feet across. It felt like sitting inside a family-sized yurt.

Valor dropped to one knee, sweat dripping from his forehead, his eyes closed, taking shallow breaths. He used the staff to steady himself.

Brenda was about to ask if he was all right when he stood and began again.

This time, he chanted louder, and the vibrations rumbled through the ground. The dome expanded. New runes appeared. Others merged like bubbles. There was a high, metallic screech, as if the air itself was straining to follow the elf's commands. Finally, he slammed the staff down again, and now, they were sitting inside a dome the size of a house. Plants sprouted at its edges. It must have been a hundred feet wide.

Valor shook. His eyes were shut tightly, his breathing ragged, his clothes soaked.

Brenda opened her mouth to speak, but he raised his hand to silence her. A small flower at his feet brushed against his ankle, like a cat offering affection.

Still, with closed eyes, Valor took another deep breath and began his dance for a third time.

His voice was louder now, and the pulses hit Brenda's body and mind like a large timpani drumbeat. Every step sent rocks leaping from the ground. Every word tore the air around them. He moved so quickly he blurred before her eyes.

The dome grew again. The runes burst into colors and merged into thousands of orbs, each glowing with magic. The deafening sound thundered. The dome was now nearly a thousand feet wide.

Valor lifted his staff one final time and slammed it down. Fist-sized stones flew into the air, hovered for a moment, and then crashed down.

Thousands of tiny butterfly-like creatures burst from the dome of light, emerging like sparks from a bonfire. They were translucent and glowed with the same bluish hue as the dome itself. The creatures dispersed and flew out into the desert night, spreading in all directions like messengers carrying urgent news. One fluttered close to Brenda, and she could have sworn the blue butterfly creature looked like a tiny human with wings. It hovered near her face for a moment, studying her with intelligent eyes, then winked at her before zipping away to join the others disappearing into the darkness.

Valor dropped to his knees, pale, his eyes wide open.

Brenda stared at him. He didn't look like the Valor she knew. His pupils had expanded to fill his entire eyes. He looked both ancient and young, like a soldier after a hard-fought battle. His eyes crinkled at the edge, as though a smile waited to dawn.

He turned to face her and in a voice that was not his own, a voice that sounded to Brenda like the voice of gods, he spoke a single word. This time, she didn't need a translation. She *knew* what it meant.

"*Casatius,*" he said.

Home

CHAPTER THIRTY-THREE

Ben woke up after what felt like ten minutes after falling asleep. This was unusual for him. He was accustomed to sleeping through the night. Ben might have been the on-call Redstone Springs park ranger, but nothing interesting ever happened in Redstone Springs at night.

Yes, from time to time, there were tourists who got lost in the wilderness, and once, there was a group of ten young female Australian backpackers who had been very thankful when he'd rescued them after they had gotten stuck upstream in the middle of the night.

But usually, there was nothing of interest going on, and Ben really liked his sleep. It was one of the reasons he never transferred out of Redstone Springs. It was far from everything and everyone. Luckily, the few people in the park felt the same way and kept to themselves most nights. Most days, too, come to think of it.

Tonight, though, something felt off.

He sensed an oddness in the air, like a buildup of static electricity before a lightning storm or something like it. Then, he noticed the sound or, rather, the lack of it. Redstone Springs was far from any signs of civilization, yes, but it was never completely still. The rushing water from the falls, the buzzing of bugs, the rustling of nocturnal animals... these were the sounds Ben loved. They calmed him and helped him sleep.

But not tonight.

Tonight, there was silence.

A deep, eerie quietness hung in the air, and it sent shivers up his spine. He dressed, laced up his boots, grabbed a flashlight, and stepped to the door of his cabin. The damn thing squeaked as he opened it. It was the only sound he heard besides his own breathing.

Ben started down the path toward the waterfall. He didn't turn on his flashlight, wasn't sure why, but he didn't want to. He knew the trail ahead well enough to walk it at night.

The moonlight cast soft shadows from the bushes and trees along the path. Nothing moved. There was no wind, and even his footsteps were barely audible on the soft earth. The silence felt unnatural, as if the desert itself was holding its breath.

The closer he got to the falls, the more creeped out and afraid he became. There were whispers all around him, barely audible, more like sensations than sounds, like the feeling of a fly about to land on your ear.

Then, he saw them.

Tiny, glowing, butterfly-like creatures filled the air. They surrounded him, whispering urgently. He tried to listen, but it was just a blur of repeated sounds in his head, unintelligible and insistent. Was he dreaming? He must be dreaming.

He quickened his pace. The whispers intensified, more urgent, more pleading. One of the creatures landed on his hand. It was larger than a typical butterfly, he realized.

He raised his hand for a closer look. The creature resembled a tiny woman, no more than half a finger long, slim and lovely.

Her wings were paper-thin, and she shimmered with faint blue light. She was semi-translucent, as though she was made of glowing mist.

The being was trying to tell him something. Ben was sure of that. It was high-pitched and feminine, like an angry mosquito with almost intelligible words. Her tiny hands were waving angrily at him, gesturing frantically as if she were giving him a piece of her mind. The sounds came in rapid bursts, urgent and frustrated, clearly meant to warn him about something, but all Ben could make out were fragments that sounded like miniature shouting.

He brought his hand closer to his ear.

"Get the fuck out of here, human! This is elvish territory now," she snapped.

Ben jerked his hand away from his head, staring in astonishment at the tiny creature who now frowned at him, her hands on her tiny hips.

He swiped at her with his other hand, but she was crazy fast. Ben was proud of his fly-swatting reflexes. He'd smacked more mosquitoes than he could count out here, but this creature was faster than any flying thing he'd seen, and it disappeared.

Shaking his head, he pressed on, more determined than ever. The whispers grew louder and more frantic. Several more creatures tried to land on his head and shoulders, but he brushed them off.

"Leave now!" they demanded.

"Turn around!" they warned.

"Get out of here, please!" they begged.

Then he saw *her*.

Beautiful and regal, she hovered inches from his face. She was twenty percent larger than the other flying creatures, her face long with a narrow chin and flowing hair that covered her shoulders. Her eyes were striking, the kind that demanded obedience without question. A tiny crown sat atop her head, glinting with what looked like microscopic jewels, and she wore a magnificent blue gown that seemed to shimmer with its own inner light.

She raised one hand in front of his eyes. "Stop." Her voice was calm, royal, and commanding.

Despite his better judgment, Ben stopped and stood straight. Strong-minded women always scared him a little, another good reason he'd picked a job in this secluded place.

How funny, Ben thought in a daze, *that someone so small can sound so authoritative.*

"Who are you?" he asked.

"None of your business. You are trespassing. This is elvish land," she said.

Well, that's rude, he thought.

"No, I'm not. Who are these 'elvish'? This is a public U.S. park," Ben said, his voice rising. "And I'm the ranger!"

"I do not understand the stupid words coming out of your silly head, but you shall not pass," she said, lifting her chin.

She frowned in a way that reminded him of his mom when he'd come home with bad report cards, which had been quite often. The same disapproving expression, the same tone that said he'd disappointed her beyond measure. Even at his age, that look still made him feel like a scolded child.

"Oh, for fuck's sake," Ben muttered, raising his hand to swat her out of the air.

Before he could make contact, a tiny stick like a wand appeared in her hand, and she touched his approaching finger with the point.

His hand froze. Not just in place but cold. Dead cold. It dropped limply to his side. He tried to move it, but it was completely unresponsive.

She scowled at him. "You are a bad, silly human," she said,

wagging her tiny finger. Then, she waved her wand again, and Ben's cold, dead hand slapped him across the face. Hard.

His knees wobbled, and he saw stars. It took a few seconds for the spots in his vision to fade.

"Get the fuck out of here! These are elvish lands now!" She was no longer a lovely, glowing sprite. She had become something out of a nightmare, her eyes red and blazing, her wand pulsing with ominous light.

Ben turned and ran. He tripped twice, scraping his knees on the rocky path. His dead hand flopped uselessly at his side. He didn't look back, and he didn't think. He just ran.

A truck roared down the path not far from his cabin. It zipped by, not bothering to avoid the ruts. It was his old friend, Geoff Marshall, in his truck racing toward the paved road.

Ben burst into his cabin, yanked open drawers, and scrambled for the keys to his classic Jeep. Scratching sounds came from the back door. Then, tiny fists started pounding the windows.

His good hand shook as he found his keys. He bolted out the front door and ran for his vehicle. Starting the Jeep took forever. He had to awkwardly twist his body, reaching across with his left hand to turn the key in the ignition.

The creatures now swarmed the windshield, shrieking in a terrible, high-pitched chorus.

Small cracks started to appear in the windshield where their tiny fists pounded relentlessly against the glass. The thuds of more tiny fists came from the rooftop of his vehicle, like supernatural hail beating down on him. Through the spreading web of cracks, he could see their furious faces pressed against the glass, their eyes blazing with rage.

An old sedan shot past him, followed closely by another. The first was the chapel minister Lucas and his wife Berta. Ben had never seen them drive at night. Hell, he wasn't even sure the old man could *see* at night. The second car belonged to the backpackers who had come into the park this morning. A weird-looking hippie couple, they had seemed far too cheerful at the time.

As far as Ben could tell, apart from himself, everyone in Redstone Springs had now fled.

Finally, his engine roared to life. Ben shoved it into gear, slammed on the gas, and sped down the dusty path, hitting the paved road hard. The lights from the other fleeing vehicles were already far in the distance.

Thus ended the human habitation of Redstone Springs.

CHAPTER THIRTY-FOUR

Brenda didn't remember falling asleep, but she would never have believed that waking up after sleeping on the ground could feel so good. The cushion of grass beneath her was soft, warm, and comfortable. This was the second time she'd woken up on this kind of grass bed. It was such a different experience from the few times she'd been on camping trips, when she'd always woken up stiff and aching all over. She made a mental note to ask Valor about that.

The scent of flowers filled the air. She stood, stretched, and looked around.

She remembered the photos of Redstone Springs from her mother's computer, images of a beautiful desert park with a waterfall as the main attraction, an oasis in the middle of the desert, a park inside the Grand Canyon.

That was not how the place looked now.

The waterfall was still there, and the general landscape was the same, but everything was even more green and lush. Trees stood everywhere, taller and greener than Arizona's climate could naturally support. Flowers bloomed, and a large green mesa dominated the center. The changes clearly radiated outward from a central point. About five hundred feet in every direction, the greenery tapered off, returning to desert. The waterfall was within the lush zone, and small birds flitted in and out of the spray.

Valor climbed out of the clear water, naked.

Brenda couldn't look away, and her cheeks heated. Well, that answered the question of whether elves were anatomically compatible with humans. She concluded that they definitely were. *Very* compatible, biologically speaking, of course. She finally tore her gaze away before he spotted her staring.

"Good morning, Brenda!" Valor was as cheerful as ever, sounding remarkably refreshed after the night's exertions. He had found some clean clothes—she wasn't sure from where—and began dressing. "Did you sleep well?"

"Yes, um, thank you." She was still flushed, keeping her face turned away long enough for the heat to subside.

"Wonderful! We have a lot of learning to do today. Tomorrow is the big day!" He grinned like a kid on his birthday, and Brenda found herself smiling back. "Let's start by teaching you about magic." Valor began stretching like someone warming up for a run. He looked happier and calmer than she'd ever seen him. "First, you need to understand that magic isn't what humans today think it is. I read so many speculations and theories online. It was quite funny to see what modern people believe."

"Then what is it?" she asked, taking a seat on the ground.

"Magic is energy. A form of energy that powers life, the universe... and everything, so to speak," he said with a sheepish smile. "I believe what Kador did was radically reduce the amount of this energy on the surface of the Earth so that magic could no longer be sustained. That's only a theory, though, since I don't know the details of his spell. Some creatures need only a very low level of this energy to live. These are called 'non-magical' creatures, though that's actually misleading, since all life requires magic. Other beings need a higher level of magical energy to survive. These are magical creatures, like unicorns for example."

"Wait, what? You mentioned that before, and I thought you were joking," Brenda said skeptically. "Unicorns are real?"

"They are." His expression darkened. "They're benevolent in theory, but I strongly recommend you don't mess with them. It's an ancient understanding that unicorns are... how do you say... assholes."

"Unbelievable," Brenda muttered to herself. "Unicorns are assholes. Good to know."

"Then, there are magic-wielding creatures, beings who can use magic as a utilitarian energy source. You and I are examples of this," he said, gesturing to her with a smile.

Brenda raised her eyebrows but said nothing, waiting for him to continue.

"It's not so strange when you think about it. Humans have progressed with science over the last six hundred years, moving from trying to create gold from other metals—which was utterly silly—to exploring many forms of energy. I really like science. It's freaking fantastic."

"Right... it's *freaking* fantastic," Brenda repeated, amused by his choice of words.

"Yes! So in their scientific explorations, humans discovered electricity, another form of energy. All creatures have some level of electric current in their bodies. Some, like electric eels, use it intuitively, and then, there are humans, who are electricity-wielding masters, using it in a utilitarian way. It's the same principle. Magic doesn't conflict with science. It conforms to it. Again, these are all assumptions, of course, but ones I hope can be tested using your scientific methods, which are truly quite impressive."

Valor radiated so much joy now that Brenda felt like she needed sunglasses. He reminded her of some extra-happy Californian friends who'd pissed her off in college by being too cheerful on Monday mornings. Upon reflection, though, she decided she liked this version of Valor better than the sad or worried one. All his emotions, she realized, seemed a little more intense than most regular people. Then, she reminded herself that he was not regular, or a person for that matter.

"Go on," she said.

"Magic-wielders, more commonly known as spellcasters or wizards, use magic with their minds. I'm not entirely sure how to explain it scientifically, but I'm confident that, in time, humans will figure it out. Magic can also be stored in objects, just like batteries store electricity. The same is true of many types of energy; and there are many. It would take years to cover them all. To become a proficient spellcaster, one must study for about ten years," he added.

Brenda's eyes widened. "So I need to learn it all in one day?"

"No," he said with a calm smile. "For tomorrow, you'll only need to perform a very simple task, which I'll teach you. You are a fantastically intuitive spellcaster and will become a formidable wizard one day. To control magic, a top wizard doesn't need to do anything more than think about it, but that's only the top ten percent. Most spellcasters need to say a word or use an object like a wand or staff to channel magic and bend it to their will. All you'll need to do is say a specific word again and again while I open the gate. That word will channel energy into my spell and unlock the requirements for the gateway."

"What's the word?" Brenda asked.

"*Tempus,*" Valor replied.

"Time," Brenda translated.

"Indeed. You'll say it every ten seconds. I know that might sound boring now, but it'll be very exciting and very dangerous. You'll have to concentrate for a long time. Every time you speak the word, it will syphon energy from you, making you tired and more prone to losing focus."

"Wait. What do you mean 'dangerous'?" Brenda asked. When Valor said something was dangerous, she suspected, he probably did not mean dropping-your-phone-in-the-toilet-level dangerous.

"You'll be feeding my spell with energy tied to time. You'll be drawing time from the universe and converting it into power. Your scientists haven't figured it out yet, but time is a form of energy, and it behaves similarly to other forms. This is important. You must focus on objects, like a mountain or the waterfall, and pull the time from them. If you lose concentration, the spell will take time from the closest available source... which would be you."

"Me?"

"Yes," he said evenly.

"What do you mean 'take time from me'?"

"Make you older." He looked her straight in the eyes. "You need to know the risks involved."

"Shit, I don't want that!" Brenda snapped.

"Working with energy always has risks, just like electricity can electrocute you."

"You don't get old when you get electrocuted!"

"No. You die," he replied. "I've seen dozens of videos and reports about it on the Internet."

"Right, well, your plan for tomorrow sounds *very* fucking dangerous," she muttered.

This didn't feel like a good idea at all.

"I understand your fear, Brenda, but please believe me, tens of thousands of lives are at stake. I'm confident you can handle this. It's no different from life in general. Your human lives are short. If you don't concentrate, time flies by without you noticing it."

Brenda nodded. There was truth in that. "How long will I have to do it?"

"The spell will take about five minutes to stabilize the gateway. Once that happens, you can stop. You won't need to concentrate or say anything more."

"That's not too long," she said.

"No, it's a drop in the sea of time," Valor said. His voice didn't sound so young at that moment.

A small blue bird landed on his shoulder. He smiled at it and gently scrubbed its head with a finger.

"Does that happen to you a lot?" she asked. He glanced at her, puzzled, and she pointed at the bird. "Birds landing on you. Letting you pet them."

"Oh, yes, all the time. Animals are drawn to positive magic. You should see porcupines. They're a really friendly, prickly bunch."

She shook her head in disbelief. "You really are something else..."

His glow seemed to increase just a little. "Will you do it, then? Will you join my quest to save my people?" he asked, suddenly serious.

Why is he asking this question again? This is getting old.

"I'm already here," she said, trying not to sound annoyed.

"But you must verbally agree. It must be consent born of free will."

"Okay, okay. I'll do it," she said.

The moment the words left her lips, warmth bloomed in her chest like embers catching fire. The sensation spread outward through her limbs, carrying with it an unexpected confidence that settled into her bones. What had felt like Valor's impossible mission just moments before now pulsed in her mind as their mission, something that belonged to her as much as to him. A sense of rightness, of destiny, washed over her with surprising intensity. The word Quest materialized in her vision, glowing softly like text on a screen, then faded as the magical bond solidified between them.

"Finally! The Quest spell is working today!" he said cheerfully. "That bond you're feeling will help us coordinate our actions and thoughts much better."

"Is that why you kept asking me to join your quest? It was starting to get quite repetitive," she asked.

"Yes, the spell was not working until today," he answered sheepishly. "Members of a quest need to consent for the Quest spell to work and bond them together."

A tiny part of her brain wanted to object to being blindsided, that he should have told her about this spell and its consequences, but then Brenda realized his happiness was more contagious now. She could feel his joy in her body.

She nodded, smiling at him.

"Fantastic! Thank you, Brenda." He looked truly pleased. "Here's how it's going to work. See the big boulder next to the waterfall?"

"Yes," she said. It was about three feet tall and seemed easy enough to climb.

"You'll stand on that boulder with my staff in your hand. You'll say the word *Tempus* first, and I'll begin casting the spell around you. Count to ten between each word. Use the staff like a metronome. Don't worry if you miss a second. The gateway might flicker, but it will stabilize if you keep going. I won't be able to answer any questions during the casting. My eyes will be closed, and I can't pause for a single millisecond."

"When will I know to stop?"

"When elves start coming out of the gate," he replied.

She laughed. "What a trip."

"Yes. A trip through time," he said with a smile, "an exodus for survival."

For a moment, neither of them spoke. The sound of the waterfall made the silence peaceful.

"All right," Valor said after a long moment. "Let's practice. Take my staff and climb onto the boulder. Say 'Time' instead of '*Tempus'* for this round. By tonight, we can do a minute or two of real practice."

She took the staff and climbed the boulder. The top was flat and wide enough to stand comfortably. "What do I do now?"

"Now, with confidence, begin saying 'Time' while focusing on the ridge in front of you. You'll draw time energy from those mountains," he instructed.

It felt strange to be looking down on Valor. Brenda smiled briefly. Then, her expression turned serious, and she tapped the boulder beneath her with the staff. *Here goes nothing...*

"Time... Time... Time..."

CHAPTER THIRTY-FIVE

Mary stepped out of her vehicle, leaving her teammates in the car. It had been a long drive, and they had driven the distance as fast as they could, taking turns at the wheel, with everyone but Mary sleeping in shifts. Using her new powers, Mary had clouded the minds of every police officer they'd passed, making their radar guns malfunction and their eyes slide away from their speeding vehicle, but they'd still had to run a few slow cars off the road when the drivers wouldn't move fast enough. She liked her newly acquired skills, the effortless way she could bend human minds to her will. She also hated herself for it.

At least Kador accompanied her, speaking to her in her mind.

As they pulled off the paved road near Redstone Springs, she noticed the lingering effects of the elf's magic. Her driver looked concerned about the road conditions and suggested they turn back. The other passengers agreed. It might have been a mistake to come here, they said.

But Mary saw through the cheap tricks.

"The vile elf has woven runes of protection against his enemies," Kador's ancient voice whispered in her mind, his knowledge flowing into her consciousness like ice water. "Any who approach with harmful intent will feel an overpowering urge to flee. Even neutral visitors will feel uneasy and be compelled to turn away." His voice grew more urgent. "Be warned, my child, you may encounter magical barriers and sentinel creatures as part of these protective enchantments the elf has cast."

That only strengthened her resolve. She had all of Kador's knowledge now, paired with her own iron will. The runes would have little effect on her.

Unexpectedly, her driver screamed in terror and yanked the wheel hard to the right, sending the vehicle veering off the road. The car lurched toward a massive tree, missing it by inches as he overcorrected, his knuckles white on the steering wheel. His breathing came in rapid, panicked gasps, and sweat streamed down his face.

Mary cursed him, ordered him to switch places with her, and took the wheel herself. As they neared the epicenter, even she began to feel the pressure of the spells the elf must have cast. Her colleagues looked terrible, pale, trembling, scared.

This is humanity under the rule of magic—crushed, fearful, deprived of willpower, helpless by mere proximity to elvish power, Mary thought grimly. Her people, God's chosen, would be reduced to trembling children by unholy power. She steeled herself for the fight ahead.

"Stay in the car," she told her team, contempt sharp in her voice.

Relieved, they agreed easily.

Useless bunch, she thought. They lacked her determination

and her willingness to sacrifice. She was already gone, beyond saving.

It will all be worth it if we can save humanity, she whispered to herself as she checked her sidearm and grabbed a case from the trunk of the car.

"Facing a powerful elf alone is not the wisest nor easiest thing to do. You will need to be cunning," Kador's voice echoed in her mind.

Mary could feel the elf's strength. It was palpable, a putrid taste of vomit in her mouth and fear in her heart.

She climbed carefully to the top of a small ridge and crouched behind a rock, making sure she remained unseen. She pulled out her scope, and...

There. They. Were.

The bitch was standing on a boulder, chanting with a stick in her hand. The stinking elf was dancing around her like some deranged Karate Kid. It was disgusting and sad.

They were about twelve hundred feet away. There was virtually no wind and perfect visibility. The range was well within her weapon's capabilities, the targets stationary and unaware. Through her scope, she could see every detail with crystal clarity. It would be like shooting at a practice range.

She could end it now.

Mary opened the case she'd brought with her, her fingers moving over the precisely cut foam that held each component. She assembled the rifle with the efficiency of someone who'd done this hundreds of times—barrel to receiver, bolt carrier sliding smoothly into place, stock locked tight. The scope mounted with four precise clicks, and she made minute adjustments to the windage and elevation. She chambered a round with barely a whisper of sound before carefully taking aim.

The rifle had a silencer, but she doubted she needed it. She was lightning fast and an excellent shot. She was confident she could take them both out before they even knew what hit them. Kador told her that Redstone Springs had been emptied by the elf's unclean magic spells, so the noise would not draw outside attention.

The traitor bitch had to go first. The elf might have a body-protection spell, but without the girl, Mary knew he couldn't open the gateway and get the rest of the filthy elves here. Once the girl was dead, Mary could handle the elf one way or another. Her mission would be a success, and the elf's would not.

She aimed at the girl's head, inhaled, exhaled slowly, and, without hesitation, pulled the trigger.

Using her enhanced senses, Mary's consciousness rode alongside the bullet as it cut through the desert air. She felt its trajectory, its spin, its deadly momentum, until suddenly it struck something that shouldn't exist. The bullet simply ceased to be, dissolving against an invisible barrier.

Disappointing.

Mary had been looking forward to seeing the girl's head vanish in a cloud of red mist. She'd chosen special bullets for the job, ones that were not legal in the U.S., but she didn't care about man's law. Only God's law mattered.

She cursed.

"The elf has managed to put up a defensive dome around them. That is impressive. This spell usually requires three elves," Kador said in her head. "Nothing metal or fast-moving can pass through the barrier."

Mary wanted to scream. She had come so far. She had sacrificed everything that had once made her human. This was her life's mission, the culmination of centuries of preparation by the Bellum Sacrum, the one battle that every generation had trained for but never faced. Humanity's future was on the line, and the weight of all those who had come before her pressed down like a crushing burden.

Was she about to fail?

“Do not worry, my child,” Kador said, soothing her. “Look at them. They’re practicing the Gateway spell. This kind of spell is best done at dawn. Tomorrow is one of the optimal days of the year to cast it, and I have a plan.”

She waited.

He said nothing.

“What is your plan?” she asked, trying to remain respectful.

The sky grew darker as the sunlight waned.

"You will need to get close just before dawn," Kador replied. "There will be several wards, but I can help you bypass them. When the time comes, I will teach you to forge a blade of pure light, a weapon that can cut through any elvish magic, any protective spell they might weave. Once the casting begins, the elf's full attention will be on the gateway spell. You only need to break his focus. Strike him down with the light sword or push him off balance, anything to disrupt the ritual. Once the spell breaks, the girl will die, and the elf will be weak. You can finish him then. You *must* stop them at all cost."

“You are the light of God, Kador,” Mary whispered, relief washing over her.

All was not lost.

She could still save humanity, even if she could not save her soul. She felt closer to Kador now, his divine purpose flowing through her flesh. With absolute certainty, she knew her sacrifice would give humanity many more generations to flourish in God's light, uncontaminated by magic. Her damnation was a small price for such glory.

The return walk from the ridge to the car was peaceful. The wind was warm and dry, and the views were breathtaking.

Around one of the corners, she nearly collided with a tall

man she didn't recognize. He was hiking up the path with a bat in his hands.

In a split-second decision that was as automatic as breathing, she shot him in the face with her sidearm. Then, she dragged his body off the path into the brush. He was heavy, but she was strong. Her sweat dried quickly in the desert wind.

Two to go.

CHAPTER THIRTY-SIX

"This is taking too long. Are we there yet? Maybe we should go back?" Chris suggested.

Richard was so tired of Chris by now that he wanted to strangle him. "No," he bit out.

They had been driving for two days straight and were only just now reaching their destination. Why had Valor chosen such a remote location?

The drive had been mostly uneventful, mile after mile of empty desert highway, with nothing but endless expanses of sand and stone stretching to the horizon. Richard had found himself marveling at the sheer size of this country. How could you drive for two solid days and still be swallowed by the vastness of the American southwest, surrounded by nothing but sagebrush and the occasional gas station oasis?

The monotony was broken by one terrifying moment when an insane driver in a car with dark windows had blown past them at what had to be a hundred miles an hour, nearly running them off the road. The close call had left Richard's heart pounding and his temper flaring, but his instincts and the fact that he'd been driving at a steady sixty had saved them. If he ever saw that car again, he thought, he would give the driver a piece of his mind.

After the near-accident, Richard and Chris had started taking turns behind the wheel, one driving while the other slept or helped navigate. At the moment, Chris was driving, which only made Richard more annoyed that he was also complaining about the trip.

As they neared their destination, Chris became increasingly agitated. He kept repeating that he had a bad feeling, that he hadn't signed up for *this shit.* Richard was tempted to kick him out and leave him by the side of the road, but he was fairly certain Chris wouldn't survive alone in the Arizona wilderness. Besides, they were just about two minutes from the turnoff to Redstone Springs.

The AC was blasting, but Chris was still sweating like crazy. He mumbled nonstop to himself, and he'd gone pale and jittery. When they left the paved road, Chris began to truly lose it.

"No, no, no..." he whispered, breathing rapidly, clutching his chest.

Then, during a turn, instead of hitting the brakes, Chris slammed on the gas. *Floored it* would probably be a better description.

Richard bellowed as the car careened off the road and crashed into a boulder. The front end crumpled, definitely totaled. Steam billowed from beneath the hood. Dusk had fallen, and only one headlight lit the large rock they'd rammed.

"What the..." Richard turned to Chris, who was clearly unraveling. The panic on Chris's face was real, and Richard felt a flicker of genuine concern.

"I can't. I can't... I'm sorry, Richard. I don't know what's wrong with me, but I *know* I'm going to die here. Please don't ask me to keep going. Please, please, I'm sorry!" he begged. The stench of urine filled the car.

Chris had completely lost it. He started to sob.

Richard gaped at him with a mix of pity and disgust. "I'm sorry, Chris. I can't deal with you right now. Stay in the car, and try to call a tow truck. I'm heading out to see if I can find Valor and Brenda. Please don't make a bigger mess than you already have."

"Don't leave me here!" Chris shrieked, his voice high and broken. "Please, Richard, this is a mistake! This place... it's evil. It's wrong. I can feel it crawling under my skin! You're going to die out there. We're both going to die! Let's come back in the morning. I promise it will be better in the morning!" His sweaty hands shot out and clamped around Richard's wrist with desperate strength.

Richard had to pry Chris's fingers away one by one, feeling how they trembled with fear. Even after he slammed the car door shut, he kept hearing Chris's pleas.

Richard pulled the baseball bat from the trunk, the one they'd picked up along the way. He'd learned the hard way that this country gave guns to criminals but not to tourists.

The gun store owner had refused to sell him one. "At least the criminals we sell to are honest Americans."

Richard hadn't seen the logic in that twisted patriotic reasoning, but arguing with a gun salesman who'd already made up his mind seemed like a waste of time they didn't have. Luckily, owning a solid baseball bat was still legal for anyone in this country, and Richard knew that in the right hands, a heavy wooden bat could be just as deadly as any firearm with the added benefit of making no noise.

He started climbing up the path.

Chris's desperate cries followed him. "Richard! Richard, please! Don't leave me alone!"

The path was steep, but the dry air helped, and his sweat evaporated quickly. The temperature was dropping with the coming night. The landscape was breathtaking. Long shadows stretched across the distant towering orange stone pillars painted gold by the dying light.

For the first time since losing his wife, Richard felt something other than grief. Maybe when this mission was over, he could come back here and take some time off. He deserved time to mourn properly, to heal, to remember what life felt like before everything fell apart.

Turning a corner, he spotted a figure descending the ridge toward him, a redheaded woman in black leather tactical gear picking her way down the slope with practiced ease. She carried a briefcase like she was heading to a business meeting, but something about her movement set off every alarm bell in Richard's military-trained mind. When she raised her head and looked directly at him, her eyes were an impossible shade of light blue, too bright, too cold, too inhuman.

Then, came a loud noise, and everything went dark.

CHAPTER
THIRTY-SEVEN

Brenda woke up, feeling Valor's hand tugging her shoulder. The pink of dawn danced behind the horizon.

"It is time," he said, grinning. The light blue glow of the dome illuminated his face.

He took her hand and led her back to the boulder by the waterfall, gently helping her climb onto the stone. It was still dark, but he moved with confidence, and his steadying hand warmed her.

He retrieved his staff and handed it to her. It, too, was warm to the touch. "I added a small spell to help you stay focused. If you feel tired, just squeeze the staff. It'll give you a little boost," he said.

She beamed at him and leaned down to kiss his cheek. "Thank you, Valor, for thinking of that."

He blushed and smiled back. "Thank you, Brenda, for helping save my people."

With that, he returned to the same spot he had used during all their practice sessions the day before. He planted his feet and looked at her with quiet intensity.

She felt genuinely excited about today despite everything that had led to this moment—the terror, the violence, the impossible choices. In five minutes, they should have a gateway with magical creatures coming out of it. After a lifetime of feeling like she was drifting through other people's plans and expectations, she was finally doing something that mattered on a cosmic scale. She would not just be witnessing history. She would be making it.

Brenda took a deep breath, fixed her eyes on the mountain above, and began. "*Tempus... Tempus...*"

Casting this complex magic in real life was very different from yesterday's practice. Every time she uttered the word, a wide stream of white light was pulled from the mountain and concentrated into a thin, dense stream of blazing energy in the center of her chest. The power flowed through her like molten silver, cold and intense, vibrating through her body while drawing from her stamina. From her, the concentrated beam shot directly to Valor's outstretched hand. His part was to weave the light like a master craftsman working with threads of pure energy, starting with broad strokes that outlined the gateway's frame before spiraling into intricate patterns that would stabilize the portal.

It was breathtaking to see Valor's fingers move like a master tapestry maker, pulling her dense stream of energy into broad, sweeping patterns that formed the gateway's foundation, and then spiraling inward to create a delicate lacework of power that shimmered with blue light.

It was really happening.

"IT IS TIME," Kador said in Mary's head.

She checked her companions, the remaining members of the

Bellum Sacrum. They were still sleeping in the car they'd arrived in. She was pleased. They would hate her for what she was about to do. They would never forgive her for what was coming, for what would destroy their souls.

With Kador's help, she cast an Eliminate-Fear spell followed by an Enchant. Then, in a loud voice, she called out, "Good morning, Bellum Sacrum. Rise. It's time to do God's work."

Her team was under her control now, and she could feel their minds like chess pieces arranged in her consciousness, small, moveable fragments of will that responded to her slightest mental pressure. Their eyes, which had been wild with terror last night, were now empty vessels awaiting direction. They retained their intelligence and skills, but their capacity for independent choice belonged entirely to her. The power was intoxicating, and she despised herself for it.

They made their way in the dark. Each of them wore top-tier tactical gear, dressed all in black, night-vision goggles strapped in place. Mary knew the goggles would be useless once they got close to the dome, and the sky was already beginning to lighten in the east.

Then, the whispers began, soft all around them. Hard to parse but unsettling.

Kador told her it was part of the defensive spell. *Keep going.*

A few hundred feet later, a small figure appeared in the air in front of Mary. It looked like a butterfly with a humanoid body made entirely of shimmering blue light.

The figure hovered, raising a tiny glowing hand to signal her. "Stop. Go back. You are trespassing. This is elvish land."

"A fairy-like sentinel. Part of their layered magical defenses," Kador explained in her mind, his ancient knowledge flowing into her consciousness. "These creatures are bound to the elvish magic protecting this place. Cut it down quickly before it can alert the others. Time to carve your way through their evil enchantments."

Mary reached into her pocket and pulled out a small canister she'd prepared under Kador's instruction. She spoke the word, "*Espadus*," and the device transformed into a sword made of light. The weapon was cold in her hand despite its radiance, with runes etched along its wide blade and a hilt that molded perfectly to her grip.

With a flick of her wrist, she sliced the little creature's head off and continued walking before its body even hit the ground.

Sword raised, she marched forward. It felt right. She was God's agent now, an angel with a blade of light and her soldiers following behind her.

After a short while, they reached a dome made of strange blue light. The sun was rising, and bright rays started to hit the stone pillars around them with orange heat. At the dome's edge, energy hummed in the air.

Raising the sword again, she cut a large hole in the dome's light-fabric. It resisted, but she forced the blade through. Her team followed silently behind her, glassy-eyed and numb. She felt more alive than ever.

Kador had warned her that nothing metal could pass through the dome. He couldn't help her with that. No matter. She had her magical sword, her will, and her faith.

As they stepped through the breach she had carved, Mary felt her watch dissolve against her skin like sugar in rain. The sensation was unsettling, not painful but wrong, as if reality was editing itself around them. Glancing at her team, she saw them patting themselves in confusion as belt buckles, weapon parts, and even the metal eyelets on their boots had vanished completely. Only their flesh, fabric, and her divine blade had survived the magical barrier.

They moved slowly toward the waterfall. The human traitor

girl stood on the boulder, tapping a staff lightly against the stone. The elf was dancing again, but this time, it was different. This time, it was real.

She could *feel* the energy. She could *taste* it.

They were just a hundred feet away now.

Then, she heard a branch snap behind her.

A cold stab of fear hit her. None of the Bellum Sacrum would have made that kind of mistake. This was someone else!

CHRIS WAS ABSOLUTELY HYSTERICAL.

It had been hours since Richard left, and there was still no sign of him. The suggestion to call a tow truck had been, of course, completely idiotic. There was no reception out here, and after hours of trying, his phone battery had died.

He'd tried to sleep in the car, but he was thirsty, and he'd run out of water.

Finally, the thirst and his stink drove him out of the car. It was cold and dark, and he was scared, but he needed to move.

He wandered up the path aimlessly. As the sky began to lighten, he spotted the silhouette of someone sleeping off the trail.

"Thank God," Chris whispered, stumbling toward them. Maybe they had water.

But as he moved closer, the realization hit him.

He froze, his hand rising to his mouth. A scream formed but never came out. Instead, he bit down hard on his knuckles. It felt like the pressure of the silent scream burst veins in his eyes.

The body in the brush was Richard's. Or what was left of it. The clothes were the same, yet there was nothing above the shoulders but a pulpy mess.

Chris staggered backward, tripped, and fell hard, hitting his head on a rock. His vision blurred, but he managed to find his way back to his feet. His head was wet. Confused, he reached up to wipe away the sweat. Instead, his hand came away covered in blood.

Shit!

Chris started running. He didn't know which way to go. He didn't care. He just ran.

Then, something strange happened. His belt buckle evaporated. So did his watch, and his pants began to slip.

"Oh no, oh no, oh no," he rambled.

There was a figure ahead, dark and human-shaped holding something glowing in one hand. Others stood behind her, shadowy.

Chris stumbled toward them, nearly tripping over his pants. As he got closer, he stepped on a thick branch and fell once more.

As he was falling, the figure turned with feline grace and swung the glowing blade at him. For a split second, Chris was struck by her terrible beauty—those impossible light-blue eyes that seemed to burn with inner fire, her red hair catching the dawn light like flames. The sword missed his head as he tumbled but sliced cleanly through his outstretched hand, severing it at the wrist.

His severed hand hit the dirt beside him.

Chris screamed. The glow filled his vision.

And then...

Darkness.

Brenda thought she heard a scream, but she didn't stop. She couldn't.

Her heart pounded like she was sprinting in a marathon.

Sweat dripped down her face, her neck, and her body. This was taking longer than she had expected. Or maybe not. Maybe time was slipping by unnoticed. The spell was working. That much was clear.

But it was *slow*, and it was *painful.*

Every time she said the word *Tempus*, her whole body shook. The energy drained out of her, diminishing her power and her vitality so much that fear crept in.

The scream returned to her mind. Was someone out there? Was Valor in danger?

After whispering another, "*Tempus*," she glanced sideways, still tapping the staff on the rock, still mouthing silently, "One, two, three..."

Valor's face was tight with pain and concentration, his eyes squeezed shut. Above him, a great shining arc of light formed, inscribed with runes. The shape was familiar. It reminded her of a smaller version of the Washington Square Arch in New York City but one built from light and magic instead of marble.

The gateway.

Then, behind him, she spied a dark figure, holding a glowing sword.

The figure was dressed entirely in black tactical gear, her red hair blazing like fire in the dawn light, but it was her eyes that truly terrified Brenda. The electric blue orbs glowed with unnatural light, like stars burning in a human face.

"Nine, ten..." Brenda's lips kept counting, but her heart pounded in panic.

The gate's light flickered. She forced herself to focus again and stared up at the mountain.

"*Tempus*!" she shouted.

The gate brightened.

"One, two, three..."

The figure was almost upon him, covering the ground

between them with terrifying speed. Brenda could see the woman's face now, cold and determined, beautiful in the way that lionesses focused on their prey are beautiful. The light sword raised higher with each step, and Valor remained completely oblivious, trapped in the spell that demanded his total focus.

Brenda couldn't speak to warn him without breaking the spell. What could she do?

"Nine... ten!" Tears blurred her vision. She blinked them away. "*Tempus*!"

The gate solidified, full of light and glory. The figure drew near.

"Nine..."

The sword was rising.

Then, it hit Brenda, what she had to do.

It was all up to her now. There was no one else to fix this situation, no one else to stop the approaching sword, no one else to save Valor and their entire mission. She could stand by helplessly and watch disaster unfold, or she could seize control of the magic flowing through her veins.

The choice was clear—be a passive witness to tragedy or become the agent of change who rewrites reality.

With tears streaming down her face, she shifted her focus to the figure instead of the mountain.

"*Tempus*," she screamed.

The attacker aged centuries in the span of a heartbeat. Flesh turned to dust and blew away, clothes crumbling to nothing, leaving only bleached bones that tumbled across the ground with hollow clicks. The strange glowing weapon fell from skeletal fingers and struck the earth, shattering into countless shards of pure light that scattered like broken glass.

A shockwave hit Brenda instantly.

The magic, having devoured the assassin's time, turned on

her with ravenous hunger, drawing from her life force what it could not extract from dust and bones. It felt like crumbling from within, like her life force was being siphoned away to satisfy the spell's relentless demand.

A lock of Brenda's hair turned gray before her eyes. Her vision blurred. Her lips went dry.

The sun rose behind the mountain.

The gateway was complete. Brilliant doors shimmered across its span.

Brenda was still counting. "Nine... ten..."

Her voice cracked. Her back ached. Her hands on the staff became ancient, wrinkled and spotted with age.

Another figure rushed toward Valor with a rock raised high in their hand, ready to strike.

"*Tempus*!"

The wave hit harder. Her knees gave out, and she tumbled. One knee shattered on the stone beneath her. Pain exploded through her. A tooth fell loose in her mouth. Her fingers looked like gnarled twigs.

The attacker collapsed mid-stride, flesh crumbling away as they fell. What hit the ground was nothing but a scattered pile of bones, the stone still gripped tight in the cage of their skeletal fingers.

"Nine... ten..." Brenda's lips moved, but sound barely escaped. She couldn't see the mountain. Couldn't remember the word. "Ohhh," was all that came from her toothless, dry mouth. Her white hair whipped in the wind.

She studied Valor with blurred vision. She didn't remember why she cared for him. She just wanted to sleep.

His face twisted in pain. The magic was fading. They were so close.

Brenda no longer knew where she was. The world tilted, and

her consciousness slipped. She clutched the staff as best she could.

Then, it happened.

A jolt of power shot through her, and she remembered. The staff erupted with brilliant blue light that spread from her withered hand up through her arm like liquid starlight, flooding her entire body with energy her aged flesh could never produce. The magical boost cut through her exhaustion and confusion, giving her the strength to continue.

She remembered the spell.

She remembered him.

She remembered their quest.

Five more black-clad figures emerged from the shadows, moving with deadly purpose as they formed a tightening half-circle behind Valor's dancing form. The rising sun illuminated their faces. She could see the murderous conviction burning in their eyes, the absolute certainty that they would complete their mission.

Brenda focused and screamed with a voice not her own, "*Tempus!*"

The five attackers dropped like dolls. Turning old and crumbling in a heartbeat.

The final shockwave struck, lighter but no less devastating to her fragile body. She fell from the boulder. Bones snapped—arm, shoulder, ribs.

Her mind was too slow to process it. Her vision dimmed.

Just before the dark closed in, she opened her eyes...

...and saw elves emerging from the gate.

It was the most beautiful sight she had ever seen.

CHAPTER THIRTY-EIGHT

"You have done well, my son." The voice was rich, royal, and familiar.

His father stood before him in all his ancient majesty—the King of the White Elves, tall and broad-shouldered despite centuries of life, draped in deep forest-green robes that seemed to capture and hold the morning sunlight. His weathered face bore the weight of ages, but his eyes blazed with pride as he extended a graceful hand toward his youngest son.

Valor limped toward his father. He tried to stand tall, but the strain of performing the gate spell had drained nearly all his life force. His clothes were soaked with sweat, his face streaked with dust, tears, and exhaustion.

He bowed and fell to his knees before his father, his ruler. "Thank you, my king," he said.

The gathered elves burst into celebration. Children's voices rising in pure delight, adults offering prayers of thanks in his ancient language, all of them surrounding their prince who had brought them safely home. Their joy filled the air like music, a symphony of survival and hope that echoed off the canyon walls.

The elvish queen, his mother, stood beside her king. She wore a flowing gown of pale green silk embroidered with crimson flowers that turned their delicate faces toward the rising sun as if they were alive. Her face was a masterpiece of elvish beauty, combined with centuries of loss that had carved lines of sorrow. “We have lost so much,” she said softly. “Sacrificed so many lives, so many friends... so many sons...” The last words were barely a whisper.

“Indeed, my queen,” Valor said, bowing his head.

“Rise, Valor, son of Valor,” the queen proclaimed, her voice iron once again. “Greet your people. They have worried for you and prayed to the ancient trees for your safety.”

The gate had opened fully now, and the elves were still arriving by the hundreds. Some were already chanting, expanding the dome, reinforcing it. Others were removing the skeletons of the men in dark clothing, clearing them from the sacred grounds of their new home.

Then, Valor spotted something that made his blood freeze. Brenda's small form had collapsed at the base of the massive boulder, where she had stood so bravely just moments before. Several elves approached the fallen form with the gentle care of those who had seen too much death. His heart clenched with devastating realization.

“Stop!” he shouted, breaking into a run.

Her body had crumbled to the ground like a broken doll. She looked so brittle, so impossibly fragile that a breath might scatter her like dust. Her skin was parchment-thin and cracked like dried earth, her once-dark hair now wispy white strands that barely covered her scalp. Even her clothes had aged, the fabric faded and threadbare, as if the time magic had drained the very life from the fibers themselves.

He dropped beside her, brushing her ruined face gently with his fingertips.

A strong hand gripped his shoulder. “Son, let me near,” his mother said.

Valor moved aside.

The elvish queen kneeled beside the broken human girl, her movements reverent as if approaching a sacred altar. With the tip of her finger, she caught an elvish tear at the corner of her own eye, powerful beyond measure, for the tears of elvish royalty carried the essence of life itself. She placed it softly on Brenda's cracked lips, whispering words in the old tongue as the tear began to glow with healing fire.

Brenda exhaled a tiny, fragile sigh.

“She will live,” said the queen.

Valor's face collapsed with relief so profound it left him shaking. Tears streamed freely now, wetting his cheeks as all his carefully controlled emotions finally broke free. She was not lost. He hadn't asked too much of her, hadn't sacrificed the one person who had believed in him completely. She would live to see the wonderful world she had created, to know that her courage had saved them all.

“It will take her months to recover,” his mother said gently. “We will heal her injuries. Mend her body. Humans who live among the elvish people tend to grow younger with time.” She smiled faintly, her voice now full of quiet wisdom.

“What are a few months but drops in the infinite sea?” she asked Valor.

“Indeed, my queen,” Valor answered, holding Brenda’s delicate old hand in his.

The queen looked at her son, deep, dark green eyes meeting his tear-filled ones. "You have so much to do, my son." She reached for his hand, steady and strong.

"The world will be changing now that we are here," she said, her eyes glowing blue with the power of a prophecy. "This marks the start of a new era, different from anything the world has known."

She gazed out over the expanding dome. "This is just the beginning. We are only getting started."

EPILOGUE

Og stirred.

It had been ten thousand years since he had last moved, and his back ached.

Someone was manipulating time.

Og's scales quivered in the dark under the mountain. A shiver ran from the pointed tip of his head, down his wings, and all the way to his long, powerful tail.

Time was sacred.

Time was not to be manipulated.

Change was coming to the world again. It smelled of magic. And death.

Og did not like change, though he knew it was inevitable.

But manipulating time? That was *not* inevitable.

Manipulating time was an avoidable blasphemy, and blasphemy had a punishment.

The punishment usually involved getting eaten.

Getting eaten... by Og.

ACKNOWLEDGMENTS

To my wife, Deby Shevat, who supported me from the moment I said "I have this idea for a book," all the way through to publication.

To my sons, Daniel and Jonathan, who read draft after draft without complaint. Your patience never wavered, even when you could probably recite entire chapters from memory.

To my editor, Bokerah Brumley, who took a rough manuscript and helped me shape it into something I'm genuinely proud of. Your patience with my learning curve was extraordinary, and this book wouldn't exist without your guidance.

To my alpha readers: Tal Sarig-Avraham, Nicole Zoltack, Jennifer Jones, Rotem Boker Michaeli, AJ Glasser, Eli Klaiman, Tal Shohamy, Razi Briga, Anat Ben Yosef, Yochay Kiriaty, Olga Kogan, Shirley Marom, Kate Reading, and Lindsay Galloway. Your feedback made this book immeasurably better. Every note, every question, every suggestion pushed me to dig deeper.

And finally, to everyone who picks up this book and gives Brenda and Valor a chance. Thank you for taking this journey with them. I hope you enjoy reading it as much as I enjoyed writing it. See you in book two.

Fun fact: People who write great book reviews online or share good books with friends live longer, happier lives.

What's Next?

Continue the adventures of Brenda, Valor, Lixi, and other beloved characters in book two, *The Catalysts* (Book Two of The Time of Magic series), available at:

TheTimeOfMagic.com/booktwo

Want More?

Join our community, explore The Time of Magic lore, and discover other books at:

TheTimeOfMagic.com

ABOUT AMIR SHEVAT

Like my characters, I'm far from perfect. I'm dyslexic and dysgraphic, learned English as my second language, and spent my career in tech before turning to fiction. I probably worked on several of the pieces of software you use every day. I'm a D&D enthusiast, food lover, and compulsive traveler who's endlessly fascinated by humanity's contradictions. My stories explore what happens when flawed people face extraordinary circumstances, because the most interesting characters are the ones who struggle beautifully with being human, even when they are wizards.

www.ingramcontent.com/pod-product-compliance
Lightning Source LLC
Chambersburg PA
CBHW020542020726
47494CB00006B/1880

* 9 7 8 1 9 7 1 2 9 5 0 6 0 *